ANGELA DANDY

The Silver Dagger

Gaia
Fenrir

Acknowledgement

Special thanks to my friend, Phil. for working his way through the first draft word by word and to Jane for providing me with invaluable feedback. Thanks also to my copyeditor, Claire Cronshaw, Cherry Edits, for doing a brilliant job.

And thanks to all The Silveries who have made this series possible!

One

All old buildings have history – stuff long since buried and forgotten that has a way of coming back and kicking you in the teeth when you least expect it. Magnolia Court is no exception. It sure does keep us on our toes.

"ST JOHN'S COLLEGE CLOSES

"...The closure of the school follows on from the so-far unsolved murder of mathematics teacher, Mr Vincent Palmer, on 5th June 1985. Detective Chief Superintendent Garry Seymour was unable to confirm that the boy who went missing at the time of the murder had been found. The public is reminded that any sightings should be reported to the police. The boy should not be approached.

It is rumoured that the site has been acquired by a property developer as a future investment. The name of the developer has not been revealed.

That's how an old newspaper report read, and that's almost how it all started this March.

By the way, my name's Sam; Miami born and bred, like my beautiful wife Jas. We upped sticks and moved to England in the early seventies.

Bought our cottage at Magnolia back in April 2019. It was a wildcard, the biggest wildcard we have ever played. I was stressed and frankly worn out; Jas persuaded me it was time to retire and move out of the big city. So, one day, we just got in the car and drove up to Gloucestershire. Why Gloucestershire? you might ask. Well, we had friends in the county and had visited them over the years. It kind of grew on us – the diversity of it. From the beautiful Cotswolds, down to Cheltenham, with its magnificent Regency buildings. To Gloucester, the county town on the River Severn. Something for everyone.

We made a weekend of it. Hopped from town to town checking out estate agents. Frankly, we didn't know what we were looking for. It could have been a thatched cottage in a village, a terraced house in Cheltenham, or a flat in Gloucester Docks. One thing's for certain: it had never crossed our mind that we might end up buying a cottage in a retirement community. We saw it advertised in an estate agent in Stroud. I remember saying to Jas: Did you ever see anything like that? It was the Mansion House that first caught my eye. *'Built in the Regency period in a Tudor Gothic style, this magnificent house sits within extensive grounds. Two new cottages have recently been constructed within the grounds, bringing the total number of residences to twelve. Known as Magnolia Court, it derives its name from the extraordinary sweep of magnolia trees that line the drive and extend a quarter of a mile from the main road up to the house. A small retirement community; potential buyers should be over fifty-five years of age.'*

Well, we were that alright. I'd recently turned sixty-five and Jas wasn't that far behind me. If I'm honest, I just wanted to take a look at that old house. So, we made a last-minute appointment to see the new development. We giggled and sang along to Bob Marley all the way there. We teased each other mercilessly about sitting around like nodding donkeys – excuse the expression – and drinking endless cups of tea before a seven o'clock bedtime.

We couldn't have been more wrong. Not about the Mansion House, you understand – that was awesome. But about the whole setup. No sooner had we parked than we saw a woman with long red hair waving wildly in our direction. That was the one and only Jennifer, as I learned later. There was a whole bunch of them. That welcome was very surprising; it wasn't something we were accustomed to from previous visits to the country. We're what are called 'people of colour'. Personally, I prefer the term black.

None of them were a day under seventy, and one of them – Amy – was in her early nineties. If you closed your eyes and listened to them, you'd have thought they were no more than a bunch of teenagers on a night out. That's the way they behaved – but responsible teenagers, if you know what I mean.

Magnolia Court, they told us, was both a home and a business; that helped keep costs down. If you wanted to buy into Magnolia, you had to be prepared to muck in. Otherwise, no deal. Cool, I thought. They were fast reeling us in.

We looked inside the cottage and then wandered around the grounds before being given a right royal welcome down at the Mansion House. Pity I had to drive; it could have been quite a party. Maxy – I think he's got used to me calling him that – ran me through the history of the place. Built for none other than Sir James Fotheringay in the early 1800s, he said, as if I was sure to have heard of the man. He reckoned the family went broke about the middle of the century because it was then turned into a school, then a hospital, and then a monastery. And then a convalescent home for World War Two vets, and then a school again. Considering what it had been through, it looked in pretty good shape to me. Those ceilings, those stained-glass windows, blew me away.

By then we were pretty much wriggling in the net. And then they closed the deal. Jennifer told Jas about the Magnolia theatre company, the weddings, then the group outings, and finally the nightly cocktail hour in the Mansion House. Well, we fell in love with the whole setup, lock, stock, and barrel. As good as signed on the dotted line there and then. That was almost three years ago, and we've never regretted a day of it.

My retirement didn't quite work out the way I'd planned. You see, I was a medical man, a specialist in tropical diseases in London at University College Hospital back in my day. We'd been lucky with SARS and MERS and even Ebola, but Covid caught us out, caught the whole world out. No one could have predicted how far and wide that virus would spread and how deadly it would be.

I volunteered immediately to help out – in Gloucester Hospital and down in London advising government departments on the best ways to contain the spread. Eighteen months I spent away from Jas, returning on the occasional weekend when the rules permitted, to recharge my energy cells before diving straight back in. I'm still working a bit, but not so much now. Thank God, we're now back to normal, or the 'new normal' as they now call it. It was a wake-up call like no other.

I worried about Jas during that time, worried about everybody back here at Magnolia, but I didn't need to. They rallied around and worked together. No sooner had the Tesco van delivered the weekly shop than the girls busied themselves with the cooking. Jas made eighteen portions of her famous Jamaican chicken curry complete with rice and peas in the first week and hand-delivered them that same day. The phone didn't stop ringing. Everyone wanted more. No one starved at Magnolia Court; no one had time to be bored. And no one was lonely – a bit isolated, yes, but lonely, no. Duncan insisted that everybody should have an iPad and know how to use it. In what might otherwise have been very long evenings, residents enjoyed quizzes, recitations, play readings, and music evenings. TVs were rarely switched on. The doors to the Mansion House and the cocktail bar remained firmly shut until just over nine months ago when the final restrictions were lifted.

I have to hand it to them: they followed the rules to the letter, took no chances, but if you were vulnerable, you would, wouldn't you? And none of them went down with Covid. It wasn't until all this happened that we all really understood how lucky we were, especially the older ones among us. Once the lockdowns were behind us, we were able to get back to more or less normal. The same couldn't be said for all those poor folk in care homes who still weren't allowed out and couldn't have visitors either. There's a huge case for retirement complexes like Magnolia where residents support one another and are trusted to make decisions for themselves. That's me – getting on one of my soapboxes again.

But it's March now. The magnolia trees are strutting their stuff – huge pink-and-white buds have just blossomed. There are God knows how many weddings booked in for the summer and I'm to be in charge of the discos. Jas and Jennifer are locked together, deciding on the next theatre production. I hear tell that there's love in the air at Magnolia as well, but that's all Jas will say. The rebuild of the Old Forge is just about complete. And Paul, our next-door neighbour, is being a pain in the ass. That's life.

And just when everything was starting to get back to normal, along comes that kick in the teeth I mentioned earlier...Never a dull moment at Magnolia.

Two

Jaipur. 6.30 a.m. The sun, a magnificent golden globe, rises above the distant hills and wakes the pink city.

Cars, vans, trucks, tuk-tuks, rickshaws, and bicycles jostle for space on the jam-packed roads, meeting head-on at intersections, missing one another by a whisker, while swerving to avoid the sacred cows oblivious to the mayhem. Collisions are a rarity. Collisions with sacred cows are unheard of. To the uninitiated, the whole of Jaipur is an accident waiting to happen.

The streets are buzzing. The bazaars are coming to life. Market stalls piled high with clothes, shoes, fabrics, bags, rugs, and souvenirs of every colour, assault the eyes. The choice is endless. Sellers take time out to rest before the day begins.

The air is rich with spices. Steam escapes the cooking pots and floats in whisps up through the dust into the blue sky far above. Braziers glow red and sizzle, their smoke mingling with the steam, mingling with the aroma.

Everywhere is chaos, but organized chaos.

This is Ahmed's city – the pink city, a city of palaces and magnificent architecture, a city of commerce, a city of bazaars, a city that embraces and enriches the rich and the poor, a city that beckons tourists, a city that excites all the senses.

It is October, a comfortable twenty-one degrees. By noon, it will reach thirty-three degrees, the perfect day.

* * *

Surefooted and lithe, Ahmed navigated the narrow streets. Ever aware, stepping left and right, right and left, he let neither cows, tuk-tuks, bicycles, nor other traffic impede his way. It was a game, a game of chance, a game in which he was an artful player.

On his way to the Rambagh Palace, Ahmed revelled in the hustle and bustle. One of the most prestigious hotels in Jaipur, and in times past, the residence of the Maharaja of Jaipur, it was where Ahmed had set up his base. Where the rich and famous – and tourists with deep pockets – stayed. It was surrounded by crenellated walls, and overhung by rugged hills crowned with forts. The Rambagh dominated the middle of the city.

Ahmed walked the two-mile route from his home to the palace. Never varying his route, there were few people he did not know. Greeting each one of them by name and as friends; offering a helping hand when it was needed – he was popular and well-liked by men, women, and children alike.

"Hey, Ahmed, wait for me."

Ahmed slowed and looked over his shoulder. He had just spent fifteen minutes helping an elderly man mend the broken wheel of a rickshaw. He was running behind time. "Where are we off to this morning?" his friend asked. "As if I didn't know. Rambagh again? You set your sights too high, my friend. How many days do you go there to wait all day and get no work? Come with us – we find tourists. Not rich, maybe, but with money."

"Today will be good, Gadhar. I feel it in my heart and soul. Four coaches, a hundred or more American and British, arrived late yesterday. I saw them come with their luggage. Today they will be seeing the city. I will share our beautiful city with them."

"You'll not get near the palace, Ahmed. You know what security is like there. The nearest you will get is to wave to the coaches when they leave the gardens," Gadhar replied.

"I can but try," Ahmed replied. "And you, my friend, where will you be today?"

"The railway station, on the platform, ready to unload suitcases from the train. Ready to help provide solace to visitors after their journey. Ready to protect them from the sacred cows that will greet them as they step down from the train. Ready to guide them safely around the cow pats." Gadhar grinned. "A few paise here, a few paise there. It all adds up, Ahmed."

"You are right, but I will take my chance," Ahmed replied. There were some things that he would not share with his friend. Better to let him believe his daily quest was rarely, if ever, successful. "I wish you well today." Ahmed glanced up at the sun and checked the shadows cast over the buildings. It was time to make haste. "Good luck, Gadhar"

* * *

Fariq was his key to success. It had taken time, money, and effort to win him round but eventually, he had succeeded.

Ahmed and Fariq were now firm friends and business partners. A long-term, respected employee of hotel security, Fariq was able to open doors, but at a price. Through sheer hard work, determination, and charm, Ahmed had finally brought Fariq around to his way of thinking. Were those guests who were determined to see the city on foot not safer with him than walking the streets alone? Would Fariq not enjoy a share of his earnings for the day?

Long ago, Ahmed decided he would not be one of the street kids. His offering to tourists would be genuine. With him, they would ride the tuk-tuks, ride in the best rickshaws and horse-driven carriages, and visit the best sites in Jaipur. The price would be stated upfront. There would be no haggling. There would be no inflating prices. He would negotiate good prices for rides around the city. Only if they specifically asked would he take them to merchants, and then they would visit only the most reputable, those merchants Ahmed knew well. His mother had taught him manners. It is manners that maketh a man, she said, more often than he cared to remember. It was manners and a good business head that would distinguish him from the rest of the street kids: manners, honesty, knowledge, and personality. Ahmed had personality in spades.

He knew he had to separate himself from other street kids not only by his offer but by his appearance. Unlike most, Ahmed wore sandals. Old and worn as the sandals were, his feet were covered and were as clean as they could be in spite of the city's dust. Most of his earnings he gave to his mother; a small amount he kept for himself to buy essentials for the trade: T-shirts, shorts, underwear, sandals, and soap. Each day before leaving the home he shared with his mother, he stood under a cold tap high on the wall in the kitchen courtyard, washed from head to foot, and then dressed in a fresh set of clothes. Each evening, he scrubbed and washed his clothes under the same tap and, smoothing them flat, hung them over a balcony to dry. He appreciated that he was fortunate. Few of his friends had ready access to cold running water and instead made their way daily down to the Banganga to bathe. The paise and the rupees that he saved were kept in a small metal box alongside his bed rug.

Tall at twelve years of age, Ahmed was of a slight build, which worked well and to his advantage. He chose clothes that were on the large size so that they would last a long time, and so that they hung loosely about his frame. He might be mistaken as in need of a meal, a picture that could elicit a small amount of sympathy, helping to secure a day's work.

Ahmed had plans for the future. One day he would work for the Jaipur tourist board as a listed guide. One day he would have his own tourist company.

Standing well back from the gate close to Fariq, he watched as, one by one, coaches loaded with day-trippers glided down the long drive and out into the city beyond. Ahmed watched carefully as more adventurous guests set off on foot. He knew their confidence was skin deep. Everyone was warned that venturing out on the streets of Jaipur was a precarious occupation. Beware of street kids, they were told. They will lead you on a merry dance and take you only to their fathers', brothers', and uncles' factories. You will be plied with tea and spirits until, in desperation to get away, you buy something that you do not want at an extortionate price. And they will still not leave you alone until, eventually, you give them money so you can be on your way.

Ahmed listened carefully to their nervous chatter. He was wary of the Americans. They were by no means all made in the same mould, but some were loud, over-confident, and stupidly flaunted their wealth, wearing gold chains around their necks, and rings about their fingers. It was always a hard sell to persuade them that a guide, a boy at that, would be able to show them the city and keep them safe. The British were altogether different. Mostly reserved and unsure of themselves, they followed the rules but were not bound by them. If they preferred to see the city on foot, then that is what they did, but they took the appropriate precautions.

Straightening his shoulders, and brushing his hair away from his eyes, Ahmed glanced towards a man and woman approaching the gates. He nodded to Fariq. They were sensibly dressed, wearing open-toed walking sandals and sun hats; matching loose cotton tops and chinos. They had bum bags strapped around their waists and water bottles bulging from their pockets. They held hands and spoke little. Ahmed could feel their excitement and their almost palpable fear. They were about to leave the safe confines of this magnificent palace and walk out into the unknown. "Have a good day, sir and madam." Fariq stepped forward. "Please enjoy our beautiful city, but take care. Have you decided where you will go first today?"

The man glanced at Fariq and smiled. "Yes, we're headed for the City Palace and we'll see what happens after that, I think." He waved a tourist map in the air. "I'm no good with maps. Which way should we go?"

"It is a way from here. If you cut through the streets, you'll be there in forty-five minutes. If you take the main routes, it'll take you an hour or more. You could take a tuk-tuk or a rickshaw taxi," Fariq suggested.

"You know, I just don't know. What would you do?" The man took off his hat and scratched his head. "It's all new to us and I have to admit it's a bit daunting. My wife and I like to see the real city. Get to know the people. Understand how they live. Soak up the culture. One palace is more than enough, however beautiful it might be. Tours just aren't for us."

Fariq waved Ahmed forward. As if from nowhere, Ahmed appeared beside the couple and held out his hand. "How do you do, sir? How do you do, ma'am. My name is Ahmed. If I can help in any way, then I am at your service. I will feel privileged if you would accept me as your tour guide for the day."

"I can vouch for him." Fariq wrapped his arm around Ahmed's shoulder. "He's a good boy, honest. If you need a tourist guide, then Ahmed is your man. He knows the city like the back of his hand. He knows people, and places, and he's not so bad at history either. And if he doesn't behave, then I'll be right here to sort him out when you get back."

The lady looked at her husband, the worry lines leaving her face in an instant. "I think we should, dear. I would feel so much happier."

"Act in haste, repent at leisure, my dear. Isn't that what we always say?" the man said, thinking it over. Ahmed listened intently. The man had an accent, one that was hard to follow. "We've been warned about imps like you, my son. Read the riot act to us, they did. Don't do this and don't do that. And don't be led on by street kids. You know, young Ahmed, I don't like being told what I should do and what I shouldn't do. I've got this far in life and here I am, still in one piece. And what's more, I don't like being told what to do when I've come all this way to see your beautiful city. We want to see the real Jaipur, warts and all."

Ahmed nodded. He had not heard of warts before, but by the end of the day, he was sure that he would have made friends with them as well.

"I don't suppose you give your services for free, young man?" the man asked.

"No, sir. My charge is five hundred rupees for six hours' work."

"What's that, Nancy, in real money?" the man asked his wife.

"If I am not mistaken, it is less than five pounds," she replied.

"Seems reasonable. How much did they want for that walking tour back at the hotel, dear?"

"Twenty pounds, if not more," she replied.

"Then we'll shake hands on it. My name's Bill, Bill Hathaway. You call me Bill. This is Nancy, my wife of twenty-five years today. And before we set off, young man, let me tell you that we don't want to ride on elephants, and we don't need any new rugs. I may want to buy a little something gold or silver for my Nancy. Not that she wants it, but I am going to insist. You better back me up."

"Fine. And one palace, you said? Gold and silver bazaars, no rugs, no elephants," Ahmed confirmed.

"We want you to show us the real Jaipur," Bill continued. "Ride those tick tacks, do the markets, eat local food, and, if we have time, do that palace so we can take some pictures and tell them back home that we went there."

"I think you mean tuk-tuks, sir. We can do that, and we'll take a horse-drawn carriage as well. It will save your feet. That comes as extra, but you'll pay only the local going rate. You like hot curry, sir?" Ahmed grinned.

Bill licked his lips. "Bring it on, boy, as hot as it comes."

"I will take you to the best street food in the city. You must try our pani puri. It is expensive. Fifty rupees. I will order for you, bring it to you, and wait while you eat," Ahmed said.

"Fifty rupees? That's not going to break the bank, son. Back home, it would be no less than five hundred rupees. And there'll be no waiting while we eat. You'll eat with us – at my expense. We're family today." Bill turned to Fariq. "Cheers, pal." He slipped a few notes into Fariq's hand. "We're looking forward to this. Lead the way, son."

* * *

The day flew. Loaded down with parcels, Ahmed returned Bill and Nancy to the Rambagh in a magnificent horse-drawn carriage. Instead of five hundred rupees, it had cost just two.

"Come in, Ahmed. Join us for afternoon tea," Nancy said.

Ahmed smiled gratefully. "No, ma'am, I will not be allowed into the hotel. The gate is as far as I will be allowed to go with you." The day had been a revelation for all of them. While he had spoken endlessly about his beloved Jaipur, Bill and Nancy had narrated endless stories about their home in a town called Birmingham.

"Then you'll take this today," Bill said, putting his hand in his pocket and withdrawing a wad of notes. "Five hundred that we owe you, and five hundred as a bonus. Worth every penny, son. We're here for three days. If you're not doing anything else, then how about we go out again tomorrow and the day after that? Same price, mind."

"I could do you a reduction for three days." Ahmed grinned.

"You'll do no such thing. Same time, same place. We'll look

forward to it."

The three days were over before they knew it. As they said goodbye to one another, Bill gave him his business card. "If you're ever in England, don't be a stranger. There will always be a welcome at our door." Ahmed walked the two miles back home, his thoughts of England, a place on the other side of the world that he was as likely to visit as the moon. That night, he tucked the card away safely in his precious box.

Three

1985

"We have been friends for twenty years, David. We have shared the good times and the bad. I have never asked for your help in the past, but I am now." Fists clenched, knuckles white, Francis rocked back in his chair and stared at his friend.

"Anything. You only have to ask. You've dug me out of so many holes, I have quite lost count." It was so true. Francis was fifteen years his senior and closer to David than his own father. It was Francis who had persuaded his father he had no passion for trading gold. It was Francis who fought his corner when he decided he wished to study law. It was Francis who nurtured him through his studies, and it was Francis who helped him set up his own business and introduced him to his first clients. Without Francis, he would not have the successful law practice in Jaipur that he now had. He would be ever grateful to him and owed him a great deal. Over the years, their relationship had grown and matured, and they counted each other the closest of friends. David knew from the moment he had received the call that morning that there was something seriously wrong. He had heard it in his friend's voice. There was no cheery good morning, none of the usual

17

debate about the Iron Lady and what steps she might take next to resolve the nationwide miners' strike back home. I'll be with you in an hour, he had said, asking no further questions.

* * *

"What is troubling you, my friend?" David sat opposite Francis. Unusually, he had not been offered tea or something stronger.

"One of my servants died last night. Her name was Indira Singh."

David heaved a sigh of relief and laughed. "My God, Francis, you had me really worried for a moment. A servant dies. It happens all the time. It shouldn't, but it does. I am sorry. Will you replace her? I know of several women who would be more than happy to work in your household."

David knew, almost before the words had slipped out, that he had said the wrong thing. He had angered Francis in a way he had not done for years.

"She was not just a servant to me, David," Francis snapped. "She was a woman, and a very beautiful woman at that. Beautiful, kind, and caring. She was just thirty-two. Words cannot…"

Francis stood and walked towards the window, lost in a world of his own. The view over the pink city never failed to inspire him, but that day it held only sorrow. It was as though an unknown, unseen presence had swept in and torn his heart out, torn his soul apart, leaving nothing but an empty shell.

"You can tell me, Francis," David cajoled.

"We were close, as close as two people can be. We were in love."

18

"You don't mean...?" David said, unable to hide his shock. It was an unwritten law in India. Men broke it at their peril.

"Yes, I do mean. We were lovers. We have been lovers for the past thirteen years."

"You never told me. You could have confided in me. All these years," David said. "I am lost for words. It was you, was it not, who drummed it into me that one should never fraternize with the servants? Respect them, treat them fairly, you said, but never, ever get involved. I remember your words as a mere youth."

"This is my penance." Francis pulled a pristine white handkerchief out of his pocket, wiped the corner of his eye, and sank into the worn old armchair from which he had conducted business throughout the years. Where on many an occasion Indira had sat at his feet while they talked.

"Why, what made you get involved in the first place? You could have had your choice of English women? What made her so special that you broke all the rules?"

"She was different. I knew her father long ago. Sajiva. He was a good man. A clever man. Indira was his only child. Sajiva made the most exquisite Bagru you have ever seen. His fabric was sought worldwide. He was the oldest of two sons – just – and inherited the business from his father and his grandfather before him. When Sajiva inherited the business, his twin, Jahi, was left with a house and a tidy sum of money. Sajiva offered him work in the business, but he was too proud or lazy to take it. You wouldn't credit it if you knew him, but Jahi means bright. He was far from that."

"Did you know the daughter, Indira, I mean, as a child?" David asked.

"I did. I first met her when I went to the factory to help

Sajiva finance a warehouse. She was no more than ten years old. As bright as a button. He allowed her to roam the factory at will. Indira was oblivious to castes. Even as a small child, she resolutely refused to accept that those of a more lowly birth should be labelled or that their destiny had been written on the day they were born. To her, the men, women, and children who worked in the factory were just that – men, women, and children. They loved her. They all loved that little one. She'd sit side by side with them, learning the process of creating Bagru. I remember that first day I set eyes on her. She was sitting alongside one of the carpenters carving her own little wooden block. Nothing fazed her. I heard her say to her father that she'd look after the factory once she'd grown up. It seemed he never had the heart to tell her it could not be. He never told her that on his death the business would pass automatically to Jahi. Nevertheless, Sajiva made sure that Indira had a good education with private tutors. She learnt English, mathematics, and history. He wanted her to have a future, a good future."

"So, what happened?" David asked. Little by little, word by word, Francis was drawing him into the story. He needed to hear the rest.

"Once Sajiva died, Indira was on her own. Her mother had died in childbirth. She was seventeen, not much more than a child herself. Javi took her in – not out of the kindness of his heart, but because he had plans for her. On her eighteenth birthday, she was to marry his younger son. An arranged marriage. It was quite legal. But Javi's son had his own ideas about who he wanted to marry, and it wasn't Indira. But he was given no choice. So he went out of his way to make

Indira's life unbearable. He took it out on her. I heard all this from Indira much later. They were living under the same roof and, with no choice in his partner, it seemed he decided there was little point in waiting for the marriage. He raped her. More than once. He threatened her with her life if she ever uttered a word. When she could take it no longer, she ran from the house with a few belongings and lost herself in the streets. I don't know what she would have done if there'd been a baby to consider, but thankfully it never came to that."

"I'm sorry, Francis." Deeply fond of his friend, David shared his loss and understood. Francis had always been a kind man, too kind. He hated the poverty in Jaipur. He hated seeing children, dirty and ragged and stealing; women with babies wrapped up in blankets begging for a few paise to feed a child and often going hungry themselves; cripples, all skin and bone limping around on makeshift crutches with nowhere to go and no hope for the future. Never setting foot outside the house without a purse of paise, he rarely passed by on the other side of the street, always offering a kind word and a little solace. He was incredible. "And how did you meet up with her again?"

"By chance, or maybe God was looking down on us both. She was sitting cross-legged on the pavement, her shawl drawn up around her head and face, her hands held out begging for money. I bent down to talk to her and then I recognized her. I could hardly believe my eyes. Little Indira on the streets. I brought her home with me that very day and told the servants to clean her up. I wanted to give her everything, but she would accept no charity from me. She would work in the house alongside all the other servants; that was her condition for staying with me. We stole time with one another after the servants had retired for the evening. First talking endlessly, sharing our past, sharing our dreams for the future. And we simply fell in love."

"I am so sorry, Francis," David said. "But you must move on. She would want you to move on, put the past behind you."

Francis sighed. "The past will not be left behind this time, David. There is more. There was a child…"

"But you said there was no offspring from the rape."

"I did and that is true. A boy was born a year after Indira came to live in this house. My child. I arranged for her to go away for the last three months of her confinement, after which I invited her to return to the house with the baby. I told the other servants she would take up her former position and that a child would be living in the house. I gave them no chance to object. I told them if they wanted to find a job elsewhere, it was their decision. My mind was made up. She came back. She stayed below stairs. The boy had his mother's dark eyes and colouring. No one would ever have guessed that the child was mine."

"A boy. How old is he? Where is he?" Suddenly he understood his friend's melancholy. Francis had always wanted a wife and family, but it had not come to pass. And now a son – a son that he could not acknowledge as his own.

"His name is Ahmed. He is twelve. He is a free spirit, strong-willed and bright. His mother schooled him all these years. Two hours every evening without fail. He speaks English fluently. He reads and writes in English, and he has a way with figures. I see him leave in the mornings and return at dusk. I have followed him from a distance. I have seen him start conversations with tourists and lead them away. I have even sat in those very same hotels and had conversations with those who have spent the day with him. I needed to know that Ahmed was honest. He excelled my expectations. They sang his praises – of his knowledge of Jaipur, his honesty, his enthusiasm, and his love of life. Since his mother died, I have seen him leave the house, his clothes dirty, his hair dishevelled, his shoulders slumped as though he carried the weight of the world on them. Once he had his mother to live for and now he has nothing."

"You can't tell him you are his father?" David asked.

"It is too late, too late in so many ways. What would he think of a father who had ignored his son all these years? How would he handle finding out after all this time that he was a bastard? It would not be fair to the child. And there is something else…"

"Did he ever ask his mother about his father?" David asked.

"Many times. Indira had a whole storybook about the heroic father who had been killed in a tragic accident just months before he was born. She would paint a picture of him. It was almost as if she believed he had existed as well."

"What is it that you want me to do, Francis?"

"I want the boy to have a proper future, a career. I want the boy to be educated in England. I want to see him rise to fame, to be given every chance in life. I want you to be his legal guardian, David."

"Me? What do I know about bringing up a boy?" David's mouth flew wide open in astonishment. "You can't be serious, Francis?" Francis's face was set in stone, his eyes steely, leaving no doubt that he was in dead earnest. "Surely you should be the one to do this. If you can't acknowledge him as your own, which I understand, then the least you can do is look after his welfare yourself. I know how much you value your reputation, but there are times—"

"My reputation," Francis bawled. "My reputation. You think I care about my reputation? I am asking you this because there is a good chance I shan't be here for much longer." Francis strode back to the window.

A deadly silence hung over the room as Francis's words sank in. "Dying?" David whispered.

"Cancer. I have seen specialists. The chances of me surviving for more than a couple of years are remote. How could I tell the boy he is my son and then leave him again so soon? You will draw up the paperwork. Tomorrow you will find I have transferred sufficient funds into your bank account for his education and expenses that will see him through until he comes of age. And then he will inherit my wealth. Tomorrow you will meet up with him and explain. I will tell one of the servants that he is to run an errand for me. He will deliver an envelope to you."

"Explain what? How?"

"You'll find the words, David. And there's one other thing I need you to do for me. Make sure that he has this." Francis opened a drawer and placed a parcel on top of the desk.

Four

"Message for"—Ahmed glanced at the envelope and reached for the door pull—"Mr David McMasters. I was told to deliver it. I have to wait for a reply."

A woman servant opened the door and eyed him with disdain. Dressed from head to toe in a turquoise blue sari, edged with gold, she wrinkled her nose. She held her hand out at arm's length and took the envelope between two fingers. "Wait there," she said, pointing to the bottom step.

Ahmed stepped back down the wide-sweeping steps and took a seat. He glanced up at the house. It was a fine house of pale pink stone, built on three levels, each surrounded by a balcony. Not as fine a house as the one he and his mother lived in, but it spoke of history and wealth. Ahmed corrected these thoughts. Not as fine as the house he and his mother *had* lived in. It was two days since his mother *had* died and still, he could not speak of her in the past tense, could not think of her in the past tense. She had been his world, his reason for getting up and earning what little he could to help her. The world was suddenly a different place. Without meaning and purpose.

25

He had lost interest in his personal appearance, not washed nor changed his clothes since the moment she died. It had been an unexpected and painful death. He had not left her side. He could still smell her death on him. It was both revolting and comforting, and he could not bring himself to part with it. He was sad and he was angry. Broken-hearted to lose his mother, angry at the so-called all-loving, all-caring gods that had taken the one person in the world he loved beyond all others.

Their small room in the servant's quarter of the big house was empty, soulless without her. Her rug lay on the floor beside his. As he reached out in the night, her rug was cold, empty, devoid of life. It was now a temporary shelter but nothing more. Soon, he would find himself on the streets.

His study books remained unopened on the long wooden trunk that was the repository for all their possessions – clothes, shoes, soap, and a few toiletries. He knew that she would have been angry with him. The one thing that she had always insisted on was his two hours of study every evening – two hours during which they spoke only English. Together they read the great classics, books that had been loaned to her by the master, she said. Together they wrote their daily diaries, always in English. Together they did sums. And then she would tell him stories about the great moguls and maharajas of India and Jaipur and the many battles they had fought. It was her wish that one day he would do well for himself. One day he would have a family of his own and live in a fine house. And she taught him values, values that he did all in his power to live by.

"Ahmed?" Thinking only of his mother, he had neither seen nor heard the man descend the steps and sit down beside him. He was not old. He wore pale cream trousers and an open-neck shirt. His eyes were shaded by Gucci sunglasses and they were not fake. Sorting the wheat from the chaff and the fake from the genuine article was one of the first things he had learnt as a tour guide. "I'm David McMasters," he said. His voice was soft, his eyes kind.

"Thank you for delivering that letter to me. Sir Francis told me you would be stopping by this morning." David wrinkled his nose and gently shuffled a few feet away from Ahmed. The boy needed a wash. He needed clean clothes. Could this really be Francis's son? They bore no similar features, other than one. Francis and Ahmed had the same nose. Most if not all Indian noses were short and rounded. This one was unmistakable. All doubts that he might have had were set aside.

Ahmed jumped to his feet. He should not be sitting side by side with an Englishman on that Englishman's own doorstep as if they had been made equal. He should have known his place. Ahmed stood up straight and waited. The man slit open the envelope, his fingers long and fine, his nails clean and manicured. "Hmm. This is important. Come with me, Ahmed. We can talk and then you can take my reply to Sir Francis. That is if you have the time to wait for it?" David said, rising to his feet and turning back to the open door. He was fair-haired, tall, six-foot, slim, and agile.

"I will wait here, sir," Ahmed replied. "It would not be right for me to enter your house through this door."

It was not difficult to see why Francis wanted more for this

27

boy. He was polite, respectful, and spoke English like a native. Few street boys had such a command of the English language. His pronunciation was almost perfect.

"Call me Mr McMasters, and follow me. No arguments."

Wide-eyed, Ahmed followed him back up the sweeping stone steps across the threshold into another world. Stepping from eighty-five degree heat into the air-conditioned house, he shivered, but it was not unpleasant. Transfixed by the ancient wall hangings that contrasted starkly with the marble floor and colonnades, Ahmed gazed around in awe. He wondered whether 'above stairs' in the house he had lived with his mother shared the same opulence. He had never seen it. Ahmed lived with his mother in the servants' quarters in the basement of the grand house. Their room was located off the kitchen where his mother worked throughout the day. A door from the kitchen led out into a tiny walled courtyard with steps up to the streets of Jaipur. It was unthinkable that he might enter one of the great houses from the front steps.

He had not known what to expect. He had seen picture postcards of rooms such as this. The walls were hung with portraits of men, old and young, in civilian clothes and uniform, together with pictures of horses and country scenes where hills towered over fields of green, and mountains, purple and green, towered over valleys and lakes. It could be no other than England.

"That's my grandfather," David said, noticing the direction of Ahmed's eyes. "He was an admiral in the British Navy. Died in service in World War Two. A U-boat. I never knew him. Sit down," David said.

Ahmed looked at the plush Indian carpet – it was one of

the best. He realized he had not washed his feet nor bothered with his sandals, and he brushed the worst of the dust off before treading carefully on the rug. It felt soft and warm. Lowering himself quickly to the floor, he crossed his legs and straightened his back. "No, not there, Ahmed. Sit in that chair," David said, pointing to the plush red leather armchair opposite the one in which he had already seated himself.

With his feet dangling in the air, Ahmed wondered if it would not be better to run.

"It's a bit old that chair but leather matures with age and it could tell many stories. Now, Ahmed, we are going to talk man to man. You're probably wondering why you are here..."

"To take a reply to my master. Isn't that what you said, sir?"

"Mr McMasters. I've told you. Call me Mr McMasters. 'Sir' makes me feel old and I may look it to you but I'm not. There's a small matter we need to discuss."

Ahmed coloured crimson. If he was in trouble, he didn't for the life of him know what he had done. He hadn't left the master's house for the past two days.

"I'm a lawyer, Ahmed, and a friend of Sir Francis. You know what a lawyer does?" Francis had said the boy was bright, but it was unlikely he had ever crossed paths with a lawyer. Baby steps, he reminded himself.

"Contracts, property, prosecuting people, defending people, probate. Those sorts of things?" Ahmed whispered quietly.

"You are well informed, young man. Right on all counts. I shall not underestimate your knowledge again. At times we are called upon to do more unusual work. Do you know what a benefactor is, Ahmed?"

"No, sir," Ahmed replied.

"It's probably best if I use the dictionary definition." David reached for the dictionary on his desk, selected B, and ran his finger down the page. "'A benefactor is a person who gives support to a person or cause. That support is often financial.' You have a benefactor, Ahmed." Picking up his pen, he started doodling on the blotter and waited. Would he recognize the enormity of the statement?

"You mean someone wants to give me money?" Ahmed replied open-mouthed. "I don't understand, Mr McMasters. Why would anybody wish to be my benefactor? I think you must be mistaken if you will forgive me saying so," Ahmed said.

"No, I assure you, young man, I am not mistaken. You have a benefactor who wishes to remain anonymous. 'Give' is not necessarily a word I would use; there will be conditions. Your benefactor is prepared to be extremely generous both now and in the future. You will not need to worry about money again."

"I do not worry about money." Ahmed looked puzzled. "I earn an honest living. Most of my earnings I give to my mother – or I did when she was alive. A small amount I keep for myself for clothes and soap; and I am still able to save a little each week. I have over a thousand rupees. I do not need a benefactor." He paused. "I apologize, Mr McMasters. I spoke out of turn," he added.

"I see you have your pride, Ahmed, and that is a good thing. I admire that, and so would your benefactor. It would not be charity. Your benefactor loves this country, and he is wise enough to know that it needs clever men like you. Let me explain a little more." David crossed his arms and gathered his thoughts. His next words would be crucial. "Your benefactor wishes you to continue your education in England and hopefully go on to university and obtain a good degree. Your expenses will be paid. I spoke of a condition. It is that when you have qualified, you will return to Jaipur to put your learning to good use for the benefit of the people. Your profession will be your choice. On your return, you will be given sufficient funds to set yourself up in the business of your choice. I repeat, Ahmed, your choice of profession must be one that is of benefit to the people. Do you understand, Ahmed?"

"Yes, I have listened to what you have said, but I still think there must be some mistake. My name is Ahmed Singh. My mother is – was – Indira Singh. She was a servant. I am her son, no more. My friends are street boys. I earn my living on the streets."

David cut in. "That's not quite what I hear, Ahmed. I hear you earn your living by being a tour guide and a very good one at that. Have I been misled?"

"No, Mr McMasters, you have not."

"Your command of the English language is excellent. Can you read and write in English?" David asked.

Ahmed nodded.

"And can you do maths, sums?"

Ahmed nodded.

"Tell me, what is seven times eight, subtract six from the result and then divide by four?"

"Twelve point five," Ahmed replied instantly.

"You'll do." David grinned. It had taken Ahmed less time to work it out than he.

"Who is this benefactor, Mr McMasters? Who would possibly do all this for me? Do I know him?"

"I have already told you, your benefactor wishes to remain anonymous, so I cannot reveal his name. I promised I would not do so but I can tell you that your benefactor knows or knows of you and has been observing you closely. I can also assure you he is sincere in his offer. You should ask no further questions about him."

Could it be true? Was somebody really going to make his dreams come true? England. He had always wanted to go to England, where people like Bill and Nancy lived. The green land they'd described to him just a few days earlier; the land depicted so vividly in the pictures that hung from the walls of this very house.

"What would your mother wish for you, Ahmed?"

"A good life. To use my talents honestly and well. To make something of myself. To have a family…"

"So, now you have that chance. Show her the love and respect she deserves in her passing. I am assuming you will accept your benefactor's offer?"

Dumbfounded, Ahmed nodded.

"I will write my response to Sir Francis and you will take it back to the great house." Ripping a sheet off a pad, he wrote, 'Done', folded the sheet, and put it into the envelope. "We'll be seeing a great deal of each other in the next few weeks, young man. We have much to discuss. I suggest a wash and a change of clothes before next we meet. I will send word for you."

Ahmed felt the blood rush to his face. It was no more than forty-eight hours since his mother had died and already he was letting her down. It would not happen again.

Five

William Rutherwood, born March 1940, learnt discipline from the cradle. If he cried when his mother was otherwise engaged, he was left to cry. If he failed to eat his meal, it was there for him for the rest of the day and the following day. If he wandered into his parents' private quarters uninvited, he was removed without explanation. If he spoke when he had not been spoken to, he was silenced. Discipline was a way of life. Without routine and discipline, there was nothing. Love had no part to play in his childhood. He had not resented his upbringing; he had known no other. The rules were clear; the boundaries set. Provided he operated within both, life was straightforward and held no unwanted surprises. It was a model within which he found comfort and one that, as the years passed, he adopted without question.

He'd had an unremarkable academic career. He managed to achieve a respectable second in physics – a subject in which he had no interest whatsoever. He abhorred the laissez-faire attitude of tutors and students alike. He abhorred the meaningless frivolity of the way of life. He kept himself to himself.

33

At age twenty, he signed up to Sandhurst Royal Military Academy. It felt familiar and he excelled in all aspects of military life, graduating as a second lieutenant. Rising to the rank of major after nine years, he had his own company of officers and men – men in whom he could instil discipline, in much the same way as his parents had instilled discipline in him. He set the bar high for each and every one of them. Failure to deliver was not an option if they wanted to remain part of his company.

A man's man throughout his life, he had no time for women. One brief dalliance in his university years had been sufficient to persuade him that women were eminently dispensable, best avoided. Since that one encounter, they had never been further from his thoughts. He could well do without a wife and a family to drain his resources. Both were incumbents; unnecessary distractions.

Deployed to Cyprus on active service in 1974, he had been tasked with safeguarding the British base of Dhekelia following the Turkish offensive. To his dying day, he would hate the Turks and the Greeks. Had it not been for them, their tanks, and their guns, he would still have been in the army and probably would have reached the dizzying heights of colonel, brigadier, or even major general. One stray bullet in the leg was all it had taken to put paid to an auspicious career.

Discharged on medical grounds and with only his degree in physics to fall back on, William Rutherwood, turned to teaching. Bitter at the hand that he had been dealt, he set his sights on restoring himself to his former glory. He was born to be a leader, a commander of people, an officer. As a teacher, he demanded commitment from his pupils. It was results that mattered and results that got him noticed. The welfare of his pupils came a very poor second.

When offered the position of Headmaster of St John's College, a private boarding school, located not far from the town of Stroud in June '79, he accepted it with alacrity. At last, he would have his command again. It had pleased the school governors to find a man that would lead from the front, instilling discipline in teachers and pupils alike. It would be his task, they said, to eradicate the previous incumbent's proclivity for freedom of speech and freedom of choice. It was manna made from heaven.

It was he who had laid down the conditions for his appointment, not the governors. If they wished him to turn this school around, he must have complete freedom to select his staff and dismiss others whom he believed to be lacking in some respect: in fibre, in that all-important quality of self-discipline, in the ability to instil discipline in others. Salaries would be set by him alone. He would expect to be well recompensed for his work, including a significant bonus at the end of each academic year. He would not welcome interference from any of them. In return, he would deliver academic excellence and turn in an acceptable profit at the end of each school year. The governors had raised their eyebrows at his blatant demands. With a measure of reluctance, they had agreed to his terms and conditions with one exception. Vincent Palmer was to be retained as the head of mathematics. A brilliant mathematician, he was well respected in academic circles and by parents. Indeed, he was the reason that so many parents chose St John's College over other private schools.

The moment he set eyes on Vincent Palmer, he knew he was looking in the eyes of an adversary. A long-haired insolent individual who did not, and would never, know the meaning of discipline.

Within the month, he interviewed and assessed every member of staff. It surprised him to find the majority of teachers were reasonably competent, acquiescing without question to work under the new regime with a new set of rules and regulations. They were none of them young. There were two exceptions. The head of history, a free-thinker who strongly believed in allowing pupils to form their own views, was dismissed with a month's notice. Mr Ian Walker replaced him, a man Rutherwood knew and trusted. The head of English with equally liberal views chose to depart of his own accord rather than comply with new ways. Mr Brian Stanwell took his place; another man with whom he had worked in the past and with whom he shared common interests and values. Neither Walker nor Stanwell was married nor showed any signs of interest in women. Both good, solid men who knew the meaning of discipline.

Finally, Rutherwood added a new caretaker to his list of employees. Adrian Grzeskowiak.

Six

1985

Ahmed glanced up at Mr McMasters as they stood side by side at the floor-to-ceiling windows, watching the planes take off and land. Neither the airport nor the planes seemed to faze him.

"How are you feeling, Ahmed?" David asked. "A little nervous?"

"As though I've just stepped out of one century into another," Ahmed replied. "Am I really going in one of those? It's huge, bigger than a palace. That," he said, pointing to the Air India 747, "cannot possibly leave the ground and fly through the air."

"Look up in the sky, Ahmed. See those vapour trails. The same that you see every day. Each one is made by an aircraft as it rises into the sky, or descends to land, or simply passes through our airspace. It is the safest form of transport in the world. It is a simple matter of physics. You'll learn physics in your new school and then you'll understand."

Ahmed fought to find the words he wanted. "There is so much I don't know, Mr McMasters. So much I want to learn. This is a chance in a million, but it frightens me that I might fail – fail you and my benefactor."

"You won't fail either of us, Ahmed. The art is to keep each day in a watertight compartment. Deal with one day at a time. Your first and immediate challenge is to get yourself to England. You will change planes in Delhi. A ground stewardess will be there to guide you to your next flight, which will be direct to London Heathrow. What time is it now?"

Ahmed looked at the watch Mr McMasters had given him as a parting gift. 'This watch,' he had said, 'will be your best friend. You will be expected to be on time. All the time.' In Jaipur, the ever-present sun had been his timekeeper; he had had need of no other. "It is eight of the clock," Ahmed replied, checking the small hand and then the big hand.

"It is eight o'clock, Ahmed. That is the way you will speak of the time in England. And what day is it?"

"Sunday," Ahmed replied, marvelling that such a small timepiece could tell him the day of the week, the date, and the time.

"You'll arrive in London at about ten fifteen tomorrow, Monday, morning. The time difference between London and Delhi is five hours, thirty minutes. So you'll arrive earlier than you would otherwise expect. When you come out of the airport, you will be met by a driver who will take you to the school. All that clear, old chap?"

Ahmed took a deep breath. Nothing was clear. "Yes, Mr McMasters, quite clear, and thank you."

* * *

Ahmed squeezed his eyes tight shut. The engines roared and the plane gained speed before the nose lifted and slowly but surely rose in the air, levelled out, and purred her way through the skies high above the clouds. The whole journey was one awesome experience after another. First food and then drinks, then more food and more drinks, all the while mesmerized by the small TV screen on the back of the seat in front. He had been invited to visit the cockpit and sit alongside the captain. He had watched disbelievingly through the window as the plane crossed oceans and traversed the world below as if by magic. Armed with the documents Mr McMasters had given him before he left, Ahmed had presented his passport at immigration as he'd been instructed and, word perfect, answered the questions asked by the uniformed official. He had found his own suitcase on moving platforms that they called carousels, both at Delhi and then again at London Heathrow. He had passed through 'the green' at customs, just as Mr McMasters had told him. Mentally and physically exhausted, he carried his suitcase out into the arrivals lounge and looked out for the sign, 'Ahmed Singh, St John's College'.

* * *

It was two and a half hours before he noticed the signpost. The driver left the motorway at Junction 13 and veered right towards a place called Stroud.

It had yet to sink in that he, Ahmed Singh, had been singled out for an education in England and had just flown halfway across the world. It had rained constantly since they left the airport. In all his twelve years, he had never seen so much rain. When the rains came in July and August in Jaipur, it was cause for celebration. Here there was no sun. He had left it behind. The sky was grey. Angry black clouds raced across the sky, stopping only to alleviate themselves of their load.

The school, St John's College, so Mr McMasters had told him, was in the county of Gloucestershire. Three miles outside a town called Stroud and set in its own grounds. It was, he had said, one of the most beautiful counties in England, boasting an area of natural beauty called the Cotswolds, where villages of ancient yellow stone buildings and thatched cottages dotted the countryside. It was not far from McMasters' hometown of Cheltenham. Ahmed had painted a picture of it in his mind.

He was not at all sure that he liked what he had seen of England so far. The land was green, just as Mr Hathaway and others had described it, but not that emerald green that he had been led to believe. Trees, skeletal and bare of leaves, crowded hills and valleys and lined roadsides. Hedges divided expanses of grass and brown soil. Cows grazed in the grassy enclosed fields; their freedom denied. Everywhere there were warning signs. Keep left, keep right, stop, bend ahead, do not overtake. There were rules for everything. Was this the land of the free that Mr McMasters and the tourists spoke so highly of? Maybe it was the land of plenty as he had been told, where its people had opportunities, jobs, brick-built homes, a health service, and free education, but there were no palaces, at least none that he had seen. Ahmed set aside his doubts.

Shivering, he picked up his new brown leather satchel and stepped out of the car. A bitter wind threatened to blow him off his feet as he lifted his suitcase out of the boot. His eyes watered in the wind and with the memory of Jaipur. Momentarily, he wished he were back there, standing at the gates of the Rambagh, excited at what the day might bring.

Jaipur seemed so far away, so very far away.

"In there," the driver said, pointing to a forbidding-looking Gothic-style door. He was a man of few words. These were the first words he had spoken since the airport, other than that the time in England was then 11.00 a.m. and that he should now put his watch back. Ahmed recalled Mr McMasters' words of wisdom. 'Speak when you are spoken to and you'll not go far wrong.' Did nobody speak until they were spoken to? If that were the case, then how did anyone ever converse in this strange land?

Fighting against the wind and rain, Ahmed pulled down his cap and trundled his case towards the door. Tired, dismayed by everything he had seen so far, he stood back and took a deep breath. There was no going back now. This was it.

Leaking puddles on the polished oak floor, Ahmed glanced around at the stained-glass windows set high in the far wall, the dark wood panelling that surrounded the room, and the wide staircase that swept up towards a second level, and said nothing.

"Has the cat got your tongue?" a bespectacled woman wearing a tweed jacket over a cardigan over a jumper snapped, looking up at him from a desk. She was old, her face lined, her grey hair drawn back in a severe bun.

It was another expression he had not heard before, but the gist was clear. "No, ma'am. I was told to speak when I was spoken to. Did I get that wrong?" Ahmed replied politely.

"We'll have less of that cheek for a start, young man. Take those damned shoes off and hang that wretched coat up over there, and then come over here," she said, pointing to a row of coat hooks high up on the wall, under which a tray had been strategically placed, too late, to prevent the puddles he had already created. It was no hardship to rid himself of the already sodden woollen coat or the brown brogues that he hated with a passion. A fleeting moment of well-being followed as the weight on his shoulders and the lead on his feet were no more. Returning to the desk, he removed his cap in deference to the lady – another tip that Mr McMasters had given him.

"Singh, I presume? Couldn't be anybody else, the colour of your skin. Indian, aren't you? Well, you're the first. We've never had an Indian in this school before. I sometimes wonder what it is all coming to. But now you're here, I suppose we will have to make the best of it."

"Ahmed Singh, ma'am. My home is in Jaipur, in India. It is a very beautiful city," Ahmed said.

"No Christian names here, young man. You'll be known as Singh and nothing else. Behave yourself or we'll send you straight back." Ahmed was sorely tempted. But there was Mr McMasters and his benefactor to consider. He couldn't and wouldn't let them down. It was a matter of honour. "Sit," she said, pointing to a wooden bench beside the door. "I will inform the Head that you have arrived."

Ahmed sat down, crossed his legs, and looked longingly at the woollen coat that now hung on one of the coat hooks. A cold draught blew in under the door. He shivered and reluctantly wished that his feet were still in his new shoes. His eyes closed and his chin dropped onto his chest, as he finally gave way to sleep.

* * *

"Singh, wake up, boy," a voice bellowed in his ear. "Follow me. Shoes on. Bring that case and coat with you."

Ahmed stood to attention, found his shoes, slipped them on his feet, and fumbled with the laces. He had yet to learn how to tie a bow. "Yes, sir," he said automatically. So this was the Headmaster, yet another man of few words. Tall and broad, he wore a dark brown double-breasted suit with a white collared shirt and tie, under a black flowing gown. His feet were clad in brown brogues not dissimilar to those that he wore himself, but a hundred sizes larger. Struggling to keep up, Ahmed followed him down a long corridor. Either side were rooms with strange names on them: The Chalford, The Dursley, The Nailsworth, the Stonehouse, The Woodchester...Inside each sat rows of boys, silent, their eyes trained on a blackboard at the front of the room and their pens poised. The classrooms, Ahmed quickly realized.

A brass plaque on the door ahead announced to the world that this was the domain of Mr Rutherwood, the Headmaster. Ahmed glanced at the floor-to-ceiling bookshelves that covered the walls around the room. His eye caught the almost threadbare Indian rug that all but covered the polished floor and he was tempted to smile, remembering how often he had steered his tourists away from the rug makers who were eager to part them from their money. A huge map of the world hung over the oak fireplace in which glowed the coals of an electric fire which flickered in the darkening afternoon but emitted no heat. The room was as cold as charity and bleak. A large mahogany desk cleared but for a telephone, the leather desk chair behind it, and a small wooden chair with no arms were the only pieces of furniture in the room. The small chair was placed away from the desk in the far corner of the room, under one of the two leaded windows. Mr Rutherwood sat down. Ahmed stood in front of the desk.

"Stand up straight, boy. No slouching," he said.

"Yes, sir." Ahmed straightened his shoulders and looked straight ahead past the Headmaster to the rain which hammered on the window.

"You address me as Headmaster, Singh. I hope we will not be meeting in here too often," he said, pulling open a drawer in the desk and extracting a blue file. "I have to tell you that I had great reservations about accepting you into this school. We can't do with backwards boys here. I am, however, assured by your guardian, Mr McMasters, that you are of good stock and that you can at least read and write in English."

Ahmed kept his mouth firmly shut. Of good stock? Quite what did that mean? Cows, goats, and animals were described as of good stock – not men and boys.

"Well, speak up. I asked you a question."

"I'm sorry, Headmaster, I didn't realize it was a question. Yes, I speak, read and write English, and I am from good stock." He hoped it was the right answer. "I am also very good at maths."

"Are you indeed? We'll see about that. History, geography, physics, chemistry, biology, religious studies?"

"History, sir – the history of India," he replied. His mother's tuition had not stretched further than that.

"You will join the Nailchester class. It's for boys aged ten years old. Academically, that is your level, and you will stay there until you catch up in all subjects and prove me wrong—"

"But, sir, I am twelve years old. I'll soon be thirteen. Surely I should be with boys of my own age?"

"Insolence. You do not question anything I say to you.

My word is God, do you hear me?" he said, banging his fist down on the desk. "You will report to Mr Frobisher, your class teacher, at 9.00 a.m. precisely in the morning in The Nailchester."

Ahmed nodded. The conversation that had never started was over. Not a word of welcome, not a word of comfort to a boy who had just travelled from the other side of the world, not a word of encouragement. He had never met an Englishman like this before.

"Matron will show you to your dormitory. That is all."

Dismissed, Ahmed turned and left the room.

He had not expected a welcome committee, but neither had he expected his first encounter to be quite so daunting. The Headmaster had made it quite clear that he had been admitted to the school under sufferance, and that he would be made to pay for it. Matron strode out in front of him, uncaring of the boy who hadn't slept for the past only-God-knew how many hours, whose arms had grown three inches at least under the weight of his suitcase, and whose legs were ready to give way under him.

The dormitory was a soulless space with three metal-framed beds either side of the small room, each covered in a blue candlewick bedspread. Ahmed carefully unpacked his belongings into the small closet beside the bed. Tired and hungry, he climbed up on the strange bed raised high above the ground, lay down, buried his head in the pillow, and sobbed quietly to himself.

"Singh? Ahmed? I've got something for you," a voice said.

Ahmed turned his head towards the voice and almost smiled as the boy unwrapped a strange-looking slice of bread and handed it to him. It was his first taste of English bread and the first time he had tasted corned beef. "My name's Bright, but you can call me Ed."

Seven

1985

"Name?"

"Grzeskowiak, Adrian," he replied, tapping his fingers on the desk.

"Age?"

"Forty-eight," he replied. "It's all down there in that bleeding file. Why ask the same bleeding questions every time I come in 'ere?"

"It's my job," she replied. "And to put the record straight, it is not me who has asked you these questions in the past. Your case has been passed to me, and it's high time, Adrian, that we found you a job. Nationality?"

"British."

"With a name like that?"

"My old man was a Pole. Fought alongside your lot in the war. Me mam was English. I'm British."

"Address?"

"10, The Run, Polefields Estate – prefabs up Holly Lane."

"Have you lived there long?"

"What's that got to do with you, missus?" Adrian asked sharply. "I was born there, if you must know. Work it out for yourself. If you're going to ask me what it's like up there, it's shit. But none of us is going to move into them council 'ouses. Rubbish piled high outside every door, kids running riot, druggies. We're better off where we are."

"Sorry I asked," she said. "I have some sympathy with you. Now let's turn back to this matter in hand. You have been on the dole for the past six months. You have attended twelve interviews but have been unable to secure any of the jobs. Before that, you served as a street cleaner for the local council. Why did you leave that job?"

"Because, missus, no sooner did I clean the streets than some prat would throw 'is bloody chip papers on the ground right behind me. It were a waste of my bleeding time and a waste of the bleeding council's money. It got right up me nose so I cuffed one of them litterbugs, not 'ard, not 'ard enough. But he complained to the council, and I was out."

"I see," she replied. "I think I might have done the same thing, but don't tell anybody I said that. So, tell me, what is your preferred profession?"

"Cleaning, I just told you," he replied. "I like cleaning. And if the money's right and I ain't got to travel miles too far, I like me cleaning even more."

"Good. I think we have something that might be just up your street, if you will excuse the pun. There's a caretaker post at a school just three miles on the other side of Stroud, and before you ask, there is a regular bus service. I take it you have a bicycle, should you need it?"

Adrian nodded.

"I see there are no formal qualifications required. The applicant must simply be prepared to undertake light cleaning work, carry out simple maintenance work, and be prepared to assist in the gardens." She looked up at him. "I take it you can wield a hammer and use a screwdriver, Adrian? And that you know one end of a lawnmower from the other?"

"You do your own maintenance work up at the prefabs. The council ain't interested. We don't have no lawnmower and we don't have no grass, but who's going to know that?" Adrian replied, a smile spreading across his face.

"Nobody, Adrian. I shall tell nobody. As far as I am concerned, you are the ideal candidate. You will have an interview with Mr Rutherwood, the Headmaster, at 10.00 a.m. tomorrow morning. I will set it up. Don't get your hopes up too high. I've already had three good candidates turned down for the job. Why, I don't know. Best foot forward, Adrian."

* * *

Adrian sat on the doorstep of his prefab home, smoking a roll-up. Unusually, he was almost looking forward to the following day. Caretaker? Sounded posh. Step up in the world from cleaner.

Cleaning was what he knew about. Cleaning was what he did and did well. Didn't mind getting his hands dirty. He'd had no choice. Neither his mum nor dad had ever done any. If it had been left to them, the whole family would have lived in squalor and died of dysentery or some such thing. Books hadn't done anything for him. School had done even less. With cleaning, it was different. You started in a mess, and you worked your way through it until everything was back the way it should have been in the first place. It was satisfying. It gave you 'job satisfaction' as they called it. There was only so much cleaning you could do in a small prefab, and he was bored with cleaning for the sake of it. Adrian wanted a job and a reason for living.

* * *

"Name's Adrian Grzeskowiak. Up from the jobcentre," he said.

"Sit over there. I shall deal with you in a moment," a bespectacled woman wearing a tweed jacket over a cardigan over a jumper snapped. She muttered under her breath and otherwise ignored his presence.

"Repeat, my name is Adrian Grzeskowiak. Ten o'clock is the appointment and I ain't going to be late because some sourpuss like you tells me to wait."

"Caretaker job, no doubt," she said, looking up at him as though a bad smell had entered the building. "I very much doubt, Mr Grzeskowiak, that we shall be seeing you again."

"Mr Rutherwood. Headmaster," a voice boomed from across the hall. "Grzeskowiak, right? This way."

Surreptitiously pointing two fingers at the bespectacled woman behind the desk, Adrian picked up the old tweed cap that he had dug out especially for the appointment, and followed the Headmaster down a long corridor and into an office.

"CV?" Rutherwood said.

"C what?" Adrian replied calmly, rolling his eyes.

"Your CV, man, Curriculum Vitae," Rutherwood snapped. "It's Latin. The qualifications you achieved at school and your career history."

"Ah, that one," he said cheerfully. "Don't go in for them

things. No qualifications, no career history, ergo – that's a good word – no CV. I come 'ere for a cleaning – no, let me correct that – the caretaker job. Since when 'as a cleaner got to know Latin? Ain't no bleeding good to you when you're cleaning, now is it?"

"Then your last job, Mr Grzeskowiak?"

"Cleaner, street cleaner. Little bastards kept throwing litter down right after I'd cleaned the streets. Let's just say we 'ad a reckoning and I left."

Rutherwood smiled. The man was beginning to tick the boxes. Not too intelligent, if intelligent at all. Not fond of children, particularly those who disobeyed the rules. Not afraid to wade in when circumstances warranted intervention.

"Family?"

"Dead and buried. No wife, no kids."

"Hobbies?"

"Chess, I play meself."

"I'm looking for a man who doesn't mind getting his hands dirty. There'll be some light cleaning to do – boys' toilets and showers, corridors, classrooms, dormitories, et cetera. Simple repairs and maintenance. Some minor works in the gardens, assisting the full-time gardener, but only rarely will that be necessary. And you'd have responsibility for security throughout the school. We have a CCTV system which operates at all hours. You'd be instructed in how the security system works. Can you do that?"

Adrian raised his eyebrows and nodded. It sounded very much like he had just been offered a job. "Don't sound like rocket science."

51

"There's accommodation thrown in. You'll live on-site. Keepers Cottage. That is a condition of the job. It's a six-days-a-week job. You'll get two days off each fortnight. You'll be paid four hundred pounds a month and your accommodation and food will be found for you, free of charge."

Adrian sat back and scratched the stubble on his chin. Sounded too good to be true. There would be a catch. There was always a catch. "What's the catch, gaffer?"

"You call me Headmaster. I am not your gaffer," Rutherwood snapped. "There is no catch. If you do your job well and I am satisfied with your performance, there's the possibility of an annual bonus. You will understand that I demand absolute loyalty from my staff. If I say jump, you jump. If I say jump higher, you jump higher. If I ask you to undertake specific small tasks for me, you will do them, with no questions asked. I run a tight ship. I don't hesitate to hire and fire. And no students are to be allowed in your home."

There was no way that he would ever get to like this man, but, hell, he wasn't going to marry him. Jobs like this didn't come along every day. No rent on the prefab, no travelling expenses, no bills, food chucked in, and time off that he wouldn't know what to do with if he had it. But he hadn't missed that bit thrown in about doing things, no questions asked. Keep his nose clean and he was laughing all the way to the bank. For that sort of package, he'd be happy to jump over a mountain.

Rutherwood neither expected a reply nor waited for one. "You will start at the end of the month. I assume you can get yourself moved in by then. Take it or leave it. I don't have time to discuss it further."

Grzeskowiak took it.

Eight

1985

"Come in. I'm not bloody well going to open the door for you," Vincent yelled. "Damn and blast." He swore as the ash from his cigarette fell onto a drop of wet ink.

Ahmed gingerly turned the handle, opened the door a fraction, and stuck his head around the door.

"Well, don't just stand there. You're letting the cold in, boy. Shut that bloody door. Plonk yourself on the bed. Sorry about the mess. Not enough room to swing a cat in this place."

His back turned away from the door. Vincent Palmer sat hunched over a desk, a cloud of smoke drifting up towards the ceiling where it hung in a bluish, grey cloud. Ahmed coughed. "If you don't like the smoke then open the bloody window. It goes with the territory, Singh. No fags all day, so I have to build up vitamin N in the evenings. Do you want one?" Vincent turned and studied him. The boy looked uncomfortable, worried, as though he were about to go up against a firing squad. "It was a joke, Singh. I really don't encourage boys to smoke. Bad habit. Call me Vincent. I've had my eye on you."

"Yes, Mr Palmer. I mean no, Mr Palmer. I mean, I don't

smoke." Ahmed stuttered, taking a deep breath, trying not to choke.

"Vincent, spelt V I N C E N T."

"Vincent," Ahmed whispered.

"Right. I'll just finish marking this book and then we'll get down to business, and will you stop looking so glum? Anyone would think I was going to eat you. Come on. Lighten up, Ahmed. This is going to be fun. Say after me: This is going to be fun."

Ahmed had never met anybody quite like him. With long blond hair falling across his eyes and resting on his shoulders, he looked like one of the hippies that his mother had told him about.

Vincent got up and sat down on the bed beside Ahmed. "Finished. Last of the marking for tonight. Some of these boys haven't got a brain cell between them. Plenty of money but no brains...Okay, Ahmed. Why don't you think that we're going to have fun? Spill the beans. What's going on in that little head of yours?"

"Nothing, Mr Palmer, Vincent. Nothing at all." It was not a subject he had ever expected to come up. He was quite unprepared to start a conversation about it with a man – a teacher – he hardly knew. "It's just that some of the boys, some of the boys..." Ahmed stumbled over his words. He couldn't say it out loud, not to himself and not to anybody else.

"Boys been talking, have they? Rascals. I'll skin the lot of them, and I know who I'll start with. How old are you, Ahmed?"

"Thirteen, just. A few days ago."

"Well, you're old enough to know about the birds and the bees, then. They tell you that I'm gay – I prefer men to women?

You don't need to answer that. It's written all over your face. Well, look, Ahmed, it may be frowned upon – even a hanging matter where you come from – but here it is legal. Men with men, women with women, man with woman, woman with man. Take your choice. Some of us are made that way. It's God's way. Well, maybe God wouldn't approve either, but it happens. We don't choose our sexuality, but we live with it and make the best of it. Any questions?"

Ahmed shuffled his bottom on the bed and bit his lip. He understood the basics as well as any other thirteen-year-old, but it was the first time he had come face to face with – and was sitting no more than six feet away from – a man who openly admitted he was gay. What his mother would have thought about it didn't bear thinking about.

"Look, Ahmed, I'm interested in your brain, not your body, and just for the record, I don't do kids anyway. That's called paedophilia and I'm not one of those. I'd shoot the lot of them if I could catch them. So shall we get to business?"

"Yes, Mr Palmer."

"Vincent. Spelt V I N C E N T. Last time! Where'd you learn maths, Ahmed?"

"My mother taught me, and I needed it for my business," Ahmed replied.

Vincent laughed. "Get you! And what business was that, young man?"

"I'm a tour guide back home. I show visitors around my city, Jaipur. I have contacts and I negotiate the best deals for everything. None of my tourists has ever paid over the odds for anything."

"Negotiator, as well, then. Mummy and Daddy got plenty of money then? Must have to send you halfway across the world to a private school."

"My mother died last year. My father died not long after I was born. We were poor but happy. I have a benefactor."

"That's a first, son. Plenty of kids with silver spoons come here. But a benefactor...Well, that's a new one. Nice guy, is he?"

"I don't know. I've never met him. I don't even know his name," Ahmed said. He didn't add that he had his suspicions. He could neither prove nor rationalize them. And he knew that Vincent would latch onto anything he said and dig for more, of which there was little or none to tell.

"You must know, Ahmed. Who pays the bills? Who are they going to send your reports to? Must be someone out there interested in what they're getting for their money."

"A man called David McMasters, my legal guardian, pays the bills on behalf of my benefactor. That's all I know."

"Straight talking. That's good. Sorry about your mum and dad. Tough. You and me, we're going to get on just fine. Want to know why you're here?" Vincent asked, putting his arm around Ahmed's shoulders. "You're here because you're a bloody genius or you're going to be. Bloody Rutherwood. Sticking you in a class with ten-year-olds. Me and the school guvnors get on pretty well. I soon told Rutherwood what would happen if he didn't change his mind about that. You've got a quick brain. You don't just add up figures, you see a problem in your head, you analyse it, and you see the answer – no pen. Don't often meet kids like you. Ed's not bad, but you'll leave him standing. Colin – well, he's pretty smart, too, but you, well, you're Cambridge material and I'm not often wrong."

"Cambridge?" Ahmed asked. "What's Cambridge?"

"The best bloody university in England. Only the crème de la crème are offered a place there. That's where I did my degree. Churns out mathematicians, scientists, chemists, doctors, physicists, politicians even. Graduate from Cambridge and the world is your oyster, young man. Anyway, less of this chatter. For the second time, let's get down to business. First, I need to assess where you're at with your maths. If you're where I think you are, we'll get stuck into applied maths straight away. You'll come over here twice weekly. Tuesday and Thursday, five to six. Okay?"

Ahmed nodded uncertainly, not at all sure that he could aspire to Mr Palmer's expectations, nor that he liked the sound of this applied mathematics.

"Right, I've written out some exercises. I want you to do them now." Vincent thrust a printed sheet towards him.

"Do you have a pen, please, Vincent?"

"No pen, Ahmed. Use your brain. I'll ask you to give me the answers verbally. You've got ten minutes to run through them and then I'll expect the answers."

Ahmed looked down through the list and concentrated on the first. And then the second, and the third, until finally he looked up and breathed a sigh of relief.

"Answers?" Vincent said.

Ahmed closed his eyes, recalling each of the answers.

"Not bad. Not bad at all. The first – wrong, but I can see you thought it through. We'll start on Thursday. Five o'clock and don't be late. Now, off with you," Vincent said.

"Thank you, Mr Palmer," Ahmed said without thinking.

"V I N C E N T. Mr Palmer in class, V I N C E N T here!"

Nine

1985

"Griffiths?"

"Sir."

"Hunter?"

"Sir."

"Singh?" Vincent looked up from the register. "Singh? Am I talking to myself?" Ahmed started and quickly closed the book he was reading. "Singh, you're in my form now and what do we do first thing every morning?"

"Register, sir, and school notices. Sorry, sir," Ahmed replied.

"Correct, Singh. That is unless you want me to get booted out of this school. It's a bore, but it's the rules."

"Bright?"

"Sir."

"Reed?"

Vincent pushed his hair back behind his ears and looked around the room. "Where's Reed?"

"Probably sulking, sir," Bright said. "He was in detention last night."

"Reed? Detention? Reed never gets detention. He wouldn't know how to get detention. It's as unlikely as this school ever winning the schools' rugby league. No, it's even more unlikely. Which one of you lot is in his dorm?"

"Me, sir." Hunter held up his arm.

"Right, Hunter. You go down there this minute and get the stupid little sod out of bed," Vincent said. "Now."

"I don't think he's there, sir. I didn't see him this morning," Hunter said.

"He'll be there," Vincent said. "Go, and straight back."

The register completed, and the notices delivered, Vincent turned towards the blackboard. "Algebra today. One whole hour of it."

* * *

"He's not in the dorm, sir," Hunter said, breathlessly. "And all his stuff's gone."

"What stuff?" Vincent asked.

"The photographs of his parents and brother that he always keeps on his bedside table – they're not there anymore and I looked in his locker. It's empty," Hunter confirmed.

Vincent narrowed his eyes, picked up the chalk, and turned back towards the board. His mind elsewhere, he chalked up four equations, all of which were too advanced for the class but would keep them occupied while he was gone. "You've got ten minutes to work through these. When I get back, I'll expect you to have the answers."

With his gown billowing behind him, Vincent strode out of the classroom, along the corridor, through the Great Hall, and, without knocking, barged straight into the Headmaster's office.

"I'm here to report a missing boy," Vincent said. "Reed."

"Your manners leave a great deal to be desired, Mr Palmer." Rutherwood looked up with an air of contempt. "Nobody enters my study without knocking or having first made an appointment. Please see my secretary and I will see if I can fit you in today."

"Damn your appointments," Vincent began. "I'm here to report a missing boy. He's a no-show in my form this morning. And I'm reliably informed he's not in his dorm and neither are his possessions. As his form teacher, I demand to know what is going on. I have a right to be told."

"You have no rights, Mr Palmer. Let me make that clear. When it comes to decisions affecting this school, then I, and I alone, make those decisions. I do not need your interference. But since you are so concerned about him, Reed is no longer a pupil at this school. He has been taken home and will not be returning here..."

"And would you care to explain to me why Reed has been taken home?" Vincent was close to losing control.

"Certainly. He was seen running down the corridor, caught by Mr Stanwell, and given detention. Later, he proceeded to use threatening behaviour towards Mr Stanwell. I will not condone such behaviour," Rutherwood said, poker-faced. "After discussing the matter with Mr Stanwell, I asked him to drive Reed home."

"Are we talking about the same kid? Reed never breaks the rules. What sort of threatening behaviour? Did he blow him a kiss or something?"

"That is none of your business, Mr Palmer."

"You're unbelievable, Rutherwood."

"Headmaster or Mr Rutherwood, if you please. You may have the school governors under your thumb, but it does not give you the right to be insolent. We cannot and will not condone assault in this school."

Vincent glanced sideways at the small wooden chair and the cane that lay on top of it. So it was okay for Rutherwood to assault the boys, but not okay for the boys to assault a member of staff. "Assaulted?" he said sarcastically. "Stanwell's sixteen stone and that boy's six stone, if that. He couldn't assault a fly."

"I think this discussion is at an end, Mr Palmer. I presume you have a class to return to. And if you wish to share the news of Reed's departure with the form, you will tell them that Mr and Mrs Reed decided they preferred Colin to attend a day school nearer home. No more and no less. You will toe the party line, Mr Palmer. I will not tolerate bad publicity for the school. Good day."

* * *

Vincent sat on the step outside the Great Hall and lit up. It was forbidden, but right at that moment, he didn't care. It was that or go straight down to drag Stanwell out of his classroom and demand an explanation. Chain-smoking, he went over and over it in his mind. Anyone but Reed, if it had been anyone but Reed, he might have understood it, but Reed? Hardworking and diligent, he never got into fights, turning a blind eye. Bullied regularly by some of the seniors, he had long since learnt not to give them the satisfaction. Reed was one of those kids who smiled his way through life, let nothing get him down, and…religiously followed the rules.

Vincent stubbed out his third cigarette, defiantly leaving the three butts on the step, and returned to the classroom. He made a mental note to speak to Colin, if only to wish him luck.

* * *

"Mr Reed? Vincent Palmer speaking. I hope you won't mind me ringing. I was Colin's maths teacher at St John's. We got on well. I liked him. Bright lad. Miss his cheery face about the place. Could I have a quick word with him, just to say hello?"

A deathly silence hung in the air. Vincent sensed something was wrong, very wrong.

"Colin passed on two days after he returned from your school." Vincent heard the words from afar as if in a dream. "Are you still there, Mr Palmer? Colin spoke of you often. Kindly, I hasten to add. It's good of you to ring."

"Why? How?" Vincent stuttered, reaching for his cigarettes. "I'm sorry. I'm imposing on you in a time of grief. Please accept my condolences. Oh, Christ Almighty."

"The how, Mr Palmer, is quite simple. He went for a walk and jumped off the top of a cliff. He might have fallen by accident, but I doubt it. He knew the cliff path too well. You'll forgive me if I sound quite calm about it. Don't misinterpret me, Mr Palmer. The more I repeat it, the more I come to believe that he has gone and won't be returning."

"You mean"—Vincent dared hardly utter the word—"suicide?"

"I'm afraid so. Coming on to your why, that is a question to which we will never have the answer. I know my son, Mr Palmer. He was not aggressive, never lost his temper, whatever they might have said. Why he was sent down I will never know."

63

"Did you ask him? Sorry, of course you did. I'm not thinking straight. It's just not going in." Vincent bumbled on.

"It wasn't quite that easy, Mr Palmer. He never spoke again from the moment he arrived home until the day he killed himself. The verdict was that he was suffering from severe depression, anxiety – school was getting on top of him."

Rutherwood's words echoed in his ears: 'You will toe the party line, Palmer.' "I didn't notice. Perhaps I should have done. I can't find the words to say how sorry I am." Vincent heard the words come out of his mouth and almost choked on them. "May I ask when the funeral will take place?"

* * *

Dressed in a black suit and tie, he had tied his hair back for the occasion. Somehow it felt more respectful. Vincent stood at the back of the crematorium, along with twenty or more other mourners. The crem was full, every seat taken, and silent as a graveyard. Keeping a respectful distance, he had followed family and friends into the hall, relieved to see that the coffin had already been placed on the catafalque. On top of the coffin lay an arrangement of red roses made in the shape of a cricket bat. Colin loved his cricket even though he spent most of the time standing on the side-lines. Alongside the bat lay his school cap and a portrait photograph of him proudly wearing his school uniform.

Mr Reed read the eulogy to a son who had his whole life in front of him, to a son of whom he could not have been prouder. It was moving beyond words. His means of passing was not referred to. It was common knowledge. No one understood. It was a simple but touching service. The coffin slid quietly through the curtains as everyone said their goodbyes.

Invited to go back to the family estate for drinks and food, Vincent quietly and politely declined. He had other things on his mind, not least why Rutherwood had not bothered to represent the school on the day, or even tell him about the funeral.

Ten

1985

"Are you concentrating, or are you counting the birds out of that window?" Vincent demanded. "You haven't got one answer right so far and your homework was piss-poor. What's got into you, Ahmed?"

Tempted to tell Vincent the window was so dirty it was impossible to see anything through them, let alone count the birds, Ahmed kept his mouth shut. His thoughts were miles away. And he'd hardly spent any time on his homework. Vincent was right on both counts. "I miss them, Vincent. We were good together. Now...seems like I don't have any friends anymore. Colin and now Ed." It was just four weeks since Vincent had broken the news to him about Colin. He'd never understand it – fit and healthy one day, the next, dead. Deep down he knew Vincent was holding something back, not telling him the whole truth. "He shouldn't have been expelled."

"I know that and so does every other bugger in their right mind – excuse my language." Vincent exploded. "I don't trust that man. No, I'll rephrase that. He makes my blood boil. Rutherwood, I mean. Headmaster to you. Cold bloody fish.

Not an ounce of sympathy, empathy, call it what you like. How people like him ever get to run a school, I'll never know. Bloody imbeciles, the lot of them. Second chance? He doesn't know the meaning of second chance. So long as the reputation of his bloody school isn't besmirched by the boys who pay a bloody fortune to attend in the first place, he's happy." Vincent ranted on, his eyes blazing. "Sorry, didn't mean to take it out on you. I know, you and Ed were pretty thick. You're going to miss him, and so shall I. Not the mathematical genius that you are but bloody good all the same."

Instinctively Vincent knew that Ed was no thief. If there were ever a more mild-mannered lad, he had yet to meet him. Curly ginger hair, freckled face and most definitely small for his age, Ed was another sitting target for the bullies. At least he had been up until the time when he, Colin, and Ahmed had joined forces, an unlikely trio, but it worked. Tall for his age, Ahmed towered over Ed and Colin. Streetwise, Ahmed watched out for both of them. Thoughts drifting back to Colin, Vincent made a mental note to ring Ed's parents, praying that this one hadn't done anything stupid.

"He didn't steal, Vincent. Ed doesn't steal. That money they found in his locker, somebody must have put it there. On Thursday, he didn't even have enough money to buy any sweets from the tuck shop, let alone twenty pounds. And we were together all day Friday."

"I believe you, Ahmed." Vincent waved his arms in the air. "I've already been to see Rutherwood about it, tried to get the decision reversed. He wasn't having any of it. According to Rutherwood, money was stolen from Walker's jacket pocket when he left it hanging over his chair in the classroom. According to Walker, he left his jacket there at the end of class, leaving Ed to wipe the blackboard clean."

"I remember. He had it in for Ed that day," Ahmed said. "He couldn't do anything right."

"It was late Thursday evening, just before lights out," Ahmed continued. "They came and searched all our lockers. They found the money in Ed's blazer pocket in his locker. He was as surprised as anybody. You should have seen him, Vincent. He was terrified."

"Who's they?" Vincent shot back.

"Mr Stanwell and Mr Walker. Told him to get dressed and took him away. He was crying, Vincent," Ahmed said, his eyes glazing over. "He didn't come back that night. I stayed awake as long as I could and waited."

"Look, Ahmed, I don't like this any more than you do. I've done all I can, so, right now I need you to do me a favour: keep your thoughts to yourself. If you want to sound off, then I'm here. Otherwise keep it zipped. Keep your head down and stay out of trouble. It's for your own good."

"There's something bad going on, isn't there?" Ahmed probed; he had never seen Vincent so agitated.

"Nothing for you to worry your head about," Vincent said. "But if you want to help, then there something I need you to do for me, Ahmed, no questions asked. It's important." He'd thought about it. Thought hard about it. The last thing he wanted to do was to get Ahmed in deep water and end up going the same way as Colin and Ed. If he did it himself, it would arouse suspicion. Ahmed was more likely to get away with it. "How well do you get on with Grzeskowiak?"

"The caretaker? I try my best to avoid him like everyone else," Ahmed replied. "Why?"

"The very same. Well, what I want you to do is to start getting on with him really well. He's a loner. Works during the day, canteen at six, scoffs his supper, back to Keepers Cottage by six-thirty, regular as clockwork. No visitors as far as I know. Nobody."

"Why would I do that? He gives me the creeps," Ahmed said.

"No questions, Ahmed. Isn't that what I just said. The less you know, the better. Trust me. Just do it for me, for Colin, and Ed," Vincent added as an afterthought. "Make friends with him. Get him to trust you. Get inside that bunker of his. Use your eyes. Photograph it in your head. I want to know everything about the inside of Keepers Cottage. Every single detail. Use your brains, Ahmed. You've plenty of them. Report back to me, and I'll take it from there," Vincent said.

"Is it important? Something to do with Colin and Ed?" Ahmed asked.

"No questions. And if you get into Keepers, make sure nobody else knows about it. Take your time. Don't rush it," Vincent replied.

"Okay. There's something I need you to do for me too, Vincent." Ahmed bent down, reached for his school satchel, and unbuckled it.

"Ask away. One good turn deserves another. I'm sure it won't be too difficult."

"It's this. I need you to take care of it for me," he said, unwrapping a small parcel.

Vincent's eyes widened. If the boy had produced a brass jug, rubbed it, and Aladdin's genie had appeared, he couldn't have been more flabbergasted. "What the hell? Where in God's name did you get that?"

"It was my mother's, and her father's before her. She wanted me to have it, to keep me safe. I brought it with me from Jaipur. It's the only thing that I have of hers," Ahmed said.

"You carried that in your suitcase all the way from Jaipur? Are you crazy? It's a wonder they didn't lock you up and throw away the key. Or at the very least, put you straight back on a plane. And if they found that thing here in the school, you'd be back on that plane quicker than you could say Jack Robinson. And you want me to take care of it? You're not serious?"

"Deadly serious, Vincent. I've had it hidden under my mattress since I arrived back in January. Now they're searching lockers. Next it will be under the mattresses. If they find it, they'll confiscate it. I might never see it again. And then I'll be, as you say, right back on that plane to India. I can't let that happen."

"If they find it in here, they'll bloody well confiscate it as well and, no doubt, give me my marching orders to boot." Vincent rolled his eyes.

"So, you won't?" Ahmed picked up the parcel ready to stow it back in his satchel. "Then I'll have to take my chances."

"Jesus, as if I haven't got enough problems already."

"It's okay. I just thought it was worth asking," Ahmed said.

"There's never a dull moment with you around, young man. You're right – one good turn deserves another. I must need my head testing, but, yes, I'll keep it safe for you. It so happens that there is somewhere here where nobody will find it. And I'm not even going to tell you where I put it! You'll be the death of me, boy! Right, Grzeskowiak, Ahmed. Put your thinking cap on, and get on with it, and for God's sake, keep it under your hat."

Eleven

1985

He stood out in the crowd. Tall, broad-shouldered, and well-presented with a head of thick, glossy black hair that curled onto his shoulders, he exuded a rare aura of confidence. He had been drawn to him like a magnet. Their eyes met for a matter of seconds and he knew. Freshers, they were both trying to find their place in a new society and on the lookout for like-minded people with whom they might hang out. Vincent bided his time.

Vincent – medium height, slight frame, with long blond hair. They were an unlikely pair but they were rarely seen apart outside of tutorials. Trusting one another implicitly, it was a friendship that grew and that both knew would endure long after university. Harbouring silent and unspoken thoughts that one day that friendship might mature into a more intimate relationship, Vincent waited for Garry to make the first move. It happened on the last day of the last term at uni. The following day they would be going their own ways. It was a kiss that Vincent would never forget, a kiss that cemented their friendship forever, but a kiss that was never to be repeated. He was straight, he said. In the career he had

71

chosen for himself, there was no other way.

Astute, intelligent, handsome, and with a personality that drew others to him like a moth to a candle, Garry had shot up the ranks. Becoming Detective Chief Superintendent by the age of thirty-five, he was the youngest ever to reach that rank. A person of note in the county of Gloucestershire, he was rarely out of the headlines for his good deeds, particularly those of his initiatives aimed at keeping kids out of trouble and out of youth custody centres. A strong believer that prevention was better than cure, he made it his business to visit the local schools on a regular basis. The kids lapped up his visual descriptions of life on the street; lives controlled by drugs or alcohol, and lives ruined by violence. Parents and kids alike worshipped the very ground he walked on. Schools sought him out as the perfect school governor. St John's was one of those schools.

And he never forgot a friend.

Vincent was well aware he owed him. Twice Garry had bailed him out. When he had lost his temper in a pub and hit out, Garry had intervened on his behalf, poured oil on troubled water, and managed to get the case dropped and the paperwork to disappear. If it had come out, then his job at St John's would have been on the line. He had learnt to walk away when he overheard snide remarks about his sexuality, let it go right over his head, held his temper.

The second occasion might have been even more disastrous, but Garry understood and sympathized. He had been more careful after that – careful about who he approached and where he approached them.

He was late, but that wasn't unusual. Work always came first with Garry. If something cropped up at the station, then all else fell by the wayside.

Vincent blew the froth off the top of his pint and went over it all in his mind. Was he overreacting? Was he putting two and two together and making five? Or was he just totally pissed off with the whole lot of them and needing to find somebody to blame instead of himself? More to the point, what proof did he have? Sod all, if the truth were told. Where there's smoke, there's fire, he told himself. Two boys. Both well-grounded kids. Two pretty bright kids. Thirteen years of age, normal kids in every other way. Here today, gone tomorrow.

It was crazy, he knew that, but he was just one of those guys who felt responsible for everything and everybody.

"Pint?" Garry slapped him on the back.

Vincent looked up and grinned. "Half. Don't want your lot breathalysing me in the car park."

"So, how's the wife and kids, mate?" Vincent asked.

"Great, just wish they saw a bit more of me," Garry replied. "Look, Vinnie, I haven't got long. Promised I'd be back early tonight. One pint and then I have to be off. You said there was something you wanted to chew over with me."

Vincent frowned and nodded. "Look, I reckon something is going on in the school. You'll probably think I'm being ridiculous as usual..." Vincent slowly recounted the events of the past couple of months. With a grave expression on his face, Garry sipped his pint, and listened.

"What evidence?" Garry drained his glass and waited.

"None. It's a hunch. A strong hunch. But I'm sure I'm right.

There's a pattern. Once okay, well not okay, if you see what I mean. Twice, I don't buy it. That kid, Colin Reed, didn't jump off a cliff to find out how quickly he'd land on the rocks. That kid, Ed Bright, didn't get expelled for stealing anything no matter what Walker might have said. I don't trust that man and I don't trust Stanwell either. They're creeps. Bootlickers, that's what they are. So now you can see why I'm thinking this way."

"Have you spoken to anybody else about this?" Garry asked.

"No," Vincent said. "I trust you. No one else."

"You've spoken to the parents, you say?" Garry probed.

"Reed's parents, yes. Ed's not yet. It's on my list. Can't see it will do any good. Their son's been accused of stealing and the evidence was there. Sir Edward Bright will just want to bury it and keep quiet about it. Maybe I'll call them. I don't know. I wanted to talk to you first. All Reed's parents want to do is mourn their dead son. I went to the funeral. For God's sake, don't mention it to Rutherwood if you bump into him. The bastard didn't even show up."

"So, you haven't spoken to any of the other teachers either? And I'm guessing you won't have mentioned your suspicions to Rutherwood?" Garry raised his eyebrows.

"You think I've got a death wish, Garry?" Vincent laughed. "I just told you, I don't trust any of them as far as I could throw them. Especially Rutherwood – that lump of ice. No. No point. Until I know what's going on, I'm not about to go round asking questions."

"And if you're wrong?" Garry raised his eyebrows again.

"I'm not wrong, Garry. You need to get in there and start asking questions before it's too late and another boy gets hurt, maybe even dies."

Garry stretched out his legs, looking deep into his empty pint glass, and stroked his chin. "Vinnie, you know that you're far too sensitive sometimes," he stated softly. "You always have been. You get too involved with the boys. It's not healthy. You need to back off a bit before you get yourself into trouble. And that's what will happen if you pursue this line of thinking. I'd like to help, but I really don't see what I can do about it. I can't send people barging in there slinging accusations all over the place when no one has so much as reported an incident and there's not a shred of evidence to support your theory. I know you don't like him – Rutherwood – his ways, but he runs a first-class school. I should know. I'm a governor. I see the facts and figures. I know you don't like him, but maybe you should cut him some slack."

"You bet I don't like him," Vincent cut in. "The man's a zombie. Runs the whole joint like a military operation. Don't know how GCHQ survives without him. There's not an ounce of feeling in his whole body. The original iceman."

"Think about it. Let him do his job while you get on with doing what you do best – teaching maths."

"So that's telling me, Garry, isn't it? Back off like a good boy; forget all about it," Vincent barked, as heads turned towards them.

"Don't forget, Vinnie, that Rutherwood is the man who pays your salary. Not everybody would turn a blind eye…"

"To me liking men, you mean?" Vincent said.

"You know I'm not one of those, Vinnie. We've been friends for too long for you to throw that in my face. What I'm trying to say is that it's a fine school. Imagine what a scandal like this might do, if indeed anything were to be proved. It'd be the end."

"Better that than another boy, Garry," Vincent snapped. "What if I reported my suspicions – officially?" Vincent pushed. "You'd have to investigate then."

"Would I indeed, my friend? I'll tell you what would happen. If you came to me with that story not backed up by a shred of evidence, I'd probably think you were a crank or had an axe to grind. You'd need a whole lot more before I'd open up an investigation."

"So, you're not going to help me?" Vincent sat back in his chair, put his hands in his pockets, and looked the man he trusted beyond all other square in the eyes.

"Believe me, Vinnie, there's nothing going on at that school, or I'd know about it. My hands are tied. You're a friend, and you know I would help you if I could."

"Then I'll just have to find some evidence, won't I? What would it take?" Vincent persisted.

"Look Vinnie, I know you wouldn't come to me lightly with a story like this," Garry said, softening his voice. "Sorry if I was a bit short with you. Got a double murder on my hands. A child's gone missing and I'm twenty percent down on hands this year. But I can see it's worrying you. Tell you what I'll do. I'll put some feelers out. See if there's been any loose talk. You'll be the first to know and then we can decide together what's next. Deal?"

"Okay, thanks," Vincent said reluctantly. "But I'm not letting this go, you hear me. You want evidence, I'll get it for you."

"I'm late for dinner. Four times already this week. Bessie'll have my guts for garters. Let's have this conversation again in a couple of weeks. Your turn to buy. Okay?"

Twelve

Ahmed bided his time. It was a Sunday morning and that time of day when all God-fearing boys attended the Sunday church service. Church of England, Methodists, Catholics, and atheists alike assembled in the Great Hall to sing hymns, recite prayers, and listen to Father Hammond, the regular, visiting vicar, drone on about sinners and redemption. For one day each week, the Great Hall, with its stained-glass windows and polished floors, was transformed into a house of worship. An altar cloth draped across a trestle table bowed in the centre under the weight of the candles, the wine chalice, the oversized Bible, and the communion plate. The routine was well-rehearsed. Each boy collected a fold-up wooden chair from the storeroom and lined it up with others in rows of military precision, as far back from the altar table as they dared; Father Hammond was renowned for his liberal use of incense.

Casual clothes – the norm at weekends – were left in dorms and replaced with school uniforms: navy blazers, each bearing the school crest on the breast, grey trousers, white shirts, and school ties. Shoes were inspected at the door. Any boy arriving in shoes that had not been polished to within an inch of their life risked double detention and their pocket money being withheld for a month.

Ahmed was the only boy exempted from the ritual by virtue of his Muslim religion. It did not go unnoticed and neither did it add to his popularity with the other boys. He didn't care. Sunday mornings, come rain or shine, he walked the grounds, his thoughts with his mother and his beloved Jaipur.

But not that Sunday. He was on a mission, a mission set by Vincent. He was to wheedle his way into Mr Grzeskowiak's inner sanctuary, use his eyes, and report back. Vincent had said 'use your imagination'. He had racked his brains for almost a week before he struck on the one ploy that might just work.

It was ten-thirty. The great and the good were in the Great Hall, the vicar in full swing. Ahmed picked up a bottle of orange juice he had bought from the tuck shop and rammed deep down inside his pocket. Checking to make sure the coast was clear, he made a beeline for the boys' toilets, held the bottle high above his head, and let go. It smashed into smithereens across the tiled floor. The effect was even better than he had anticipated. Shards of glass shot off in all directions while the orange juice slowly found its way to the central drain, leaving behind a nasty, sticky orange mess. If he were caught out, no one could deny there was a mess that needed to be cleaned up.

Set apart, Keepers Cottage was located at the rear of the main building and was home to Mr Grzeskowiak. Closely resembling a wartime bunker, it was least like an English cottage as it could be. Ahmed squared his shoulders, drew in his breath, and hammered on the door. "Mr Grzeskowiak, are you there?" he shouted with as much urgency as he could muster. "Mr Grzeskowiak, I've made a mess in the boys' toilets, and it needs cleaning up before someone gets hurt."

Seconds later, the door opened with a whoosh. Standing four-square in the door, his hands on his hips, Mr Grzeskowiak looked decidedly grim. "Made a mess? You know it's Sunday, don't you, boy," he growled. Ahmed flinched and stepped back, momentarily wondering if this had been his brightest idea. "No one makes a mess on a Sunday if they know what's good for them. You got tummy problems or something?" Ahmed retreated another step backwards. It was the first time he had met Mr Grzeskowiak up close, and he was, just as others had described him, quite a formidable sight. Stooped in the low doorway, he was nonetheless a tall, broad man, of indefinite age, with grey wiry hair standing on end. His eyes were a pale watery blue, his face deeply lined and weathered, his chin sporting days of salt-and-pepper growth. He wore what might once have been blue-and-white striped pyjamas under a navy dressing gown, his feet bare. Ahmed wrinkled his nose. Mr Grzeskowiak smelt of stale cigarette smoke.

"I'm sorry, sir, but I've made a mess, had an accident. I was just dropping in at the toilet on my way to the common room, and...and...well you see the bottle of orange juice I had in my hand slipped. The floor is covered in it and there's broken glass everywhere."

"Slippery Singh, hey? Isn't that what they call you? Good name for you, hey, boy?" he smirked. "Thought I recognized you." Grzeskowiak was correct; that was indeed his nickname. It didn't bother him in the least – he'd heard far worse.

"Yes, sir, I do believe they do." Ahmed shrugged his shoulders.

"They like nicknames round these parts, don't they? We've all got nicknames, 'aven't we? I'm quite proud of mine as it 'appens. You know what they call me?" he said, pointing a long thick finger at Ahmed. "Grizzly. Like grizzly bear. Like grizzly – miserable," he said. "And that's how I feel right now. Nothing would give me more pleasure than to pick you up by the neck and give you a good clout. But it comes with the territory, don't it? Wait there while I put me work clothes on. Then I'll get me mop and bucket and sort it out."

"That won't be necessary, sir," Ahmed jumped in. "I made the mess, and I am more than happy to clean it up. Just point me in the direction of the mop and bucket, and a dustpan and brush."

"I'm the cleaner round here, boy. You forgotten that?" Ahmed stepped back again as Mr Grzeskowiak closed in on him.

"No, sir, but it is Sunday morning. It's a day of rest, isn't it?" Ahmed said.

"There ain't no days of rest in this job, boy. When there's dirty work to be done, theys all come knocking on my door. Good old Grizzly – he'll sort it out. Why aren't you at the house like the rest of 'em instead of messing things up in the boys' toilets?"

"I'm Muslim, Mr Grzeskowiak," Ahmed explained.

"Explains it. There's mosques up in Birmingham, but there ain't none round these parts," he said, folding his arms across his chest as he narrowed his eyes. "You ain't like the rest of them, then? Don't mind getting your hands dirty. Makes a change. That lot, they think they're too posh to clean or sort

80

anything out for theirselves."

"No, sir, I don't mind getting my hands dirty at all. I come from quite a humble family where we did the cleaning, washing, cooking, and everything else ourselves," Ahmed explained.

"So watcha doing in a place like this? Costs a pretty penny to be schooled here."

"I picked up a benefactor along the way who wanted me to be educated properly."

"A benefactor, hey?" Frowning, he scratched his head and reorganized his hair. "The mop and bucket are in that cupboard over there. The brush and dustpan round the back of it," he said, pointing to a lean-to alongside the building. "Make sure you dry the floor and clean the mop after you, and bring it straight back 'ere. And if you cut yerself, I ain't got no plasters."

* * *

Ahmed swept the glass into the dustpan, making sure there were no shards of glass left behind, filled the bucket, and mopped the floor. Ten minutes later, the mop, bucket, brush, and dustpan had all been returned, sparkling clean to the lean-to. Ahmed rapped on the door. "Mr Grzeskowiak. It's done. Sorry to get you up. Thank you for letting me do it. Any time I can help…"

"No mess? Glass in dustbin?" Shaven, hair combed, and dressed in a clean boiler suit, Mr Grzeskowiak smiled. "Good lad."

"None, sir. I'll get off now and leave you in peace," Ahmed said, fingers crossed behind his back. "Thirsty work."

"There's a pot stewing in 'ere. You want a mug of tea? They'll be a while yet before the service ends. Likes to spin it out does old Hammond," Grzeskowiak said, as he stepped aside and beckoned Ahmed to follow him.

Ahmed grimaced and put on his best smile. He hated tea at the best of times. Worse still when it had been left to stand in the pot. It reminded him of the filthy, dirty water from the Ganges, however holy it might be. "I'd love one, if I'm not keeping you from anything."

Stepping into the bunker, Ahmed held his breath. The air was thick. The small narrow window high up on the wall was shut fast. An ashtray overflowing with cigarette ends sat on a small table close by the TV and between two well-worn armchairs. Other than the ashtray, the whole place was immaculate. Not a speck of dust on the threadbare rug, cushions plumped tidily on the chairs, and not a dirty pot in sight. A small kitchenette occupied one end of the room, together with a cracked Formica table and two kitchen chairs. Two doors led off from the main room, one of which he presumed to be a bathroom and the other, perhaps a small box bedroom. A huge screen that continually cut from one view of the school to another caught his eye.

"Sugar? You park your arse over there," he said, pointing to the kitchen table. "What's your Christian name, if that's what you'd call it?"

"Ahmed, sir."

Beginning to relax, Ahmed sat down and watched as Grzeskowiak spooned sugar into mugs and topped them up with the brown sludge.

"Where you from? You don't sound like a Brummie to me?"

he asked.

"India. Jaipur," Ahmed replied. "I left Jaipur for England in January."

"You like England?"

Ahmed shrugged his shoulders. "It's cold and wet most of the time. At least, that's the way it seemed when I arrived. Back home the sun shines twelve months of the year, but I came here to learn, not for the weather."

"Mum and Dad must miss you…" Grzeskowiak fished for information.

"Both dead. My dad, not long after I was born. My mum, last year." Ahmed dropped his head and looked away.

"Tough, ain't it. So you lost your mum and dad and won a benefactor? I 'eard of them. There was a black and white film on once about some kid that 'ad one. My old man was a waste of space. Nasty piece of work. Thought nothing of taking a strap to me. Didn't care if I deserved it or not. Made 'im feel better. And there were times when 'e did other things as well, but I don't talk about them. She weren't exactly a ray of sunshine herself – me mum. Always telling me I was a mistake. It was 'er way of saying I was a bloody nuisance. Anyway, she didn't 'ave time for me and I wasn't fussed. Did me own thing. Went off the rails for a bit. That's when I got this," he said, pointing to the ugly scar that ran down the side of his neck. "'ad an argument with a bottle."

"And I had an argument with a mule." Ahmed laughed, lifting the hair away from the top left of his forehead. Grzeskowiak grinned.

"That's a good 'un, Ahmed. Looks like you and me got a lot in common, son. Don't suppose you play chess, hey?" he asked, glancing across at a set on the windowsill. "I set it out most nights and play meself. Mostly win, I do."

"I used to play with my mother in Jaipur. She wiped the board with me most of the time."

"You got time for a quick 'un?" Grzeskowiak asked.

Ahmed nodded.

"You set 'em up and I'll wash these mugs up. Can't stand dirty pots 'anging round the place."

Ahmed slowly took the chess pieces out of the box and set them down in their right places, then looked around, committing every detail of the room to memory.

"Checkmate, me little friend," Grzeskowiak said cheerfully as the queen took the bishop. "They think I'm slow, you know, but I ain't stupid."

"I can't believe that," Ahmed said, sitting back and pointing to the screen on the wall and the array of equipment that sat beneath it on the desk. "Anyone who can operate all that equipment must be very clever. What is it?"

"That, boy, is a state-of-the-art CCTV camera system. And, in case you didn't know it, I ain't just a caretaker, I'm 'ead of security around here. Responsible job it is and I takes it very seriously. With that bit of kit, it means you can see most everything that goes on without being there, if you know what I mean. Not that I watch it. It's there in case anyone wants to check back comings and goings – that sort of thing. That box," he said, pointing to the desk, "is a VCR recorder. It records pictures taken by the cameras round the school. And those," he said, pointing to a bank of shelves, "are the tapes that 'ave been recorded, eight hours on each one, so three a day. There's three months' worth of tapes up on those shelves alone."

"That's really neat, sir."

"Yep. I likes to be organized. Each one of them tapes 'as a date and a time on it. See – on the spines? I likes to keep everything in order. Never know when someone might want to check it, not that anything ever happens round 'ere," he said. "You better get along now, Ahmed, before they comes out of that service. Wouldn't do for any of 'em to see you 'ere."

"That queen to bishop was a class move." Ahmed fiddled with the chess pieces. "Don't suppose we could do this again sometime?"

Grzeskowiak's face lit up. "'ow about tomorrow? That's if you ain't got nothing on. About half six. If I'm not back when you gets here, you'll find the key under the brick outside the door. Make sure nobody sees you. And you can tell me a bit more about this India place while you're at it."

"It's a date. It's nice to make a new friend. Thank you."

Poking his head around the door, Grzeskowiak looked outside. "Coast's clear, Ahmed."

* * *

Squeezing his eyes tight shut, Ahmed described the bunker in detail. "It's all very tidy. A bit smelly, but otherwise..."

Vincent listened impatiently, drumming his fingers on the table. "Ahmed, I don't give a damn about the colour of the cushions or the state of the carpet. What else did you see? You must have seen something else. Get on with it."

Ahmed grinned. He'd kept the best for last. "There's a huge screen on one of the walls and something he called a VCR that records what goes on around the school," he said. "And across one of the walls there are shelves filled with tapes, each

85

of them dated and timed. There's three months' worth there. And three tapes a day. The top shelf, March. The middle shelf, April, and the bottom shelf, May."

"Three a day, you say, and none is missing?" Vincent asked excitedly.

"I can't be sure, but I can check it out next time I go. Might have to miss another lesson, Vincent."

"16th and 17th May. Check those dates," Vincent said.

"Tomorrow—" Ahmed said. "We're playing chess again tomorrow evening. He's not a bad old boy at all, you know. Quite pleased I got to know him."

"I knew I could rely on you." Vincent rubbed his hands together. "Anything else?"

Ahmed grinned. "When he's not in, he leaves the key under a brick outside the front door."

Thirteen

2022

"Hey, you. Paul," Stan yelled. "What the hell is your game?"

Stan stood with his legs apart and his hands on his hips, glaring at the back of the car haring its way down the drive, wheels spinning, and ignoring the ten miles per hour limit. If that just doesn't take the biscuit, Stan said to himself. He'd looked in his mirror, he was sure of that. Seen him, but still he had floored the accelerator and whipped up gravel and dust in all directions. Turning to examine the damage to the new garage doors, Stan brushed himself down and blinked hard. Eyes gritty from the dust that still swirled around in the morning air, he watched as Paul reached the main road and turned right towards Stroud. Predictably, the gravel had pitted the paint and even chipped the woodwork. No doubt he would have chipped the paintwork on the car too. Not so much as a hi or bye, not even a wave. Just a stony glare in the rear-view mirror. What the hell was up with the man? Out of the kindness of her heart, Jennifer had financed the restoration in the first place, insisting Paul should have somewhere dry to garage the Mustang. The least he could do was show a bit of appreciation and respect.

Grim-faced, Stan opened the garage doors and laid the dustsheet on the floor adjacent to the old fireplace. It was a job he should have done ages ago before the floor went down, but it was just one of those jobs that didn't happen. It crossed his mind that it was a pity that Paul had taken the car out already. A good layer of soot would have given him something to complain about.

Knees creaking like an old staircase, Stan eased his ample frame down, lay flat on his back on the dustsheet, and pointed his torch up the chimney. Thick with black soot – no less than he had expected. He inched a short rod up through the flue. No further than the length of a man's arm, the rod stopped. Withdrawing it, he shone the torch up again. Consoling himself that whatever was up there was probably long dead, he still shuddered at the thought of a handful of dead pigeons or, even worse, rats cascading down on him, no doubt to be followed by a host of big hairy spiders. Gathering his courage, he reached in and up and fingered the obstruction. It wasn't soft. It wasn't squelchy. And his nose was telling him that it wasn't smelly either. It was hard. Quite possibly a brick or rubble that had fallen down the chimney. Working it slowly left and right, he could feel it give when, suddenly, down it came, together with years of muck, soot, and loose rubble.

Coughing and spluttering, he spat out the dust and wiped his eyes. Kicking the rubble aside, Stan eyed the obstruction. It was like no brick he had ever seen. Who in their right mind would wrap a brick up in polythene and shove it up a chimney?

Picking it up, he examined it from all angles. Whatever it was, it was certainly very well wrapped, the edges taped tight together and the whole tied around with string which, by some miracle, had remained intact. It reminded him of Christmas. Christmas presents. How he hated Christmas presents; the rigmarole of trying to guess what lay inside, hoping against hope that it would be one thing only to find that it was something that he had never wanted, never asked for. Taking a penknife out of his pocket, he cut the string and carefully ran the knife through the tape.

The parcel fell open, its contents hitting the deck. Eyes wide, mouth open, hands shaking, Stan found himself staring at no other than a dagger. It was pretty, no doubt about that, and it was shiny. Running his hand carefully down the blade, he saw it was also lethal. A small notebook and an old VHS tape lay on the ground.

His stomach in knots, Stan walked out into the fresh air, sat on the bank, and placed the three articles down beside him.

"Well, Henry, what do you think?" Stan said. His confidante and housemate, long since departed, Henry knew what to do about most things. "Who the devil stuck this lot up a chimney and more to the point, why?" Four years since he had died, and just under four years since Stan had moved into his cottage at Magnolia, he was still there, if not in body, then in spirit. Other than a lick of paint, Stan hadn't changed a thing back at the cottage. If it had been good enough for Henry, it was good enough for him. Henry's chair left of the fireplace was Henry's chair. He never sat on it. Instead, he took the chair on the opposite side so they could sit and chat just as they had in the old days.

Old Henry knew a few things about him. Far more than any of the other residents. He'd told him all about his childhood, something that he had never shared with anybody. There were moments he'd pulled himself up short. How could Henry, a public school-educated gent, a classical musician, ever understand what his early years had been like? But still, he shared his life story. For the most part, it wasn't pretty, not least that moment when his father had finally pushed his mother too far. A kitchen knife had been her only form of defence against the man who abused her, slapped her, issued orders, and made their life a daily misery. Sent to trial for manslaughter and sentenced to eight years, she had died within three months. He had been taken into the care system.

"It may look fine, Henry, but it's a killing machine all the same. If there's one thing I hate more than any others, it's knives, and especially knives like this. How about I just stuff it right back up that chimney where I found it and forget about it? Can't turn the clock back, you say? Maybe not. Pity. Strange bedfellows, wouldn't you say – a dagger, a notebook, and a VHS tape? I'll take your advice and think about it. Meanwhile, I've got an unholy mess to sort out in there," he said, pointing to the Old Forge. "And then there's the painting to get on with."

They'd drawn lots on the name. It might once have been a forge. It might once have been stables. It might once have been a wood store back in its day. None of them knew for certain. The one thing they did know from the skeleton of the building was that, at one time, it had had an upper floor. The Old Forge had a nice ring to it.

Conservation was the watchword at Magnolia, and if anything could be restored to its former glory, then that was the way it would be. Other than the one wall that remained standing with its ornate brickwork closely resembling that on the front of the Mansion House, there were few clues. It was soon agreed. The one remaining wall would be retained and restored as close to its original as possible, leaving the fireplace and chimney in place, and the other three walls, little more than piles of rubble and bricks, would be rebuilt.

While Stan propped up and worked on the one-half decent wall, the rest of the men sorted the bricks from the rubble and painstakingly chiselled away the old mortar from each. The pile of reclaimed bricks grew with each passing day. A loud cheer went up when the last was placed ceremoniously on the pile. Max, Dennis, Thomas, Gerald, Sam, Paul, and Andy straightened their backs for the final time. Only Snow White was missing.

Meanwhile, back in the cottages, the girls baked from morning until night, delivering refreshments to the workers on the hour, every hour. Peter, a retired banker, was in charge of finances, while Duncan, on-site tech whizz, googled every reclamation business in a fifty-mile radius to find the additional bricks they would need together with period windows and new garage doors.

As dusk fell, they had all retired to the cottages for a well-earned rest – he, to Henry's Cottage as it would always be called.

Over the garage, they had built a small flat for visitors: lounge, one bedroom, kitchenette, and bathroom, the whole accessed through an external wooden staircase. It had been Jennifer's idea to do the conversion and Jennifer's windfall that had financed the work. The twelve cottages at Magnolia were fine but with only two small bedrooms in each, the residents were hard pushed to accommodate visitors – so a guest suite was deemed to be an excellent idea.

There was nothing Stan liked better than a good building job, whatever the size. It was he who had been foreman on the original build project for the first ten cottages and the restoration of the Mansion House. It was he who had built the latest two cottages where Paul and Ros, Sam and Jasmine now lived. And now it was he who had completed the rebuild of the Old Forge. Proud as he was of all his achievements, he couldn't help feeling a little sad that there were no more building projects on the horizon.

Stan stacked the rubble sacks around the back of the Old Forge and re-wrapped the parcel. Henry was right. No one can turn the clock back.

Fourteen

Jasmine poured herself another cup of coffee, freshly brewed, black and strong. Sam had left at the crack of dawn.

It was eerily quiet next door, unusually so. Jasmine wondered if Ros was okay. While the double-bricked and insulated walls of the two cottages prevented noise from drifting from one to the other, an open window did not. Both she and Ros were fresh air fanatics, particularly since the pandemic had started. Each threw windows open at the least opportunity, and neither had changed this habit since.

She was not one to interfere, but it concerned her to hear the loud and angry exchanges that drifted all too regularly out through Ros's windows and into their own. Up until the last week or so, and in all the years that they had lived side by side, she had never heard raised voices. Ros and Paul were quiet and reserved by nature. It was totally out of character for them to behave as they had been. Sam had heard it too and she knew he shared her concern, but suggested they stay out of it, at least for the moment. Let them work it out for themselves, he said.

They didn't live in each other's pockets, but they were good

93

friends – at least she liked to think so. Rarely a day passed without the two of them having a good natter, either over a cup of coffee or the garden fence. Ros loved her garden, but even that was beginning to look neglected. It was as if she were avoiding her, avoiding everyone. She'd tried calling, shouting over the fence, and knocking on the door, but Ros hadn't answered. And neither had she nor Paul shown their faces down at the Mansion House for any of the social occasions of which there had been more than a few. Paul had gone out, again. Same time each morning for the past goodness-knows-how-many days, so many she had lost count. She heard him leave. The whole of Magnolia had probably heard him leave. No one could mistake the racket of Paul's Mustang firing up on a cold morning, or the roar of the engine as he set off down the drive.

Jasmine emptied the coffee maker and made a fresh brew. It had gone on too long. If she'd done anything to upset Ros, she wanted to know what it was and clear it up. She'd ring her first. If she didn't answer then she'd go round and bang on the door and keep banging until Ros answered.

"Morning, Ros," she said, more than a little surprised that she had picked up so quickly. "I'm not taking no for an answer. The coffee has just brewed and there's a couple of Danish sitting on the kitchen worktop. If you're not round here in ten minutes, I'll just bring the lot round to you. I've missed you," she said.

Jas could hear the wheels grinding as Ros searched for yet another excuse to reject her invitation. "Thanks, Jas," Ros replied. "I can't right at the moment. I'm not...I'm not...I'm not dressed yet. Can we take a rain check?"

Jas pursed her lips. Not this time, lady. You're not going to fob me off with excuses this time. And it was a crap excuse anyway. A creature of habit, Ros was almost always up and dressed by nine. "Sling on some jeans and a sweater. Doesn't matter what we look like. If it makes you feel better, I'll put my PJs on. My hair's a mess, my nails are all chipped, and I haven't got round to putting my face on either. You can't look worse than me. Let's slum it together. See you in ten minutes." Jasmine cut the call and ran her fingers through her hair.

* * *

Opening the door, Jas's heart sank. Dark circles around bloodshot eyes, face drawn, and her hair lank and greasy. It was all she could do not to cry for her friend. "In you come, Ros. Sam's off to London; left hours ago. No one's going to disturb us. You don't look good, gal. Looks like you've been dragged through a hedge backwards. Isn't that what they say? Next stop for us is a good long session at that beautician in town."

"Thanks." Ros managed a weak laugh. "I can always rely on you for an honest opinion."

"Call a spade a spade, as Sam always says."

"I'm sorry, Jas, I haven't wanted to see anyone. I hoped things would work themselves out, but they haven't. I didn't want to worry you or anybody else. I'm not sure you can do anything to help anyway," Ros said, wrapping her hands around the mug of coffee.

"You won't know until you ask, Ros. Whatever it is, you can't bottle it up. Look at you. This isn't the Ros I know and love. How about you start from the beginning? There's nothing spoiling. I've got nothing else to do for the rest of the day." Jas rested her chin on her elbow.

"It's Paul. He's changed. We've been married for over forty years, Jas, and I've never known him like this. We've always shared everything, talked to each other, and confided in each other. We've never had secrets. I can see that he's worried about something. When I ask him what it is, he jumps down my throat. He's angry at something and he's taking it out on me. I can't talk to him. I can't say a word right. I never thought I'd say it, but I'm relieved when he does go out."

"Is he hitting you?" Jas said quietly, taking Ros's hand in hers. "You can tell me."

"Good God, no. He wouldn't hit me. I don't think he's ever raised a hand to anybody in his life. How can you ask that?" Ros snapped.

"Sorry, Ros, but the fact is that men do hit women, and women hit men. It's not so uncommon as you might think."

"Not Paul."

"Okay. Let's drop that line. Is he ill, do you think? Is he eating properly?" Jas asked.

"I don't think he's ill. Picking at his food, yes. He's always liked his food, but even that doesn't seem to interest him anymore. I've tried cooking his favourites, but he just shoves them away. I'm at my wits' end."

"I could get Sam to look him over when he comes back from London tonight. If there's anything medically wrong, then Sam will find it."

"No, I don't think so. If Sam starts poking around, then he'll know I've been talking to you. Probably make things worse. I don't think it's physical. Whatever it is, it's keeping him awake at night and he's keeping me awake. With the amount of sleep we're getting, it's no wonder that tempers are frayed most of the time…He's been out in that bloody car of his six days a week for the past couple of weeks, and that's out of character too. The usual routine is clean and polish three days a week, check the engine two days a week, and go out for a ride once a week. You know Paul, he has his routine. I don't know where he goes or what he's doing. He hasn't asked me to go with him once. And he won't tell me where he's been when he gets back."

"I did notice," Jas cut in. "We all have."

"He's done nothing in the vegetable garden for weeks. It's not like him. It was his pride and joy. Weeds are growing like nobody's business, vegetables are rotting away, and the seeds that he bought for summer are still in the packets. When I mention it, he just ignores me. The others must have noticed that he's letting it go to rack and ruin, but nobody's said anything to me so far."

"Probably because nobody's seen hide nor hair of you," Jas said. "By the sound of it, he's got more on his mind than weeds and a few mouldy cabbages. But you're right; it hasn't gone unnoticed. There's been a few rumblings about missing the veg boxes that everybody's got used to, but no one blames him. It's been so bloody cold. Who would want to work outdoors in all that? Put that right out of your mind. So other than not sleeping, not eating, showing no interest in anybody or anything, except that car of his – and being a bloody pain in the ass – is there anything else?"

Ros nodded her head. "He's been acting so weird, Jas. He just sits and sits each morning waiting for the post to come. The moment the letterbox clacks, he's up and off like a jack rabbit. He'll break his neck before long. I ask him about the post. Just junk mail, he says. There are bank statements and bills, Jas – bank statements and bills that come through the letterbox as regular as clockwork. According to Paul, there have been none. I can't remember the last time we had any official mail, according to him."

"You don't do online banking then?" Jas asked.

"Paul does. I've always been happy to leave it to him. I wouldn't know how to and, if I did, I'd probably get it wrong. We get paper statements of everything as well. Double indemnity, as Paul calls it."

Jas chose her words carefully. "I don't suppose you happened to look in his desk or any of his drawers to see if he might have been telling you the truth?"

"I did and I feel awful about it. In desperation, I did just that. Turned the place upside down when he was out one day. There is no correspondence anywhere for the past couple of months. And it's not just that. It's every time his mobile rings. He's on it with the first ring, and he's off into the kitchen or upstairs to answer it. Never in front of me. And then he gives me some cock-and-bull story about a surprise he's organizing for me."

"Sounds a bit unlikely, doesn't it?"

"I'm just waiting for him to come back in an ambulance or police car," Ros whispered.

"Whoa, gal, aren't we getting a bit carried away here? He's a good driver. Knows that car better than the back of his hand. Where did that come from?"

"He's drinking, Jas." Ros's eyes filled with tears. Jas took a deep breath and pushed the box of tissues towards her.

"Serious drinking?" Jas asked.

Ros nodded. "How serious is serious drinking? He's not a drinker. The odd pint or a small scotch, yes, but not like this.

It's every day and he's driving home afterwards. If someone comes home stinking of beer, is it serious drinking? He'll either kill himself or, worse still, someone else at this rate. It would be doing me and him a favour if he were caught by the police."

"That is serious, Ros. I really do think we need to get Sam in on this one. They're pals, good pals. Sam's seen it all before. He'll get Paul to open up."

"Jas. I'm his wife. I need to have it out with him first before getting anyone else involved. I've been putting off the inevitable. Hoping that things will mend themselves. I've got to man up and ask him what the hell's going on. Even threaten to walk out on him if I have to. Maybe that will get him to change his tune."

"That's better. A bit of fighting talk. You do what you have to, but you know we're here for you, whatever. More coffee? Get that pastry down you. You need some more flesh on your bones," Jas laughed.

Ros nodded. "It's good to talk. Soon. I'll have it out with him soon."

"Changing the subject," Jas said, "Hetty and Max's niece, Gabby – you know the hero of the hour back in the day – she's coming up to stay overnight at the Old Forge. Hetty's organizing a welcome party for her tomorrow. Big bash in the Great Hall. She rang earlier. Probably rang you too?"

"The phone did ring, but I didn't answer it," Ros said.

"It's a three-line whip. You'll certainly be missed if you're not there. Can you drag Paul out for it? Don't ask. Tell. It would do you good. Sam and I will pick you both up on the way down."

"I'll try."

"You'll do more than try, Ros. If he won't come, then you'll come down with us. Put your face on and let your hair down. No arguments, you hear. And don't forget, we're both here for you," Jas said.

Fifteen

2022

"Aunt Hetty, how lovely to hear your voice," Gabby said, cramming the last of a sandwich into her mouth. "I'm sorry I haven't been in touch for a while. Why is it that I always start with an apology when we talk? How are you? How's dear old Uncle Max?" Gabby rambled. "I don't know how many pairs of shoes I've worn out since I went back to work properly. I've just got back from the last assignment."

"No apology needed, dear. I know you all too well. Get a whiff of something that isn't right and you're away. What is it you've been working on this time?" Aunt Hetty asked.

"Trafficking. Women, men, children. You know, those poor people who sell their souls to get across to England. I got back yesterday – from Tunisia. No sooner do we get to the bottom of one organization than another one starts up. There must be thousands of them. If I'm honest, it's a bit of a losing battle, but that's no reason to give up. The authorities on both sides of the channel are doing their best, but they welcome our help. If we can just get some of the scum off the streets – if you take my meaning – then it's a job well done. This last assignment took nine months and that was a whole team working on it.

But we got there in the end," Gabby said.

Hetty almost wished she hadn't asked. She'd never liked the sound of investigative journalism in the first place. There were times when she worried about her niece, they both did, and they had to remind themselves she was not a child anymore and was more than capable of looking after herself. She'd proved that several times, in spades. Without Gabby's spirit and drive, Magnolia Court and the cottages would most probably have crumbled to piles of rubble by now, and Harry Trumper wouldn't be safely tucked up behind bars. And now she was happily married to a very nice man.

"To answer your question, my dear, we're both fine. Getting older by the day and a few more creaking bones. No more of that heart trouble, before you ask. I know my limits these days. We can't help getting older. I can't believe that your Uncle Max is going on eighty-four, and I'm not so far behind. Where does the time go, Gabby?"

"The pandemic hasn't helped, has it? Just when people like you should be getting out and about and making the best of life, everybody gets locked down. Let's hope we've seen the back of that," Gabby said. "You're both always on my mind, you know that, don't you? I just knew you'd both be safe at Magnolia."

"I know that. No need to fret, dear, and we have kept in touch, haven't we? Quite how we ever managed to survive without FaceTime or that Zoom thing, I can't imagine."

"How's the refurb going, Aunt Hetty? Bet that kept you all busy."

"Now, that is the very reason I'm ringing you. That and the fact you told me you'd be needing a break after that assignment. The answer to your question is that the Old

Forge, as we have called it, is complete and we'd like you and Greg to come up and be the first to stay overnight. Everybody would be so pleased to see you both."

"Just one snag, Aunt Hetty…"

"Isn't there always, dear," Hetty cut in, readying herself for a no.

"Greg isn't around. He's in India. On a tour. There's a hotel that is reaching completion and he's got to be there. Then he's off rustling up a few more mega contracts before flying home in a couple of weeks' time. So…" Gabby paused for effect, "I'm at a loose end. Yes please!"

Beaming with happiness, Hetty started a mental list of all the things that needed to be seen to – make up the bed and put the heating on to air the Old Forge, shopping, and, of course, a welcome party for Gabby. There hadn't been a real party at Magnolia for such a long time. It was a perfect excuse to throw the doors to the Mansion House open wide and celebrate. "When can you get here?"

"This evening? I'm a dab hand at packing these days. To tell you the truth, I haven't unpacked yet. I might need to put a duster around the place before I leave, but there again, what's the point? It'll all be there when I get back. No point doubling up on housework, is there?" Gabby said, checking the list taped up on the kitchen cabinet. There was nothing that couldn't wait. "Two weeks. Can you put up with me for two weeks? What a dream. Nothing to do but sit about and read."

Hetty hesitated. "Two weeks would be wonderful, but I should tell you, dear, it might be a bit of a busman's holiday. You see, something has turned up at Magnolia and we think we're going to need your brains."

"Tell me, Aunt Hetty."

"No, I think it would be far better if you concentrated on getting yourself organized and getting up here in one piece. I don't want your mind to be on other things. Amy and Duncan are taking care of things for the moment. I'll have a word with them and tell them you're coming. You can catch up with them tomorrow morning. This evening, we're going to have our niece to ourselves, if that's okay with you?"

"Sounds good, but I could probably drop down and see them later this evening." Already she had the bit between her teeth. "No, you're right, Aunt Hetty, family comes first; the mystery tomorrow," she said, sounding like she wished it might have been the other way around.

* * *

Her little Fiat 500 had been replaced by a company-provided Audi that did everything except drive itself. Automatic transmission, cruise control, automatic rain detection, automatic headlight dipping, automatic mirror folding, heated seats, remote locking and unlocking, and Bluetooth-everything, it was poles apart from the little car that she had nursed home so many times.

Turning left off the main road, Gabby slowed right down. It was a habit formed in the distant past when the drive had been one long series of potholes. Now it had been gravelled and levelled with not a pothole in sight. She could almost see Dot and Dennis out with their rakes early each morning, raking over the tyre tracks from the previous day. It was Magnolia time. The magnolias lining the drive were heavy with pink-and-white flowers. Magnolia Court was in her heart and soul, both the place and the residents. The memory of that first visit seven years ago to see Uncle Max and Aunt Hetty would forever be imprinted in her mind. The Mansion House, sad and neglected beyond words, the cottages in the grounds crumbling and crying out for attention, the drawn faces of the residents resigned to their lot; it had been more than she could bear. Gabby smiled as she looked through the windscreen at the house beyond, restored to its former glory. And the pretty white cottages, incongruous as they were, set against the Jacobean Mansion House, each pretty as a picture. She felt very privileged to have been a part of the reawakening of Magnolia Court.

* * *

"It's fabulous, Aunt Hetty. I can't believe that anyone could have transformed that wreck into this." Gabby stood back, her hands on her hips, gazing in awe.

"Mostly Stan's doing with Jennifer's money behind it. But we all did our bit. It was fun. You should have seen your Uncle Max getting stuck in. His green woolly hat perched on his head, that old green sweater of his, a padded stool and a chisel in his hand, he looked just like a little gnome," Hetty laughed.

"And I'm going to be the first to stay here? That's awesome," Gabby said, picking up her suitcase. "Lead the way."

Hetty led the way up the wooden staircase, taking her time, and holding on to the handrail. Gabby followed a few steps behind.

"Here we are, dear." Hetty threw open the door. "I do hope you are going to be comfortable here."

Gabby fell in love with it on the spot. It left her speechless. Lovingly rebuilt and refurbished by people she loved more than any in the world; each had left their mark on it. The décor spoke of Jennifer through and through. The walls were washed with the same pale grey as the woodwork, the carpet a slightly darker grey. A long purple velvet sofa, with piping the same pale grey as the walls, occupied over half of the small sitting room. The scatter cushions were a mix of pink, purple, and blue. Floor-length grey-and-white striped curtains were held back by contrasting tasselled tiebacks. There was no chintz. Gabby knew in her heart it had been furnished with her in mind, a kind of thank you for all she had done for them in those years past. In her mind's eye, she saw Jennifer draping fabrics this way and that until she found just the right contrast, Jennifer changing her mind a dozen times, Hetty and Dot standing by with their sewing machines awaiting orders…The bedroom was an equal work of art. Tiny as it was, with just room for a double bed with the narrowest of side tables on either side and a small built-in wardrobe, it was comfortable, cosy, and welcoming.

"It's beautiful, Aunt Hetty. I'm so happy to be the first here," Gabby said.

"Right, unpack your belongings. Uncle Max will be beside himself if you are more than ten minutes. He's cooking tonight and"—Hetty checked her watch—"dinner will be on the table in fifteen minutes precisely."

"And the little mystery you mentioned?" Gabby asked.

"Something that Stan found up this chimney, only yesterday. He did say that he was tempted to leave them exactly where he found them but then curiosity got the better of him." Hetty pointed to the small fireplace. "A dagger, a notebook, and an old VHS tape. Strange place to put things, wouldn't you say?"

"You're an old witch, Aunt Hetty," Gabby laughed. "You know more, but you're not telling, are you?"

"Tomorrow is soon enough, dear. Family first, isn't that what we agreed?"

Sixteen

2022

"I'm here," Gabby called through the letterbox. "Amy, it's me."

She had hardly stepped foot across the threshold before Amy was taking her by the hand and leading her into the lounge, leaning slightly more heavily on her walking stick than she had done in the past. "We've missed you, Gabby. This damned pandemic. I hope you had all your jabs. We all had ours. No dissenters at Magnolia Court. Well, you wouldn't expect it, would you? And none of us went down with Covid. I'm so glad you've come. The timing simply couldn't be better. Now, I've got something to show you. Did Hetty explain?" Amy paused for breath. "Well, be a good girl first and put the kettle on. I haven't had a cup of tea for hours."

Gabby kissed Amy on the cheek, picked up the mug off the table, and took it out to the kitchen. It was full to the brim with tea and still hot. It was part of Amy's charm. At ninety-five years of age, a little memory loss was easily overlooked.

"She did say something. Something about a dagger and a notebook. Oh, and a VHS tape," Gabby replied. "They both resolutely refused to tell me anything else. Said I was to wait until I saw you and Duncan this morning. Well, here I am,"

Gabby said, eager to hear more.

"I can understand that. They probably wanted you to have a good night's sleep rather than worry about whether you were going to be murdered in your bed," Amy said calmly.

"What?" Gabby stared at Amy open-mouthed. "Why would anybody possibly want to murder me in my bed? They'd have a job on their hands, I can tell you that."

"I'm perfectly serious, Gabby. You see, Duncan and I have been doing some checking up. It seems a man was murdered in the Old Forge. Possibly a man called Vincent Palmer, but I'll come back to that later. Of course, in those days it was called the Annexe. We're pretty sure that it's the same place. Duncan will tell you when you go down there. He's expecting you in about half an hour, or was it an hour? Maybe it was an hour and a half. Whatever."

"I think I need some sugar in my tea, Amy, assuming you're not winding me up," Gabby said.

"Me? Would I ever do such a thing? Did you forget the tea, Gabby? It's usually me who does that." Amy grinned.

"No, as it happens, I didn't. You just stopped me in my tracks for a moment. Don't go away," Gabby said, retreating to the kitchen.

"Very nice, dear. Thank you. You haven't forgotten how to make a good cup of tea. I like that." Amy sipped her tea, with a naughty grin on her face.

"Well, I'm waiting, Amy. I'm guessing there's more to tell."

"Oh, yes. I shan't tell you all of it. That would spoil Duncan's fun and he's been so busy on that computer of his, he's hardly come up for air. So, Thomas and Gerald have the dagger. They've got contacts in the business, you know. I might be entirely wrong, but it looks as though it could be quite valuable; we'll have to wait and see. They're trying to find out more about it, where it was made, et cetera. Duncan has the VHS tape. I don't suppose you remember those; you were probably too young. Big black things with two tape reels in them. We used to rent them from Blockbuster's if I remember correctly. I've probably got some old ones up in the attic. But none of us has a machine to play them on anymore…Anyway, I've got the notebook, or rather, diary. I really can't decide which one it is. It's the format of a diary, but there's hardly anything in it – just half-a-dozen or so entries." Pottering unsteadily across to the sideboard, Amy returned with a small yellowing book in her hand. "It's got the most beautiful cover. Made from calf's leather, if I'm not mistaken. It was exceedingly well wrapped up, which is why it's in such good condition."

"Is it old?" Gabby asked, taking the notebook from Amy.

"1985. That's when it was written and that makes it thirty-seven years old – about the same age as you, my dear."

"Looks pretty ordinary to me." Gabby shrugged her shoulders.

"The last entry is the most interesting. Dated Monday 3rd June, 1985, it simply says, 'God help us'. Well, that sounds quite significant to me. Of what, I don't rightly know."

"Sounds like someone might have been in a bit of trouble," Gabby said. "And the rest?"

"Very difficult to decipher, dear. The initials AS, CT, EB, and AG crop up a few times in individual entries against specific dates with the odd word alongside. If you check Tuesday 16th April, you'll see one such entry, 'CR Left'."

"No names, then?" Gabby asked.

"No, that would be too much to ask. Not in the diary, dear, but AS we believe to be Ahmed Singh, a young Indian boy. Again, Duncan will fill you in on that one. CR and EB, we haven't a clue. CR died – at least we think so. There's an entry in the diary on 22nd April, 'CR funeral'. Whoever EB was, from another entry, it looks as though he might have been expelled."

"Expelled," Gabby said. "Where do you get expelled from?"

"School. You get expelled from schools," Amy said. "And what was on this very site before Magnolia Court was built? A school."

"So EB was probably a pupil here. What about CR?" Gabby asked.

"No idea, but AS was most certainly a pupil," Amy confirmed. "Duncan will confirm that when you see him."

"And we don't know who owned the diary?"

"Our guess is it belonged to the man I was telling you about, Vincent Palmer, the man who died in your flat. That is only conjecture. We have no proof that it was written by a man or a woman, let alone Vincent Palmer. Whoever it was, they were certainly no literary scholar and no Samuel Pepys either."

"What does your instinct tell you, Amy? When you forged documents during the war, surely you would have used a different style for a man and a woman."

"Surprisingly not so, Gabby. It's a well-known fact that gender cannot be determined from handwriting alone. It tells us plenty about the writer's mental state, but that's probably about all," Amy said. "But I would say that the writer was very agitated about something when he or she made that last short entry. The writing is spidery, almost unreadable, an emotional scrawl in comparison to earlier entries. The writing, I would say, is that of a doctor or a scientist, someone who has a very active brain and very little time. This person didn't normally keep a diary. There's no consistency in the entries whatsoever. You know what it's like. You make a New year's resolution to keep a day-to-day diary and then forget all about it the following day. Then, after that, you just record those things that must not be forgotten. And that's what I think this person has done."

"I guess it's not an unreasonable assumption to say that whoever owned the notebook, also owned the dagger and the tape? Otherwise, why would they all have been hidden in the same place up the chimney?"

"More to the point, why hide them up a chimney?"

Gabby shrugged her shoulders. "Can we just backtrack a bit, Amy? What are we trying to do here?"

"That is a very good question. Frankly, when Stan found the dagger, we simply thought that we ought to try and find the original owner and return it to them. But when we started to look at the notebook and Duncan did some research, we began to think that we might have stumbled across something far more serious."

"You mean evidence relating to this so-called murder?"

"Quite so, Gabby," Amy said.

"And you've spoken to Uncle Max about it? I can't see him being too keen on any of us getting involved in something like that. You know Uncle Max – he doesn't like to take risks unless he has to."

"Well, yes, Duncan and I both spoke to him before you arrived yesterday. And, yes, you are quite right. He was most definitely of the opinion that we should just take the whole bundle to the police and wash our hands of it. We managed to persuade him you'd know what's best to do. So, he agreed to wait and hear what we all had to say."

"Have to say that my initial reaction is much the same as Uncle Max. Withholding evidence is a criminal offence and I strongly suspect that applies just as much to old cases as it does to those that are ongoing," Gabby said.

"But who is to say it is evidence in the first place? It might just be exactly as it looks – a dagger, an old notebook, and a Blockbuster videotape. And then we'd stand accused of wasting police time. Aren't you just a little bit curious? Isn't this what you do for a living? If an investigative journalist can't sort it out, then who can?" Amy smiled, her case made. "Go on down to see Duncan now. The picture will be much clearer once you have spoken to him. And then call in on Thomas and Gerald."

"And then?" Gabby said, wide-eyed.

"You tell your Uncle Max that we're just going to make a few simple enquiries. Nothing so exciting has happened here for years. The word's out, Gabby. We have to bring everybody up to date on what we've found and what you're going to do about it. It's the perfect opportunity. You can tell them all about it at your welcome party tonight."

Gabby looked at her watch. "What time did you say Duncan was expecting me?"

"He'll be sitting there with one eye on his computer and one eye on the door. He's missed you, Gabby. We've all missed you. And don't forget to take the notebook with you. I wouldn't like to lose it."

Seventeen

2022

Duncan made himself a cup of tea, powered up his laptop, and typed 'Stroud, 1985' into the search engine. The Stroud Preservation Trust website popped up at the top of the list: 'A photographic record of change.' Scrolling down to the 1980s, he could see photographs of the reconstruction of key buildings in the town, and the forthcoming closure of Stroud High School and Marling, together with a promise of a new sixth form college. He stored this bit of information away. Mildly surprised not to find any mention of Magnolia Court with its history dating back to the early 1800s – such a fine example of a Regency period build, albeit, in a Tudor Gothic style – he made a mental note to send them an email and photographs and moved on.

Local newspapers – Stroud – 1985. Click. Duncan smiled. It was good to see that the Stroud News and Journal, founded 1957, had survived right up until the present day and that they had had the foresight to set up a digitized archive. Clicking on the archive and signing up to view the articles, he was immediately rewarded with a well-ordered and organized list of articles year on year.

It was a laborious process. A man had been charged with stealing ten pounds of groceries from the supermarket, convicted, and sent to prison for three months. Duncan shook his head. How times had changed. Nowadays it would be a rap over the knuckles and at worst a few hours of community service. That was if the police bothered to follow up on the theft report at all. Road collisions – rarely anybody killed or badly injured. The river Frome had broken its banks on two occasions; residents of the town had rallied to help with the clean-up. Garden gnomes and ornaments had mysteriously gone missing overnight. A family of gypsies had been moved on from Rodborough Common without incident. There had been several fights outside a notorious pub. A new Mayor had been appointed, replacing the previous Mayor who had been removed from office for reasons that had not been explained. It was no wonder that Stroud was rarely mentioned in the nationals.

The next article leapt out from the screen.

"TEACHER MURDERED, BOY MISSING

Police are searching for a thirteen-year-old boy named as Ahmed Singh. Originally from Jaipur, India, the boy is a boarder at St John's College. He is described as being approximately five feet three inches tall, with dark skin, brown eyes, and black hair. It is believed the boy may be able to provide critical information about the murder of a local teacher. The police can confirm the name of the deceased as Vincent Palmer, a thirty-five-year-old mathematics teacher at St John's College. The murder took place late evening on Wednesday 5th June. The deceased's body was found in his residence within the school grounds, known as the Annexe.

Mr William Rutherwood, Headmaster of St John's, described Vincent Palmer as a mathematical genius who always went beyond the call of duty to tutor the boys. Several of his pupils went on to achieve high grades and gained entry to Cambridge and Oxford. Mr Rutherwood added that Mr Palmer would be sorely missed by teachers and pupils alike. An unnamed source said the missing boy was receiving extra-curricular tuition from Mr Palmer and that they were believed to be close.

Detective Chief Superintendent Garry Seymour is appealing for any member of the public who may have seen the thirteen-year-old boy of Indian descent to come forward. The boy, Ahmed Singh, was reported missing immediately after the incident. DCS Garry Seymour added that the police and school are concerned for the welfare of the teenager, but added that if seen, he should not be approached. All sightings should be reported directly to the police."

Photographs of Vincent Palmer, Ahmed Singh, and William Rutherwood accompanied the article. Duncan highlighted the whole thing, copied it into Word, saved the file, and printed two copies.

And little more than a month later, St John's College was making the headlines again.

"ST JOHN'S COLLEGE CLOSES

The last of the boarders departed from St John's College after the doors were closed for the final time on Thursday 24th July.

The Headmaster Mr William Rutherwood said: 'This is a sad day for all of us, teachers and pupils alike. Following a structural survey, parts of the building, the old house in particular, have been declared unsafe. The funds to carry out the necessary maintenance work, notwithstanding the many appeals that have been made, are simply not sufficient. I wish all the boys every success in their future schools. I am confident they will all be high achievers, successful in their careers, and pillars of the community. We are doing all we can to find new positions for the teachers who also left us today.'

Parents were up in arms about the short notice and were concerned they would be unable to find places in equivalent private schools in time for the summer term.

"...The closure of the school follows on from the so-far unsolved murder of mathematics teacher, Mr Vincent Palmer, on 5th June 1985. Detective Chief Superintendent Garry Seymour was unable to confirm that the boy who went missing at the time of the murder had been found. The public is reminded that any sightings should be reported to the police. The boy should not be approached.

It is rumoured that the site has been acquired by a property developer as a future investment. The name of the developer has not been revealed.

Again, Duncan highlighted the article, copied it into Word, saved the file, and printed two copies. Scrolling quickly down through the archive, it surprised him to find there were no further reports about the murder of the teacher, the missing boy, or the closure of the school.

* * *

"Gabby, timing couldn't have been better," Duncan said. "Scotch? I'm about to have a small snifter myself. Keep me company?"

"Why not?" Gabby laughed. "Good to see you again, Duncan. Amy's just walked me through the diary. She's a little wobbly these days. I'm a bit worried about her. And when I leave here, I'm off to see Thomas. I have my instructions. My head's buzzing. Wow, who'd ever have thought that something like that would turn up at Magnolia Court? And who'd ever have thought that someone might have been murdered in the Old Forge?"

"Who'd have thought it indeed, my dear. Cheers." Duncan clinked his glass against Gabby's. "I've not long finished doing a bit of research myself. Started yesterday and just closed down the computer. 1985, the year of the diary—"

"Judging from some of the diary entries, we think the man who was murdered might have been a teacher at the school," Gabby said.

"As I mentioned to Amy. There's a newspaper report about it. Take a look at this. And there's one about the closure of the school as well," Duncan said, handing the printed copies to Gabby.

"So, this Vincent Palmer was murdered in a building called the Annexe. Amy seems to think the Annexe and the Old Forge are one and the same," Gabby said.

"It's possible, probable even. It's the only outbuilding at Magnolia and it's been there since we all moved in. Why don't you ask Greg? He was the architect on-site when the development started. If anyone knows, it will be him. Useful – your Greg." Duncan smiled.

"I'll do that. I'll probably call him later," Gabby said, scribbling a note on her pad.

"And while you're about it, ask him if he knows anything about these structural problems with the Mansion House? The ones mentioned in the school closure report. They must have been pretty severe to be the cause of the school closure,"

Duncan said.

"I'll do that too."

Reading the report, her eyes settled on the photograph of Ahmed Singh. A typical school photograph. Just a normal boy in his school uniform, but one that would stand out in a crowd in a private school like St John's. There was no doubting that Detective Chief Superintendent Garry Seymour was pointing the finger for the murder directly at the thirteen-year-old boy. Where were his parents? Where was home? More important, where had he gone, and had he been found? And where was he now? What possible motive could he have had for killing his teacher?

And Vincent Palmer. Long shoulder-length blond hair blowing untidily in the wind, a roll-neck sweater under his gown, he was not the archetypal private school teacher. Ahmed and Vincent – they made an unlikely pair, but that was no motive for murder.

"You know, Duncan, if I was one of those boys' parents, I'd have had my kid out of that school pronto. Who wants their kids at a school where one of the teachers has just been murdered? No fees, no school," Gabby said. "And you say there are no more press reports about the murder or the boy?"

"Nothing. I checked it out. Zilch," Duncan said.

"What do we know about this Rutherwood? A sour puss if ever I saw one." Gabby studied the photograph of the tall man in a brown suit and matching trilby.

"The Headmaster, you mean? Well, I've run some brief checks on him. Ex-Army. That's all I've found so far."

"Whereabouts?"

"Unknown," Duncan said. "That'll take time."

"And Seymour, the DS?" Gabby asked.

"Exemplary career record. Commendations for everything," Duncan replied.

"Whereabouts?"

"Likewise unknown at this time."

"I was just about to check something when you arrived. Back in a mo." In one swift flick of the wrist, Duncan turned his wheelchair half circle and disappeared to the far end of the room. "And no peeking, young lady. I never reveal my sources, as you well know."

Oh, didn't she know it? Duncan's skills for ferreting out information were well renowned throughout Magnolia. If it was out there, then Duncan would find it – his way, no questions asked.

"Just as I thought," Duncan said, "Call it second sight if you like."

"Care to share?" Gabby looked up to find Duncan beside her.

"I've just checked the National Archives at Kew. Vincent Palmer's murder case is listed. Case unsolved. Looks like it was closed in '97. Twelve years later. Pretty standard."

"No information access, I presume," Gabby asked.

"Not for the next thirty years, unless—"

"—We go the freedom of information route, and we know how long that can take. I don't think it would be wise to go down that route, at least not yet. Let's backtrack, Duncan. Palmer is murdered by Singh, or so this Seymour would have us believe. Singh disappears and is never seen again. No murderer. Case closed. End of." Gabby grimaced. "You don't mean to tell me that the whole of the British police force couldn't find a thirteen-year-old boy? I don't buy it."

"Me neither," Duncan said, draining his scotch.

"Somebody had a motive for murdering Vincent Palmer. Maybe Singh. Who knows what goes on in a thirteen-year-old's head? For some reason Palmer kept a note of – I'll use Amy's words – significant events, none of which point a finger at the boy. And for some reason, Palmer felt it necessary to hide a notebook and a VHS tape, not to speak of a dagger, up a chimney. What does that say to you?"

"Evidence of something," Duncan replied. "But evidence of what?"

"The sixty-four-million-dollar question, Duncan. In what direction might the investigation have gone if these items had been found at the time?" Gabby said. "And there's CR and EB to think about as well. One dead, one expelled. Where do they fit into this minefield? You do know, Duncan"—Gabby chewed the end of her pencil thoughtfully—"this has gone way beyond getting the dagger returned to its original owner. And it won't be until we find out why a dagger, a notebook, and a tape were stuffed up a chimney – in the very same building that Vincent Palmer was murdered in – that I'll sleep again."

"Yes, the tape…" Duncan said, reaching for the VHS and waving it in the air. "Innocent little thing, isn't it? If a picture paints a thousand words, then imagine what this might tell us. There's a date and a time marked on the spine. 16th May 1985."

"It was the following day on 17th May that EB was expelled from the school," Gabby said, checking the notebook. "Coincidence? Unlikely, I'd say. And on 1st June, not more than two weeks later, Palmer writes, 'I have the tape.' Shall we assume that's the tape he was referring to? It's got to be connected.

And I guess Amy mentioned to you about the very last entry in the notebook: 'God help us.' Written two days – correct me if I'm wrong – before Palmer was murdered. It's all here, Duncan. We just have to unravel it. That tape might be the key to it all."

"Don't get your hopes up too high, Gabby. This tape's been sitting around for thirty-seven years. It may be unreadable. I do happen to know someone who can convert it for us, but it will take time. A week, maybe less."

"Brilliant, do it." Gabby checked her watch. "Must go. Thomas and Gerald will be waiting. My first glimpse at this wonderful dagger, and then home, shower, posh frock, and down to the Mansion House for the party," Gabby said. "I do feel like a fraud, Duncan. Quite why Aunt Hetty, dear as she is, wants to organize a welcome party for me, I'll never know." She added, "Amy seems keen for us to investigate further – leaving the police out of it for the moment. What do you think, Duncan?"

"It's got my vote. What harm would it do?" Duncan smiled. "Besides, you're here now…"

"I'm not so sure Uncle Max is going to be so easily persuaded, but I'll give it my best shot," Gabby said.

"I think you might be wrong there. I rather think your Aunt Hetty and Uncle Max would like to see their Gabby as the hero of the hour again. With your brains, what could possibly go wrong? And isn't this what you do for a living anyway?"

"Funny you should say that. Amy said the same thing. What makes me think the two of you are in collusion?" Gabby laughed. "I'll see you at the party."

How could she say no to them?

Eighteen

2022

Both long since retired from their businesses, neither Thomas nor Gerald had ever dreamt that one day, they might be trading again, and from home at that. Looking back, Gerald often wondered why on earth he had paid an extortionate rent for his Chelsea-based fine art gallery when all the time he could have been conducting business online. The iPad had been a complete revelation, transforming their lives. And they had Duncan to thank for instructing them in the art of buying and selling on eBay. Gerald bought and sold artworks at the higher end of the market. Thomas dabbled happily in lower end antiques. Together they had a thriving little business.

"How's the auction going, Thomas?" Gerald shouted.

"I can't hear a word you're saying, dear fellow. I might stand half a chance if you turned that vacuum cleaner off for a minute," Thomas shouted back.

Gerald pulled the plug from the wall. "Just finished anyway. It's your turn next time. If there's one thing I hate, it's vacuuming carpets, but it had to be done. You know Gabby's got eyes out of the back of her head, don't you? She'd spot crumbs right away."

"It's countdown in two minutes. I'm ready, Gerald. Finger on the buzzer as they say. There are a few other bidders. Can't tell which way it will go but I won't go above fifty for it. I do hope Gabby doesn't turn up in the middle of the auction or I shall simply have to ignore her until it's done," Thomas said bright-eyed, staring at the screen, and with his fingers hovering over the keyboard. "How about you? Did you get that picture?"

"2.00 a.m. this morning. Yes, it's on its way. Should turn in a nice little profit." Gerald grinned. It had been a most lucrative night's work.

"Be a dear and take the scones out of the oven," Thomas said. "I've put the cups, saucers, and plates on the tray with a pot of my homemade jam. Just the kettle to go on when she arrives. It's starting now. Here we go. Wish me luck."

Seconds later, Thomas burst into the kitchen. "I won, Gerald. I did it again," he said, bursting with pride. "One second to go and I beat the lot of them. And I only paid just slightly over the odds." Gerald grinned.

* * *

Gabby planted a smile on her face as Thomas handed the plate of scones around. Silently she thanked her lucky stars that if Amy had had a cake in the kitchen, she had forgotten all about it. "I'm dying to see it," she said. "Is it as amazing as Duncan and Amy say it is?"

"Take a look for yourself, Gabby." Thomas wiped his jammy fingers on his napkin and reached down under the coffee table. "I found this little leather bag that we can keep it in, rather than that dreadful bit of polythene. Do take care. It's quite sharp."

Unzipping the bag, Gabby reached carefully in and pulled out the dagger. "Shit!" she said without thinking. "Sorry, boys, that just slipped out, but shit all the same. It's magnificent. A pity we've got to return it to its owner. What people wouldn't give to own something like this. All the more incredible that someone stuffed it up a chimney and left it there. Did you manage to find out anything about it?"

Thomas helped himself to another scone, delicately sliced it in half, and layered it with butter and jam. "Gerald and I had a most pleasant and highly informative outing yesterday afternoon," he said. "We went across to Cirencester to chat with an old business acquaintance of mine. He deals in weapons. Nothing else. Strange fellow. Archie Town, that's his name. Getting on a bit now but still has all his marbles and a magnificent collection of knives, spears, guns, and even cannons. Quite eccentric really. He's travelled the world in his time, buying and selling. He knows his onions, as they say. What were his first words when I showed him this, Gerald?"

"Not repeatable in front of a lady, Thomas, but a very crude version of bloody hell." Gerald smiled.

"Bloody hell; that will do nicely for now," Thomas laughed. "Because this dagger that you are looking at is believed to have been made by one of the finest silversmith families in the whole of India—"

"India?" Gabby cut in. It was all beginning to make some sense.

"India," Thomas repeated. "According to my friend, the skill in making such an object is one that is passed down through the generations. See those markings on the blade. Hold it up to the light and turn it around slowly."

"Got them," Gabby said. "That's the maker's mark then?"

"It is indeed. It is unique to one silversmith. Through that mark, and with a little bit of ingenuity, someone should be able to trace the precise silversmith who made it. And just maybe that will provide a trail back to the owner," Thomas said, looking like he was feeling quite pleased with himself. "I'm waiting for a call back now."

"It's not like any dagger I have ever seen," Gabby said. "Not that I have had that pleasure too many times. And the stones set in the hilt? They can't be genuine, can they?"

"They could certainly be genuine. You see, this isn't any ordinary dagger. It has a name. It is called a peace dagger. The name comes from an ancient tradition in India. When a settlement was reached between two warring families, daggers would be exchanged as a reminder of their peace agreement. Not any common or garden families, you understand, but high caste families, families of great wealth. Traditionally such a dagger is passed down through a family from one generation to the next. What is so fascinating is that the materials used all have mystical properties. The blade is made from iron – the centre of everything – like it is in our blood, transporting oxygen around our bodies. Silver is a softer metal, flexible which can be inscribed. It symbolizes the need for flexibility and adaptability. Gold is for leadership and vitality."

"And the stones? They have meanings too?" Gabby asked.

"Yes, that's quite correct, they do. Each has a special meaning in keeping with the overall theme of peace and harmony. Rubies are noble. They encourage gentleness and discourage violence. Emeralds signify love, sensitivity, and loyalty. Pearls are the ultimate symbol of wisdom. The dagger is said to have the power to guard the holder from evil, but only if the dagger is never used in anger. Once it has killed, it loses its power."

"So, I wonder if this little thing has ever been used in action? It could be our murder weapon..." Gabby said, turning the dagger over and over.

"Murder weapon?" Gerald started, his tea sloshing into the saucer and down his trousers. "Good God, Gabby. Amy didn't mention anything about murder—"

"All will be revealed, Gerald," Gabby said. "Duncan has been doing some digging and it seems I might be living with the ghost of a man murdered in the Old Forge. I'm going to update everybody on what we've found at the party tonight. Just trying to put it all together in some order in my mind first. Can you hang on for the full story until then?"

"So, this man might have been killed by this dagger?" Gerald asked, shocked.

"Unlikely, Gerald." Thomas shook his head knowledgeably. "Remember? After Archie put it under that magnifying glass, he said it was in pristine condition – not a mark on it. If there had been any evidence of anything else, I'm sure he would have spotted it and told us."

"But we can't rule it out completely, not yet," Gabby said thoughtfully. "Did your friend give you any idea of its value?"

"Archie said that if the stones are genuine, then we might be looking at a monetary value of not much less than a hundred thousand pounds," Thomas replied. "But, as he freely admits himself, he is no expert in gemstones."

"And if the stones aren't genuine?"

"Then a more modest sum of possibly five thousand pounds. The silver and gold combined with the exquisite workmanship would attract a lot of collectors of trinkets like this," Thomas replied.

"I'm just thinking, Thomas…" Gabby stroked her chin. "Greg's out in India at the moment. Some multi-million hotel for a Maharaja or some such thing. If Archie can track the silversmith down to a city, then – long shot that it is – Greg might be able to find out a bit more."

"I'll let you know just the minute I hear from him," Thomas said.

"And, if you don't mind, Gabby," Gerald cut in, "I would sleep far better without this possible murder weapon in our cottage. However beautiful it is, it gives me the creeps. Would you mind taking over as its custodian?" Gerald asked.

"I was going to ask anyway. That's no problem. I thought I'd show it to Greg when we FaceTime later on. At least he'll know what we're talking about—"

"—And, just so you know, I've taken lots of photographs of it on my iPad."

Thomas handed the leather pouch to Gabby. "She's all yours. Can't wait until this evening for you to tell us the whole story," he said.

Slipping the dagger into the leather pouch and popping it into her oversized handbag, Gabby left, hugging the bag tight under her arm. The thought passed through her mind that Uncle Max might have been right after all.

Nineteen

2022

Some welcome party. It had taken every bit of her willpower not to explode. Instead, she had retained an outward calm while inwardly she seethed with anger. Gabby raced back to the Old Forge, checking her watch as she ran. Well, whether he liked it or not, he'd just have to be woken up. Normally she timed her calls for 2.00 p.m. UK time and 7 p.m. local time in India, but this evening would be the exception. She was ready to explode.

FaceTime rang out three times. Cancel call or leave a message, it said. She did –twice, each time with the same response. Pouring herself a glass of wine, she eyed her laptop with disdain.

* * *

On the other side of the world, Greg opened one eye and reached for his phone. Five missed FaceTime calls. Somewhere in the recesses of his mind, he remembered her saying she was going to a welcome party that evening – her welcome party. Greg pushed his hair out of his eyes, propped his back up against the pillows, and called her back. "This had better be good, Gabby. Have you any idea what time it is here?"

"Yes, two o'clock in the morning and I need to speak to you," she snapped.

"I can see that. You look very nice, Gabby, but I'm not so sure about that look on your face. Who's rattled your cage?" Greg asked.

"I have just been shouted at and insulted. I was so angry I had to get out of there. How I managed to keep even half a smile on my face for as long as I did, I don't know."

"You are at Magnolia aren't you? That bunch of softies. None of them would insult you."

"There's one and he did and he goes by the name of Paul Green," Gabby said. "Nasty little man."

"Have I met him?" Greg asked.

"He's one of the newcomers. You might have bumped into him when we came up last time but maybe not. There's four of them. This creature and his wife, Ros. And then Sam, and Jasmine. They're all nice people but him…"

"What did you do to upset him?"

"Me?" Gabby exclaimed. "I didn't do a thing except tell him and all the rest of them about the dagger we found."

"Dagger?" Greg interrupted. "Am I dreaming this or are you telling me that you found a dagger. Sounds unlikely, Gabby. Have you been drinking? Maybe we should start this conversation again."

"Unlikely as it may be, Greg Olsen, Stan found a dagger up the chimney in this very place I am calling you from. And a notebook. And a VHS tape. And, for what it's worth, I have just had two glasses of wine and I'm on my third – a large one."

"Okay," Greg said slowly, a little disbelievingly. "A dagger. What has finding a dagger got to do with Paul and you getting so upset about it?"

"It's not confirmed yet," Gabby started to explain, "but the dagger may be valuable. Maybe a 100k top whacks. Paul's attitude is finders keepers. To his way of thinking, we sell the dagger and the residents split the proceeds twelve ways. All he cares about is the money. Sod the fact that a thirteen-year-old boy was as good as accused of murder. Sod the fact that there's a murderer out there getting off scot-free. Sod the fact that whoever is the real owner of the dagger might want to have it back. You'll not believe how that man spoke to me. It was so embarrassing, embarrassing for everyone. His poor wife didn't know where to put herself. It's an unsolved murder, for God's sake."

"An unsolved murder? Now I'm really confused," Greg said. "Calm down, Gabby. It's me, your husband you're speaking to. You wouldn't like to start from the beginning, would you? I'm awake now and I have the feeling I'm not going to go back to sleep too soon. How about you start at the beginning?" Greg said.

Gabby took a long deep breath and carefully ordered her thoughts. "That's the connection, Greg. The dagger is Indian. The boy is from India. Ergo, the dagger could have belonged to the boy. And maybe if we found him, we could return the dagger to him, and at the same time, maybe get to the bottom of how this man happened to be murdered. Well, that's our thinking."

"A big ask, even for you. Don't you think that maybe the residents are getting just a bit old for chasing lost boys and murderers?"

"You just try stopping them. Amy and Duncan are right up there leading from the front. Even Aunt Hetty and Uncle Max are onside. I'm beginning to feel a bit superfluous to requirements already, but they all insist I take the lead on it. I'm the investigative journalist, so they keep reminding me."

"So, what are you going to do?" It was the natural question to ask, even though he knew how she would answer it. "And I thought you were meant to be on holiday."

"The whole thing stinks, Greg. And I am on holiday, but this is just too important. An unsolved murder right here and new evidence comes to light. You don't think for one minute I can walk away from it, do you?" Gabby said.

"Nothing was ever further from my mind," Greg laughed.

"But I could do with a bit of help. A couple of questions for you. One, cast your mind back to the first time you came here with Harry Trumper. What did it look like?" Gabby asked.

"Well, there was the Mansion House right in the middle with the stables behind and two long block-built wings on either side of the Mansion House—"

"—And were there any other buildings – outbuildings – that sort of thing?"

"There was a crumbling old building – the one Magnolia used for storage all these years. And then…I vaguely remember there was a small block-built building tucked at the back of Mansion House. That was the first to be demolished if I remember correctly."

"Did it have a chimney?" Gabby interrupted.

"God, now you're asking, but I'm pretty certain that the answer is no," Greg said. "And there might once have been a block-built building near the car park – I remember a huge pile of debris that took ages to clear and, before you ask, I wouldn't have a clue if it had once had a chimney. Why are you asking me all this?"

"Just trying to confirm our suspicion that the Annexe – where the murder is said to have happened – is the same as the Old Forge. Where I'm staying. I reckon you've just confirmed that hunch," Gabby said.

"Ask me another," Greg said.

"Structural damage to the Mansion House. According to the newspaper, the school closed following a survey that declared it structurally unsafe. Ring a bell?"

"Complete crap. It may be eighteen years since I worked on the site, but I can tell you for a fact that the Mansion House was as sound as a bell right from the start. I did the survey myself. Neglected, for sure. Falling down – unsafe – no way," Greg said.

"Getting the gist of this, Greg? There's so much that doesn't add up. Did I tell you that I love you and miss you?"

"No, you missed that bit out, but I'll take it for granted," Greg laughed.

"Sorry. I've missed you," Gabby said, a warm glow spreading through her body. There were times when she missed him so much, missed cuddling up to him in bed, missed him taking her in his arms, missed dropping off to sleep after they had made love. "How's it going out there?"

"Good," Greg said. "Opening of the Raj last night. One very happy customer. And another contract lined up. Anything else, darling, or can I get a couple of hours' sleep?"

"Just one more thing. You don't happen to be going to Jaipur on your travels?"

"Tell me why before I answer that question."

"Ahmed Singh – the thirteen-year-old – was from Jaipur, so maybe that's where the dagger was made. It's got a maker's mark on it. You couldn't make a few discreet enquiries about silversmiths in Jaipur, could you? Not just any silversmith, but the best. One that's been in business a very long time. By the sound of it, it is a pretty unique piece. I can send you some photographs."

"As it happens, I'm flying into Jaipur tomorrow. Don't ask me when I'll get there. That depends on the cows. Whether they decide to take a kip on the railway line or stay in the fields where they should be. Leaves in England, cows in India. That's how it goes. You go with the tide here…It's a big city, Gabby," Greg frowned. "I'll do my best, but don't count your chickens."

"I'll let you get your beauty sleep now," Gabby smiled. Half awake, half asleep, dressed or undressed, he was always beautiful, inside and out. She couldn't do without him.

"And Paul? What are you going to do about him?" Greg asked.

"Avoid him at all costs," Gabby laughed.

"You just take care. I know you. Once you get your teeth stuck into something… And send everyone – except Paul – my love. Enjoy your holiday."

"Love you, sleep well." Gabby blew a kiss at the screen. "Did I tell you that Duncan and Jennifer announced their engagement tonight?" Gabby said as an afterthought. "How romantic is that?"

Twenty

2022

Right at that moment, he hated the woman. He loathed and despised her. Who was she to dictate what they should and shouldn't do with that little gold mine? Waltzing into Magnolia like she owned the place. Everyone fawning over her. 'You must meet Gabby,' they said. 'She's the girl who saved us from a fate worse than death.' Gabby this, Gabby that, Gabby the other. If she hadn't interfered, he wouldn't be here now. He could have brought them all round to his way of thinking. It was all very well for them: set up nicely, nothing to worry about except baking cakes, their little outings, and their stupid little coffee mornings and cocktail parties. What did they know about life? That ten grand, even eight, would have made all the difference. To hell with the lot of them, to hell with his wife and her never-ending questions, to hell with all the do-gooders. He was on his own.

Paul stroked the steering wheel and shifted up a gear. Foot down, watch the line of sight, into the bend. It was the only way to drive a Mustang. With the wind in his hair, he forgot the purpose of the journey. She was more familiar to him than any woman. His ears tuned in to the engine. If it missed a beat, he knew something needed his attention. She didn't miss a single beat. The steering was heavy and obedient, as it should be. They shared every pothole, every uneven or rough surface. She glided over them without complaint. A straight stretch ahead of him, and with no other vehicles in sight, Paul glanced at the instrument panel – fifty, sixty, seventy, eighty, ninety. With revs up at four thousand, he cast care to the wind. It mattered not one jot if he was caught speeding, today of all days. He had allowed time and had chosen a circuitous route, one that would give him the chance to say his final farewells to the car he loved more than anything in the world, besides Ros.

His destination was Rodborough Common, south of Stroud and north of Minchinhampton. It was an area he visited rarely, the last time being when he had taken Ros to Giffords Circus. Bounded by the Nailsworth Valley on one side and the Frome Valley on the other, it lay in National Trust property, in a sought-after residential location.

Too soon, he was driving across the common. Down to thirty miles per hour, it seemed he crawled forward. Glancing left and right, Paul looked out for a signpost to Rodborough Rise. He could not find it but that didn't disappoint him. He drove around in circles, passing the Bear Hotel, and the golf course several times. On the third pass, he spotted a sign, partly obscured by mature beech trees. Reluctantly, he indicated left.

The houses had no numbers. Just names. Posh names. Knights, The Pines, The Gables, Meadow View, Orchard House. And then, Hillside. Paul changed down to second gear and cruised around the winding newly built road, his eyes dazzled by the Cotswold stone that would take years to mature and blend into the surrounding countryside. Hillside was the last house in the close, surrounded by high walls and secured with an ornately carved electronic gate. Paul stopped alongside the intercom built into the wall and pressed the buzzer. The heavy gate swung open. There was no going back.

Two SUVs – a top-of-the-range Range Rover, and a Porsche – were parked in echelon alongside a shiny blue MGB. Paul parked in the last space, taking care to align his sports car with the other vehicles. Out of the window, he glanced at a middle-aged man emerging from the oak double doors, walking down the steps towards him.

"Paul," the man said, squatting beside the car. "Nice motor. Come on in. Let's have a chat. Show you around if you like?" Paul looked at him and knew he had no choice. He had to be civil. But right at that moment, he wanted nothing more than to crank the gearbox into reverse and head out the way he had come. If he ran over the man's feet as he did so, that would be a bonus. "Derek, call me Derek," he said.

The name stuck in his throat. The last thing he wanted was to have a polite, civilized conversation with somebody who was about to tear the love of his life away from him. "Derek," he muttered. "Be right with you."

"Let's go into my study and you can tell me all about her," Derek said, leading the way. Much as he wanted to hate everything about this man and his house, he found himself in awe. In awe of the man's coolness; in awe of the absolute opulence of the hall through which they passed; in awe of the views across the hills glimpsed through an open kitchen door. The study was massive. A full-size snooker table filled no more than one-eighth of the room. A huge cinema screen hung from a wall. A bank of computers, monitors, and printers occupied the middle section of a wall-to-wall desk. Patio doors led out onto the garden that swept away as far as the eye could see. On the remaining walls hung signed prints of racing drivers, many of whom had been Paul's idols.

"That's me with Lewis. Taken in 2019 at Silverstone. That's 2019. Goodwood Festival of Speed. Me with Jonny. And that," he said, pointing to yet another signed print, "is me and my mate, Riccardo, at Monte. Red Bull, you know."

It was impossible not to be impressed, but he was determined not to show it. "I've been to most of those circuits in my time with Vesper," Paul said.

"Vesper?" Derek said, "What's Vesper? Don't tell me you own a motor scooter too. That's cool." Derek laughed.

"Before your time. Vesper Lynd, played by Ursulla Andress. Casino Royale. She's called Vesper. The Mustang. If you want to get the best out of her, you'll call her by her proper name. Then she'll do anything for you," Paul explained. Eleven years old when his father had bought her in '67, she had always been part of the family.

"Gotcha. Well, we'll get round to her later, shall we? How about a tour of my garage, and then we'll do business over a cup of coffee," Derek said.

"Don't you want to take her out for a spin? Check her out?" Paul narrowed his eyes. The man hadn't once asked anything about her health or history.

"She looks fine to me. I've got a good pal who does restorations. Strips them apart and puts them back together, nut by nut, bolt by bolt. A quick visit to the spray shop and you'll not recognize her," Derek said. "Let's go out to the barn."

Paul winced. The thought of his Vesper being taken apart cut through him like a shard of glass. Paul followed Derek out of the front door and around the side of the house. The barn was almost as big as the house itself. Inside was a collection of classics that would have put those in the British Motor Museum to shame. Silently he followed Derek from one car to the other, mentally adding up the value of the collection. This matter-of-fact, cool individual was sitting on a fortune, one that he did not appreciate. He was a hoarder without passion. In that moment, Paul was sorely tempted to cut and run and take Vesper home.

"Shall we shake hands on it?" Derek asked, draining the dregs of his coffee. "The papers all seem to be in order. You can take the album back with you. A souvenir. I shan't have any use of it. The price is a bit steep, but I'm not going to haggle with you. Cheque or transfer?"

Paul picked up the file in which, over the years, he had religiously kept every photograph, every newspaper article, every bill, every MOT, and every service sheet. They belonged to Vesper, not to him. "Please keep them," he replied. "She's got a great history. One day when you come to sell her, you'll be glad you did. Transfer?"

"Sure, this way." Derek threw Paul's precious book on the desk and opened his laptop. Paul felt a stab in the heart. If it hadn't been for…that stupid bitch…

"All done," Derek said. "Money should be in your bank now or in the next few minutes. You need a lift somewhere? I could drive you in the Mus', one last time."

"No," Paul said. "But thanks for the offer. I prefer to walk."

"It's a few miles, you know."

"I know. Fresh air will do me good," Derek replied. He found his own way out. The ornate metal gates opened as he walked towards them without looking back at either Vesper or her new owner.

* * *

Three miles was nothing in a car: five minutes in a modern one, two or three in Vesper. On foot, it was endless. Legs weary and stiff, Paul pushed open the door to the Ale House and almost fell in over the protruding step. Stroud CAMRA pub of the year 2014 to 2019, they knew how to serve a pint. It was rarely crowded during the day and the staff were friendly, but not overfriendly. If you wanted to chat, you could. If you wanted to be left in peace, you were. It was his pub, his local these days. The only thing that was missing was Vesper in the car park waiting to take him home. All he wanted that day was a stool to sit on, a pint in his hand, and some peace and quiet. Time to say his final goodbye to Vesper.

"What'll it be, Paul?" The barman knew him well and addressed him by his familiar name. "The usual? Burning Sky?"

Paul nodded and threw a twenty-pound note on the counter. "Keep that behind the bar. It won't last long today," he said.

Picking up the glass, he downed it in one. "Fill it up," he said.

After downing the third pint, his foot slipped off the footrest and his body slewed sideways. Had it not been for a newcomer, he would have hit the deck, hard, but probably wouldn't have felt it. "I owe you a pint, mate," Paul said looking through a haze. Squinting, he saw a tall, broad-shouldered, elderly man with a full head of thick, grey hair and a pale face which looked as though it had hardly ever seen the light of day, and certainly not the sun. "Gerr'um in," he slurred to the barman. "Two pints of the Burning. That okay with you, pal?" he asked, turning to the long-legged newcomer who had, with ease, mounted the barstool alongside him.

"Bad day at the office?" the man asked.

"Women," Paul struck up. "Love 'em and lose 'em. That's what happens."

"Oh, dear," his new friend said. "Trouble at mill, as they say up north?"

"Big trouble, my friend. I just sold my woman after knowing her for fifty-five years. Any idea what a wrench that is?"

"You sold your wife?" The man shifted his barstool away and looked askance at his new drinking companion.

"Not my wife, my car, idiot," Paul snapped. "Apologies, you're probably not an idiot at all. It's the rest of them who are idiots. I'm not myself today. Not myself at all." Paul hesitated. "She was fifty-five years old; known her man and boy."

"But you had to let her go. It's so sad. When we get older, there are simply things that we can't do anymore. It comes to all of us."

"Yes, as you put it, I had to let her go. Needed the money you see. Paul's the name. I live up at Magnolia – the retirement place. You know, a couple of miles out of town? I bet you didn't know there was once a school out there," Paul said.

"As it happens, I did. St John's College, wasn't it?" The man moved his stool closer. "And now I hear it's a wedding venue as well as a retirement complex?"

"Every bloody weekend in the summer. Well, let me tell

141

you, they're as nutty as fruit cases up there. Lost the plot completely if you ask me..." Paul said, leaning closer.

The man leaned in close and listened.

Twenty-One

2022

Turning and closing the door behind him, Duncan filled his lungs with the fresh morning air. It was a warm spring day. A gentle breeze blew up from the valley. A few high white clouds ambled lazily across the sky. Close by, he heard the steady beat of the ride-on lawnmower. Dennis was up early. Nowhere but nowhere were there lawns to match those of Magnolia. They were Dennis's pride and joy, kept short but not too short, and mowed in perfect cricket pitch lines. No one dared walk on them after he had finished.

He had a good feeling about the day and was looking forward to spending time with the girls, as he liked to think of them. Gabby was a breath of fresh air. Nothing ever fazed her. She hadn't changed one little bit. Fame had not gone to her head. She was just one of them as she always had been – and her adventures the cause of many a sleepless night for Max and Hetty. The cup was never half empty for Gabby. It crossed his mind that the previous night's altercation with Paul might have put a damper on things, but he knew that she always bounced back. All would be well. They were making progress, albeit slow.

* * *

If he timed it right, Amy would have the kettle on and a cake ready to be cut on the kitchen table. Elevenses was always served at eleven – on the dot.

Reaching up to knock at the door, Duncan heard voices inside that sounded much like two children laughing and giggling. It made him smile. Amy and Gabby both had an evil sense of humour and had always been close. Nothing had changed that.

"Good morning, Duncan," Amy said. "I must say you're looking very dapper today. Did you borrow that bowtie from Gerald? Let me guess. A romantic assignation with the beautiful Jennifer later on?"

Duncan blushed. "As it happens, dear lady, I am off to see my bride-to-be in about an hour. We're discussing wedding plans. I rather think she might be getting a little carried away. By the end of this summer, we'll all be pleased to see the end of the season. The wedding diary is almost full and Jennifer is off to meet yet another potential client tomorrow. There's no stopping her."

"That's Jennifer, but she deserves her day. And so do you for that matter. We're all looking forward to the big day," Amy said. "Gabby's here."

"And how is she after last night's little debacle? Very embarrassing – all around. I don't know what's got into that man." Duncan shook his head. That was the truth of the matter. He'd never seen Paul behave badly in the past.

"You know Gabby. Resilient is her middle name. She's still a bit cross about it, of course, but I've tried to smooth things over. So, what have we got? Do tell," Amy asked, her eyes sparkling.

"Perhaps I can come in first?" Duncan grinned. "I thought you were the queen of suspense, Amy, wait and see," he teased. "Tea first. Two sugars if you please. And let me think. Coffee cake day. Am I right?"

"I'll get it," Gabby called. "And, you're quite right, it is coffee cake day."

Watching Amy out of the corner of his eye, Duncan took his time, stirred his tea, and carefully sliced his cake into four easily manageable pieces. Placing one piece in his mouth, he rolled it around. "A good brew, Amy," he said with a grin. "Hetty's coffee cake?"

"Oh, come on, Duncan. I can see it in your face. You've found something, haven't you? I might just take the rest of that cake away from you if you don't tell us right this minute," Gabby said impatiently.

"And I certainly won't let you have another slice," Amy added.

"Okay, you've both got me there. Well, I managed to get hold of some old information about the Vincent Palmer murder. Don't ask me how. Just thank Hell's Angels for being there for us. I've still got my contacts, you know, and very useful they are too," Duncan said.

"And..." Gabby said, conjuring up a vision of Duncan in his leathers.

"I managed to get my hands on a couple of pieces of useful information about the Palmer case. Not from the National Archive, I hasten to add. No questions asked, ladies. Like you, Gabby, I never reveal my sources. Bit disappointing really. Not as much as I hoped there would be, but after thirty-seven years, I guess we can't expect miracles." Duncan drew a plastic wallet out of the holder on the side of his wheelchair, opened it, and withdrew several sheets of paper. "Not the originals, of course, but second best. Copies. Two witness statements. That's it. Here's a copy for you, Amy, and one for Gabby too. You both have a read, and then you can tell me what you think. In the meantime, I'll finish my cake and maybe have another slice."

Gabby curled up in the armchair, her feet folded under her, while Amy searched her handbag for a pair of reading glasses before finding them hanging around her neck. Both read in silence while Duncan munched away happily and watched their faces.

STATEMENT OF WITNESS
(Criminal Procedure Rules, r. 16.2;
Criminal Justice Act 1967, s. 9)

STATEMENT OF William Rutherwood
Age of witness (if over 18, enter "over 18"): Over 18.
This statement (consisting of 2 pages) **is true to the best of my knowledge and belief and I make it knowing that, if it is tendered in evidence, I shall be liable to prosecution if I have wilfully stated in it anything which I know to be false, or do not believe to be true.**
My name is William Rutherwood. I am the Headmaster at St John's College. I have held this post for the past 5 years. On the night of Wednesday 5th June, I was standing outside at the back of the main building smoking a cigarette as I do

every night before I lock up and retire to my quarters. It was 10.20 p.m. I remember checking my watch.

I was in the process of stubbing out my cigarette when I heard raised voices. An argument of some kind. The argument went on for a minute or more. I listened but could not hear what was being said, nor did I recognize the voices. Although I believe on reflection that one of them was that of Vincent Palmer. He has a way with words, most of which I do not approve. The voices were coming from the direction of the Annexe, and I could see lights on within the building. I then heard what I thought might have been a scuffle followed by a loud groan. And then another. It was then that I became concerned that whatever argument it might have been had got out of hand. Had matters been different, I would have made my way directly to the Annexe to see for myself. I sustained an injury to my leg while on active duty in Cyprus. I walk with a stick. I knew that if there were trouble, I might be unable to deal with it myself and that the safest thing to do was to rouse somebody to go with me. Keepers Cottage was nearby, and I thought it likely that Mr Grzeskowiak, the caretaker at the school, would be awake. Mr Grzeskowiak immediately put on his jacket and accompanied me to the Annexe. It was just after 10.25 by the time we reached the Annexe. Again, I checked my watch. Mr Grzeskowiak and I hastened to the Annexe and climbed the steps to the flat above. The door was slightly open. That is when we saw him. I recognized him immediately as Vincent Palmer, the head of mathematics in the school. He was lying on the floor, face-up, his head a bloody mess. His eyes were open, but there was no movement from his chest. I could see he was dead, but I checked his pulse to be sure. There was none. I noticed a school cap upturned on the floor. The name tag was visible. It belonged to one of our pupils, Ahmed Singh. There was blood on the cap. I also noticed an exercise book that was lying on the bed. The name printed on the cover was Ahmed Singh. I asked Mr Grzeskowiak to check the bathroom to make sure there was nobody there. This he confirmed to be the case. After we found Mr Palmer, I instructed Mr Grzeskowiak to return to the school and rouse two of my teachers – Mr Stanwell and Mr Walker. He was to instruct them to go immediately to the corridor outside of the boys' dormitories and check that all boys were present and safe. I then immediately proceeded to my office to call for help. I called Detective Superintendent Garry Seymour, a governor of the school and whom I also knew to be a senior member of the police force. I made the call to him at 10.32. He told me that he would call in the incident and be at the school as soon as possible.

On return to my office, Mr Stanwell reported back to me that one of the boys was missing from their dormitory – Ahmed Singh. I instructed Mr Grzeskowiak to search the building and then extend his search to the gardens. The boy was nowhere to be found. Mr Grzeskowiak was very upset. I poured a large whisky for both of us and then told him to return to Keepers Cottage and stay there.

The police arrived at 10.50. I explained to Detective Chief Superintendent Seymour all I had seen and heard. I know of no one who would wish to harm Vincent Palmer. Ahmed Singh first arrived at the school in January of this year, and I can confirm that he was one of Vincent Palmer's protegees, one of his chosen few, to whom he provided extra-curricular mathematics lessons in the evenings. The financing of

Ahmed Singh's schooling was managed by Mr David McMasters, his legal guardian, a solicitor and a resident of Jaipur, India. I did not know the boy well, but on more than one occasion, I had reason to discipline him over picking fights with other boys and, on one occasion, for minor theft. Other than the door handle and Mr Palmer's wrist, I touched nothing within the flat.

Signed: ... *W° Rutherwood* .... **(witness)**
Date: ......6th June 1985

STATEMENT OF WITNESS
(Criminal Procedure Rules, r. 16.2;
Criminal Justice Act 1967, s. 9)
STATEMENT OF Adrian Grzeskowiak
Age of witness (if over 18, enter "over 18"): Over 18.
This statement (consisting of 2 pages) **is true to the best of my knowledge and belief and I make it knowing that, if it is tendered in evidence, I shall be liable to prosecution if I have wilfully stated in it anything which I know to be false, or do not believe to be true.**

My name is Adrian Grzeskowiak and I am the caretaker at St John's College. On 5th June, I had just changed the CCTV tape when I heard someone banging on my door. I opened the door to find Mr Rutherwood, the Headmaster. I was surprised to see him. He told me to put my jacket on and go with him. He told me that he'd heard noises and needed to check it out. I didn't ask any questions, grabbed my jacket, and followed him. He led me towards the Annexe. I knew Mr Vincent lived up there. I remember Mr Rutherwood

149

checking his watch and telling me that it was just after 10.25 when we got there.

He went up the stairs first. I followed. A light was on up there. The door was open a bit. Mr Rutherwood pushed open the door and went in. I was right behind him. I saw Mr Vincent sprawled on the floor. He was dead. It was obvious. There was blood on his head and a trickle of blood from his mouth. I watched as Mr Rutherwood knelt over him and checked his pulse. He shook his head in my direction which I took to mean that Mr Vincent was gone.

I didn't touch anything as far as I remember. Mr Rutherwood told me to knock Mr Stanwell and Mr Walker up and get them to check the dormitories to make sure that all the boys were safe and then meet him back at his office. I left the Annexe leaving Mr Rutherwood there.

Back in his office, he told me that a boy, Ahmed Singh, was missing and that I was to check all the buildings and the grounds which I did. It was a light night. If he had been there, then I would have found him. I didn't. I did not know the boy in person, but I'd seen him around. He stood out in a crowd.

I didn't know him well, but I liked Mr Vincent. Mr Rutherwood poured me a large whisky and had one himself. I remember feeling tired. Mr Rutherwood told me to go back to Keepers straight away and he'd get hold of me if he needed me. I must have fallen asleep. I didn't hear the police cars arrive.

Signed: ...*A Grzeskowiak*........................ ....

(witness)

Date: ...6 June 1985..

So, ladies, your thoughts?" Duncan asked.

"A cap on the floor smattered in blood; Ahmed Singh's exercise book on the bed. Pretty damning evidence on the face of it. Interesting that our Mr Grzeskowiak doesn't mention either one of them," Gabby said, comparing the two statements.

"In shock, maybe," Duncan offered. "He does say he was gutted, feeling sick. Not surprising. Or, simply, he's not as perceptive as our Headmaster."

"Or they simply weren't there when our Mr Grzeskowiak left the Annexe," Amy muttered under her breath.

"There are several things that puzzle me here." Deep in thought, Amy took off her glasses and stared at the ceiling. "Why would Mr Grzeskowiak refer to teachers in different ways? He refers to Mr Stanwell and Mr Walker, but when he mentions Mr Palmer, it's Mr Vincent. Otherwise, why not address him as Mr Palmer too? Doesn't that imply a level of familiarity between Mr Grzeskowiak and Vincent Palmer and yet he states that he didn't know *Mr Vincent* well? Perhaps they knew each other a little better than Grzeskowiak is prepared to let on," Amy said, looking up.

"Observant as always, Amy. A good question," Duncan said. "I hadn't picked that one up."

"And come to that," Gabby chipped in, "why would Mr Rutherwood ask Mr Grzeskowiak to wake up Mr Stanwell and Mr Walker in particular? Surely any two teachers would have done just as well. And why would Mr Grzeskowiak be so specific about them?"

"Maybe reading too much into it, Gabby," Duncan said.

"Doesn't quite ring true to me. Do you detect a little collaboration in these two statements, Amy?" Gabby said.

"Hard to tell, dear, but it's not out of the question," Amy said.

"At least we've got one good lead out of this. David McMasters, Ahmed Singh's legal guardian. If anybody knows what happened to Ahmed, then it would be him. I wonder if he still lives in Jaipur," Gabby said to herself. "I'll talk to Greg again. He's there now. I've already got him on the trail of silversmiths. It shouldn't be too difficult to track down a solicitor if he's still there."

"Your turn, Duncan," Amy said.

"Precise times. That's what I spotted. Very precise and all based on Mr Rutherwood checking his watch. It was ten twenty-five according to Rutherwood when he knocked on Mr Grzeskowiak's door. In Mr Grzeskowiak's statement, he states that he had *just changed* the CCTV tape." Duncan paused.

"I'm not following you, Duncan. What's odd about that?" Gabby said.

"What is odd, my dear, is I believe the tapes are changed at nine thirty in the evenings. At least the tape found up the chimney was dated 16th May and the time was 1.30 p.m.–9.30 p.m. Not ten twenty-five. Don't you find that a little strange? Admittedly the timing might have been changed between 16th May and 5th June," Duncan said.

"No forensic reports? No other witness statements?" Gabby asked hopefully.

"Not that I can lay my hands on," Duncan replied.

"It's just possible that our AG might be Mr Grzeskowiak. It would be rather nice if we could talk to him. It seems from the notebook that he might have known Ahmed rather better than he leads us to believe. There's an entry which simply states, AS/ AG," Amy said thoughtfully. "And I'd quite like to check out whether our Mr Grzeskowiak is a little hard of hearing. He says he didn't hear the police cars arrive. That's very odd. Well, if Mr Rutherwood's statement is to be believed, the Annexe and Keepers Cottage were not far apart."

"One step ahead of you there, Amy," Duncan said. "I thought you might suggest a little visit would be in order, so I did a bit of digging. There's a Grzeskowiak living not a million miles away. Fits the age profile. Not sure about the house though. Take a look at this," Duncan said, opening his laptop. "Street view. Pretty smart bungalow in a good location, don't you think, for a caretaker? Maybe he won the pools."

"You're completely priceless, Duncan," Gabby said. "You could charge a fortune for your skills. And Singh? I don't suppose your genius managed to find any leads on his whereabouts."

"Needle in a haystack. As common as Smith. But I'll see what I can find out about Rutherwood, Stanwell, and Walker. But right now, ladies, I must bid you farewell. I have a date with a beautiful lady. A lady must never be kept waiting, as you know full well. I've written Grzeskowiak's address down," Duncan said, handing a note to Gabby. "And if you two ladies go visiting, which I suspect you will, take care."

"What are you doing tomorrow, Amy?" Gabby grinned.

"I had nothing planned but it seems like my diary might now be full," Amy smiled. "Just like old times, isn't it?"

Twenty-Two

2022

Sitting and staring into an empty coffee cup, Ros wiped away the tear that had left streaks where her make-up had been.

He was once such a lovely man. They met at a party. She remembered standing in the corner of the room wondering why on earth she had accepted the invitation in the first place. She wasn't a party girl, preferring to spend time with just one or two of her special girlfriends. Having had her fingers burnt by a man, she no longer trusted them. Nineteen at the time and, looking back, naïve for her age, she had fallen straight into the trap. At that age, she had thought she knew everything – was invincible. He'd offered her the use of his spare room for the night after they had gone out to the theatre and for dinner. She had accepted. She hadn't known what consensual sex was at the time. She'd let herself be cajoled into it, cornered so that there was no way out. His name was Christian. How could she forget a name like that?

And then at the party, she had noticed this man standing across the other side of the room, looking equally uncomfortable and lost. Dressed in a suit and tie, he looked so out of place, it was untrue. He noticed her too and smiled across the room. He came over with two drinks in his hand and asked her if she was okay. He was nothing to look at. Not handsome. Not charming. Not pushy. Not anything really, but he was kind and attentive. She felt comfortable in his company. Safe. She fell in love with him. Four years later, they were married and saving up for their own business. It suddenly seemed such a long time ago. His name was Paul.

No TV, radio, or music, Ros waited and listened for the door. She knew what to expect. First the jangling of his keys, then the swearing as he failed to line the key up with the lock, and then his fists banging on the door at the same time, demanding that she open it to let him in. This time, she was waiting for him. Had he not gone out yet again early that morning, she would have had it out with him there and then.

Ignoring the phone's non-stop ringing, she had spent the day in silence, thinking through her options and the consequences of each. She had no idea how the day might end. Mentally, she had packed her suitcase.

Ros stood back from the front door and looked at her husband. His eyes were bloodshot and unfocused. She could see no remorse in them. Staggering through the door, he made for the downstairs toilet. Ros listened as an endless stream of urine cascaded into the bowl, closely followed by the sound of him retching until there was nothing more to bring up, all the time knowing that it was she who would have to clear up after him. She stood her ground and waited.

"Bed, I'm going to bed, woman," he said as he staggered out through the bathroom door. "Don't you look at me like that."

"No, you are not," she said, grabbing his arm and physically pulling him into the kitchen. "Sit." She pointed to the chair, her eyes stony, and stood over him. "Who the fucking hell are you?" she yelled, all thoughts of the thin walls between Bluebell and Magnolia Cottage set aside. Right at that moment, she didn't care if Sam and Jas heard her every word; she knew Jas would say it was past time. "How dare you speak to Gabby that way? How dare you embarrass me like that? How dare you behave like this? How dare you come home every day stinking of beer, drunk? Take a look at yourself, Paul, a long, hard look. Last night was meant to be a celebration – a celebration of Gabby coming back to Magnolia, a celebration of Duncan and Jennifer announcing their engagement. You ruined the whole evening for everybody. And now I can't show my face outside this house. What the hell got into you? You're a monster. A rude, arrogant monster. I don't know you anymore. And I don't think I want to know you anymore."

Paul looked up at his wife, scared, the room spinning. "What do you want me to say?" he said.

"You have one chance, Paul. Otherwise, I shall pack my suitcase and leave here today, and you'll not see me again. It can't go on any longer."

He hardly recognized her. It was as though she was someone from his dim and distant past. Slowly it dawned on him that he hadn't seen her, looked at her for the past several months. They'd been in the same room, eaten at the same table, slept in the same bed, but he hadn't seen her. Too wrapped up in his own problems, he hadn't noticed the agony she was in, the agony he was putting her through. A sense of shame swept through him. He'd bottled it up. He'd kept it all within his own little world to protect her, he'd like to think, but had that been the case? Or had he just been bloody selfish, feeling sorry for himself? This beautiful woman he had married all those years ago, the woman he worshipped, was standing in front of him with tears of anger pouring down her cheeks. She was right. It could not go on any longer. Suddenly, he was sober.

"Ros," he said, reaching out his hand to her. She snatched her hand away and buried it in her lap. "Ros, I am so, so sorry."

"You've gone too far this time. It is one thing for you to treat me like a doormat, ignore me, clear off every day without a by-your-leave, and return home sullen and drunk, but it is an entirely different matter when you insult my friends, people who welcomed us into their community. Sorry doesn't cut it, Paul." Her voice was cold.

"Please, please, Ros, I've wanted to tell you, but I couldn't. I've let you down in so many ways. I know I have." Paul stood up and reached out to put his arm around her shoulder. Ros shrugged him off angrily. "Just let me explain," he said, collapsing back down onto the chair. "I'm going to tell you the truth, the whole truth and then, if you feel that it's the end of us, I'll be the one to leave. You only have to say the word."

Ros dried her tears, fearing the worse.

"It was a phone call...I'd finished early at the vegetable plot, nothing more to do. You were out with Jas. I started playing with the iPad. God, I wish I'd never set eyes on that thing. I was just googling some seeds for next year and up popped this advertisement. It was about making your pension work for you. It just caught my interest. I clicked on the ad and read about the thousands of people whose lives had been transformed by re-organizing their pensions. I remember thinking that we were doing fine, thank you very much. State pension, the savings we had invested in our personal pension, and the rainy-day bonds. Thought about how lucky we were to have a lovely home and sufficient money coming into the bank every month to cover our expenses and spare cash for treats.

"Then a couple of days later I had this phone call – out of the blue, or so I thought. It was from a company called Sun Alliance Protected Pensions. Well, everyone's heard of Sun Alliance haven't they? Especially if they watch daytime TV. Well, the company, he said, had a great new offer for over sixties able to invest a lump sum. It was only open for a couple of weeks. The income would have doubled what we're getting now. I imagined the holidays I could take you on, a new car for you, maybe another classic for me, treating our friends here to a night out or even a weekend away...The green-eyed monster."

He ploughed on. "Stephen was his name. Posh accent, he sounded very professional. He said he'd send me some projections and he did. Emails, all looked kosher. They even linked back to Sun Alliance's head office. Looked genuine enough to me. Said that all the investments would be protected by the Financial Services Compensation Scheme and that the capital would be spread across several investments. You know that eighty-five grand ceiling and all that. He even told me that I should consult my financial advisor if I had one. I asked him if he was a financial advisor. Stupid question – he was hardly going to say no, was he? And he said that I could check out his credentials on the FCA Register. I didn't."

"How much, Paul?" Ros asked.

"Three hundred thousand. I made six payments – electronic

transfers over five days. I even read the bank warnings about scams and ignored them. I knew better. Me and Stephen – we were big mates by this time. Rang me every morning with updates on how my money was being invested. Never missed a day. I did say I'd be happy to ring him, but he said that he was out of the office most of the time – better that he contacted me. Even that didn't ring any warning bells. I was sold. He said the first income payment would be made into our bank account on the first day of the month. I checked. Nothing. And nothing on the second, third, or fourth day. Then I got really worried, and I rang the number that he had given me. Number unknown.

"I rang the bank. Okay, I'd ignored the warnings, but the bank hadn't questioned any of the payments. I had been 'unduly negligent' according to them. They were not liable for any losses. I'm not making excuses, Ros. Any half-sane man would have copped it right from the beginning. I was a fool, a stupid fool. So now you know who you married."

Betrayed, she felt betrayed. Desperately wanting to shout at him and blame him for his stupidity, she couldn't. She couldn't find the words. Before her sat a broken man. What hurt more than anything else was that he had not trusted her, otherwise he would have told her. It was only now coming out because finally she had reached breaking point and told him that she wouldn't put up with his behaviour any longer. She knew he hadn't slept properly for weeks, prowling around the house in the middle of the night. The red circles around his eyes were testimony to that. The wrinkles across his forehead and between his eyes were deeper than she had ever remembered them. His eyes were bloodshot from trying to bury it all in drink. His skin looked sallow.

"Say something, Ros. If only that you hate me," Paul said.

Ros took two mugs out of the cupboard and popped one tea bag in each, her hands shaking. "You should have told me. We've always shared everything. No secrets. Isn't that what we promised each other on our wedding day? Did you think I'd walk away?"

"You should have," Paul said.

"So, all our savings are gone, and our income's gone right down?" Ros said.

Paul nodded. "The rainy-day fixed bonds are still there but we can't touch them for the next three years. We hadn't even got enough in the bank to pay the increased service charge that will be due next month...And then yesterday evening, as if by magic, there was the chance of getting hold of some cash fast – enough cash to see us through the next year if we were careful. I wanted that dagger to be sold and for us to get our share of the proceeds, not because I felt it my right or was greedy, but because I knew it might mean the difference between our staying here or having to sell up. I saw it as a lifesaver, a lifesaver that Gabby snatched away from us. That's when I lost it."

"It was not ours to sell. It belongs to somebody. It was only you who wanted it sold. Don't blame Gabby," Ros said.

"I sold Vesper this morning," Paul whispered, the memory still raw. "I had to do something. I couldn't let you lose this place. It was the only option left, and I'd found someone who was interested."

Reaching out for his hand, she squeezed it tight. She knew how much it must have hurt him to part with the Mustang. It had been a part of him, man and boy. It was a measure of how desperate he must have been. "You stupid man, you should have talked to me."

"We've got cash in the bank to see us through now if we're really careful," he said. "I just couldn't bring myself to tell you that we might lose this place."

"It wouldn't have come to that, if only you'd spoken to me." Ros paused. She had planned to tell him one day, at the right time. "There's something that I've never told you about either. Life has a funny way of changing when you least expect it, so I kept quiet about it – for a rainy day. Remember when my great-aunt died a year ago? Well, she left me a tidy sum of money. I put it away – just in case. Whatever happens, we'll not lose Bluebell Cottage."

"I don't deserve you, Ros. You are such a wonderful woman. I've completely blown it, haven't I?" Paul said.

"You have come so very close, but I haven't been married to you for forty years to walk away now. We'll find a way forward – together." Ros said slowly, "You have to stop drinking. You have to apologize to Gabby and the rest of our friends. And you must promise me that you'll never keep anything from me again."

Twenty-Three

2022

"Where would you like me to drop you off?" Andy asked.

"Outside Leonard Walker's, please. It's a very good butcher's shop and I want to pick up a nice piece of steak for Duncan's supper. If you could wait for me outside for two minutes, and then drop me at Lavender Café in Chalford, that would be perfect. It's a lovely little tea shop. Beautiful cakes and pastries all made on the premises. There's plenty of time. I'm not meeting Mr Williams at the tea shop until two-thirty," Jennifer replied. "Do I look the part?"

Andy grinned. Whenever Jennifer had a meeting, out came the royal-blue power suit with the padded shoulders, the height of fashion in the '80s. "You look great. No older than…sixty, maybe sixty-five."

"You are a tease, Andy," Jennifer said, flicking her long hair over her shoulders before reapplying her lipstick in the mirror. "I wish I was."

"So, Duncan's in for another treat tonight, is he?" Andy said.

"I try to keep meals simple, Andy, then I can't go wrong. I'm no Mary Berry, I know that, everyone knows that. Hetty and Dot will certainly attest to that. The last time I baked cakes with them, all mine landed up in the bin. Duncan will just have to get his cakes elsewhere."

Andy stepped out of the car and went round to open Jennifer's door for her. "What time would her ladyship like to be picked up this afternoon? I've got to go to Chalford Building Supplies. I've got more Post-its stuck up on my kitchen wall than you've had hot dinners."

Jennifer smiled. What would they do without Andy and his Post-its? Mr Fix it, they called him. One Post-it popped through Andy's letterbox – that was all it took. Leaky pipes, blocked toilets, faulty locks, stains, and broken furniture – there was almost nothing Andy couldn't fix.

"I'll call you, Andy. If that's alright with you. I doubt I'll be much more than an hour, but you never know. It depends entirely upon how much of the wedding planning Mr Williams would like us to do for him."

"You've got your phone?" Andy asked. Jennifer nodded. "Right here in my bag, and it's charged. I checked it before I left."

* * *

"You must be Jennifer," he said, tapping her on the shoulder. "With a head of hair like that, I really couldn't miss you, could I?"

"Jennifer, Jennifer Buchanan. And you must be Mr Williams." Jennifer stood and offered her hand.

"Call me Ian," he said. "May I say how charming you look, my dear. Christian Lacroix if I am not mistaken? It's not often that I get to take tea with such a beautiful lady," he said.

Grinning, Jennifer wondered whether it was appropriate

to tell him that she had bought it in a charity shop a very long time ago. He held her hand in his a little longer than was necessary, but it was a pleasant sensation. His nails were beautifully manicured, his hands warm and soft. It was an elderly face, but handsome.

"I hope you didn't mind me asking if we could get together at such short notice," he said as he pulled out Jennifer's chair for her. "As I explained on the phone, my granddaughter, Sophie, is getting married, and the wedding venue has had to cancel our booking. It was to be at Burleigh Court Hotel – at Minchinhampton. Wonderful place, beautiful building. Just perfect for a wedding. Seems that royalty of some kind has commandeered the property for the weekend and wouldn't take no for an answer. Nothing they could do about it. Tried their best. They're fully booked every other weekend, just like everybody else. It was they who suggested I contact you at Magnolia. I've glimpsed the building from the road, and I have to say the house looks quite splendid. And if I'm not mistaken, the grounds are extensive as well. You have a good reputation for weddings," he said.

Jennifer smiled. It was praise indeed, but they had earned it through sheer hard work and determination. And for Burleigh Court to recommend them was the highest of praise. "I've ordered a pot of tea and a plate of fancies. I hope that is okay with you?" she said.

"There's nothing I like more than a little fancy, Jennifer," he said. "Couldn't be more perfect. And this tea shop – now how can I best describe it –old-fashioned and at the same time clean, bright and cosy? The perfect formula. Reminds me of taking tea with my grandmother many years ago."

Jennifer ignored the innuendo. "We pride ourselves on

offering a very comprehensive wedding package, Ian," she said in a business-like manner. "The Mansion House is spacious and capable of seating up to sixty people for the service. With high ceilings and almost floor-to-ceiling stained-glass windows, it provides a quite exquisite setting, if I say so myself. We do, of course, have a licence for holding wedding ceremonies performed on the premises."

"Quite how old is it, Jennifer?" he asked.

"The Mansion House, you mean? It dates back to the early 1800s, built by an industrialist with an unusual taste in architecture. Over the years, it's been everything from a hospital to a private school – that's what it was before Magnolia Court was developed. And now there are twelve pretty little cottages on the grounds occupied by the residents. There were ten originally, but we built two more a couple of years ago," Jennifer explained. "I had a little windfall and ploughed it back into Magnolia."

"And more to come, I don't doubt. Must be highly sought-after – retirement cottages in such a lovely setting," he said.

"Oh, they are. Advertised for sale one day and sold the next, but there'll be no more cottages. We like it as it is. We're all finished with the building now. We've just finished the refurbishment of the last of the outbuildings. We've called it the Old Forge. It's close to the Mansion House. It can be made available as part of the wedding package – a beautiful bridal suite for the bride and groom's first night. It's being road-tested at the moment, if that's the right way of putting it. My very good friends Hetty and Max invited their niece to come up and be the first to occupy it. She arrived a few days ago and she's staying for another ten days. A clever woman and very discerning. If there's anything wrong with it, she'll be sure to let us know, so it will be perfect for our first wedding guests. Well, she'd have to be in her profession – she's an investigative journalist."

"It all sounds very enterprising, Jennifer," he said.

"Oh, we are quite an entrepreneurial bunch up at Magnolia. But here I am prattling on about cottages and refurbishments and all you need to know is whether we have availability and what services we can offer. And, of course, how much we charge. Well, let me put your mind at rest. Saturday 30th July is free, and I've pencilled you in for it," Jennifer said, reaching into her handbag. "And I've put together a package of information which lists all the services we can offer. Priced individually, you can select those you want and leave out those that are of no interest to you. It's very comprehensive. We organize the marquee hire and catering. And we can also do all the flower arrangements, bake the wedding cake, and even organize for a celebrant if that is your wish. And don't forget that you can also book the Old Forge for the night. It's so sweet. I designed the interior myself. Small but beautiful, as they say. One lounge, a small kitchen, bedroom, and bathroom. I've popped in a selection of photographs from previous wedding events and I've included a full plan of Magnolia Court so you can see the overall layout and where the marquee will be erected."

"Very efficient. Are there any pictures of the Old Forge? I'd like to show them to my granddaughter. I rather think she'd like to take you up on that offer," he said.

"Yes, taken only last week and the plan has been updated complete with the location of the Old Forge. Our wedding service is very sought-after. I'll need you to confirm the booking by tomorrow in writing – you can send me an email

– and we ask for a deposit of five hundred pounds," Jennifer said.

"More than fair, Jennifer. You'll hear back from me just as soon as I've spoken to Sophie," he said, leaning in towards her. "You've sold it to me already. Money is no object for my Sophie. She's a lovely girl. You'll like her. Now, can I tempt you to enjoy another pot of tea – that is, unless you're in a hurry."

"That would be very nice, thank you, Ian. I should enjoy that very much." Jennifer blushed. He was flirting with her; she could see it in his eyes, and it wasn't at all unpleasant. Duncan would most certainly not approve.

"You seem to be very young to have secreted yourself away in a retirement complex, Jennifer. I doubt that it's a very exciting life," he said.

"Compliments will get you everywhere, Ian," Jennifer laughed. "But I have to tell you there's never a dull moment at Magnolia. The most surprising things happen when you least expect it. Last week we found an old dagger and a notebook up the chimney in the Old Forge. Can you imagine it? It's the very last thing you'd expect, isn't it? And it's not just any old dagger. This one is quite beautiful – silver and gold and set with the most beautiful stones. We think they might have been hidden there when the property was a school. Gabby – that's our investigative journalist friend – she's quite excited about the whole thing and turning up all sorts of information." Jennifer leant closer and whispered, "Can you keep a secret, Ian?"

"I'm intrigued. I can indeed, and I promise I will."

"Well, it seems a man was murdered in the Old Forge thirty-seven years ago and the notebook belonged to him. It's filled, from cover-to-cover, with notes about people and places and all sorts of other information. Apparently, they never caught the murderer. Gabby thinks the notebook might lead to solving the murder. Now, how exciting is that?"

"Certainly not the sort of thing that happens every day. Sounds like this Gabby knows what she's about," he said.

"Oh, she does. She is very highly respected in her field," Jennifer said, enjoying singing Gabby's praises. "She's solved far more complicated cases than this one. She's quite in her element."

"Forgive me for saying this, but isn't this the sort of find that she needs to take to the police? She's surely not intending to go it alone."

"Indeed not. She's simply going to follow up on several leads and get a better picture of what might have happened, and then she'll hand everything over to the authorities," Jennifer said. "In the meantime, she's taking personal care of both the dagger and the notebook. Keeping them both safe in the Old Forge. And just in case you're wondering, there are no ghosts there, at least none that we have come across so far."

Ian laughed and checked his watch. "Sorry, Jennifer, time for me to get going. Tomorrow, you say? You'll have my confirmation by tomorrow. And may I say again how pleasant it has been to take tea with such a charming lady."

The bell clanged as he opened and closed the door. Jennifer jumped up and called after him. "Ian, you've forgotten to give me your number."

She was getting as forgetful as Amy. It wouldn't do.

Twenty-Four

2022

"I think that's the one, Gabby," Amy said, squinting through the windscreen and pointing. "Two down on the right. And if I'm not mistaken, our luck is in. There's somebody in the garden. Elderly. Into his eighties. It could be him."

"You might well be right," Gabby said, following Amy's finger. "We'll soon find out. Now, Amy, I don't think we should mention the diary or the notebook," Gabby cautioned.

"Keep a few aces up our sleeves, you mean?" Amy grinned. "I completely agree."

Opening the car door for her, Gabby held out her hand to Amy. "I'm not incapable, you know. I can easily slide down from this seat on my own," she snapped. Frowning, Gabby stepped back. It wasn't like Amy to be quite so tetchy.

Leaning heavily on her walking stick, Amy led the way and stopped at the gatepost. "Good afternoon," she said. "I must say you keep this garden beautifully. Those roses are quite spectacular and I do so love to see that vivid blue of a Ceanothus. Summer has come quite early this year. Everything's coming out well ahead of time. I used to do

169

a bit of gardening myself, but now I leave it to others – a bit past it, I'm sorry to say."

The man looked up and nodded. "I like it. It's me hobby. 'as been for years now. There's nothing like watching the seasons come and go."

"I know a professional gardener when I see one, Mr Grzeskowiak," Amy said.

"Do I knows you?" he asked.

"Not yet, but I know of you. Would I be right in thinking that you are the same Mr Grzeskowiak who was once caretaker up at St John's College?" Amy smiled and waited patiently for a reply. "I'll take no answer as a statement that I am correct, shall I? Allow me to introduce myself. My name is Amy Wilson, and this is my daughter, Gabrielle. I live up at Magnolia Court. It was built on the grounds of St John's College some years after the school closed. My daughter is just visiting me and chauffeuring me around today. She's a bit shy. Take no notice if she's a little quiet."

Gabby smiled sweetly. "Good morning, Mr Grzeskowiak."

"I'll not beat about the bush. I am not here to talk to you about your garden, but about a young man – well, probably not a young man anymore. Ahmed Singh. I do so hope you will be able to help me. I don't want to be a nuisance – we do get a bit of a nuisance when we're older, don't we? If you could give me just a few minutes of your time, I would so appreciate it. I can see that the name rings a bell, Mr Grzeskowiak. May I call you Adrian?"

"Fuck off."

"I like a man who gets to the point quickly, but I shall not, in your words, fuck off." Amy smiled. "I do assure you it would be in your best interests to cooperate with me. I am not easily put off by anybody. We could get the police involved if that is what you would prefer."

"'ow d'you know where I live?" Grzeskowiak carried on pruning the roses, his hands unsteady.

"Adrian, if there is one thing I have learnt, it is that in this technological world there are no secrets anymore. We have no privacy. It's all out there in the ether, or is it the internet? One or the other, it really doesn't matter," Amy sighed. "I don't like it any more than you, but there are times when, used for the right purposes, it can be very helpful."

"It was a long time ago. I don't remember things like I once did. The past is best left behind, missus."

Amy stepped into the garden, gently wrapping her hand around a rose. She drew it close to her face. "The Peace Rose, is it not? Such a wonderful fragrance. It's one of my favourites…It's nothing to worry about. The very opposite, to be precise. You see, we've found something we believe might have once belonged to Ahmed and we'd like to return it to him, but he is proving a little elusive. We thought you might remember something that might help us find him. I don't suppose you could find it in your heart to make us a cup of tea while we chat about it? I am rather parched and I'm not so good at leaning on gateposts for long these days."

"Five minutes," Grzeskowiak grunted, fumbling in his pocket for the door key.

"Such a lovely, spacious bungalow and a beautiful garden as well, Adrian. You must be very proud of both. Have you lived here for long?" Amy asked, relaxing back in one of the armchairs.

"Thirty years. Maybe more. Can't remember now," Adrian

replied. "It suits me. Well, what've you found that is so important you 'ad to come all this way to see me?"

"A dagger, a silver dagger, inlaid with the most exquisite stones. Rubies, emeralds, and pearls. And worth a great deal of money. It was made in India, so we are led to believe. Not the sort of thing that anybody would just leave behind. And then we discovered there was a boy at the school called Ahmed Singh who had not long since arrived from Jaipur. We've quite possibly added two and two and made five, but it seemed he might be the rightful owner. There weren't many Indian boys in private schools in those days, were there? Did I mention we found it up an old chimney in one of the outbuildings when it was being rebuilt? I think it might have been called the Annexe in your days."

"Mr Vincent's old place, you mean?" Adrian said.

"That's correct. Mr Vincent's old place. Did you know Ahmed, Adrian?"

"Seen 'im. Like you said, missus, stood out in a crowd," Adrian replied, seeming to choose his words carefully.

"So, you didn't know him personally then?" Amy probed.

"No. I was just the caretaker. That's all. Got on with me job and kept me nose out of other people's business," Adrian replied.

"Then you wouldn't know why he killed his teacher – Mr Palmer?" Gabby cut in unexpectedly.

Adrian leapt to his feet and pointed his finger at her. "Wash your mouth out. That boy didn't kill nobody. You leave 'im out of it."

"Adrian, calm yourself." Amy reached out and rested her hand gently on his arm. "My daughter meant no harm. She can be a little abrupt at times. I've spoken to her about it on several occasions," Amy said, turning to Gabby. "Gabrielle, that was not at all subtle but, my dear, it seems your question has touched a nerve...Maybe this would be a good time to take tea."

"Thank you, Adrian. An excellent cup of tea. Can we continue with our little conversation? It does sound to me as though you might have known Ahmed quite well, if not very well. You certainly sprang to his defence quickly enough. May I also say that we share your view, Adrian? We most certainly have our doubts about the accusations that were thrown around at the time."

Grzeskowiak diverted his eyes. "'e was a good lad. We got on well together. 'e used to come round to Keepers and we'd play chess. On the quiet like. I'd 'ave got the push if Rutherwood knew that 'e came round. Mr Vincent knew. No one else."

"Keepers?" Amy enquired.

"Keepers Cottage – out the back of the school. More like a concrete bunker, but some comedian nicknamed it that."

"Did he talk about himself? Did he ever speak to you about a dagger?" Amy asked.

"Mum and dad dead. 'ad a benefactor, 'e said, who paid his schooling. Ordinary kid. Didn't mind getting 'is 'ands dirty. Made me laugh, 'e did. Kicked by a mule, 'e told me. Scar on his forehead to show for it. 'id it behind his fringe, 'e did. Never spoke about no dagger. If 'e'd been found with anything like that, they'd 'ave shipped 'im right back where 'e came from. Rules for everything in that school."

"And you've never seen nor heard of him again since he disappeared that night?" Amy asked.

"Not a word."

173

"Did he have any friends in the school? Anyone special he might have confided in? Someone who might just have a clue as to where he might have gone?" Amy asked.

"There was one. Not sure I can remember 'is name..." Adrian narrowed his eyes. "Ed, Ed Bright that was it. Little runt of a boy. Skinny as a rake. Ginger 'air. But they was the best of pals."

"That wouldn't be the same Ed Bright who was expelled from school by any chance?" EB – Ed Bright. It had to be.

Adrian nodded. "Caught stealing money. Rutherwood 'ad 'im gone and off 'ome the following day. Ahmed took it bad."

"I don't suppose you can remember anything about this boy other than that he was a thief?" Amy asked.

"Ahmed wouldn't hear a word said against 'im. Said it was all made up. Got 'imself invited to Bright's place over the Easter 'olidays. Posh place, he said. Sir Edward Bright, that was the kid's dad. We 'ad a few knobs' kids in that school."

"A great shame that Ahmed should lose a good friend," Amy said. "Ah well, that's life, isn't it? You must learn so much as a caretaker. Such an important job." Amy changed tack. "Every school needs a good, reliable caretaker. Were you working there for long?"

"Started there just after Rutherwood took over as 'ead and left the day it closed in '85. Five years. Good job it was. Not just the caretaker, you know. 'ead of security as well. Responsible job. Me own roof. Independence. Fair pay. Left me to get on with it, they did. The boys could be a bit of a handful at times, but on the whole..."

Amy started to relax. He was beginning to open up, share information she had not asked for. It was a good sign. "Goodness me, head of security. How fascinating. I can imagine you must have been very proud of yourself when you landed that job."

"I were, considering…But it weren't quite what it were made out to be. I just 'ad to lock everything up at night, unlock in the mornings, and keep the CCTV system running from Keepers."

"A CCTV system? Someone was very security conscious. I can't imagine many schools had CCTV systems in those days." Amy feigned surprise.

"School guvnors. They insisted on it."

"Indulge an old lady. I always say you're never too old to learn something new. What exactly does running a CCTV involve?" Amy asked.

"Changing tapes mostly. Three times a day. Marking 'em up with date and time, and putting them on a shelf. Not rocket science," Adrian replied.

"So, did you have to get up in the middle of the night to change tapes? Poor you. I doubt you ever got a good night's sleep."

"Eight hours a night, or as near as. First one on at 5.30 a.m. Didn't bother me. Early riser I am. Second, eight hours later at 1.30 p.m. when I were back for me lunch hour, and the third always 9.30 p.m., last job before getting me sorted out and ready for bed."

"And you never, ever varied that routine?" Amy asked.

"No," Grzeskowiak said, getting to his feet. "So, now you knows that me and Ahmed were friends and 'ow a CCTV works, can I get back to me pruning? Sorry, I can't 'elp you with finding the lad. You ever thought that maybe 'e don't want to be found?"

"I have indeed, Adrian. If I were him and somebody was accusing me of murdering my teacher, I'd make myself very scarce indeed," Amy said. "Just a couple more questions and then we'll leave you in peace. I couldn't help but noticing you referred to the teacher who lived in the Annexe as Mr Vincent," Amy said. "Most people would have called him Mr Palmer or Vincent Palmer. Did you know Mr Vincent well?"

"As good as any. 'e was a good bloke. Different to the rest. A rebel and a queer," Adrian laughed. "We got on okay."

"You mean gay, don't you?" Amy suggested. "The term queer seems so old-fashioned these days."

"Queer, gay, it's all the same to me. 'e didn't flaunt it and whatever 'e got up to, he did it outside of the school. Good to Ahmed 'e was too. Took 'im under 'is wing and treated 'im like a son," Adrian said. "Wicked shame, it were."

"You were quite fond of him, then?"

"I 'ope you're not implying..." Adrian snapped.

"Never further from my mind." Amy corrected the misunderstanding. "I was just interested in your relationship with Mr Vincent."

"We was friends, from a distance."

Amy sat back and smiled. "Well, that is good to know, Adrian. That probably counts you out from murdering him."

Gabby glanced at Amy. "So, who did murder him? And why?" she said.

"How the fuck should I know," Adrian yelled. "Time's up, missus, and take this one with you."

"Gabrielle, we should go. I do believe we have outstayed our welcome," Amy said, turning back to Adrian. "You're quite right. We've taken up far too much of your time. You've been most helpful. I fear we've hit a dead end as far as finding Ahmed is concerned, and we still can't be sure the dagger belonged to him at all. I do wonder if that boy ever sleeps, forever looking over his shoulder and wondering when he might be caught and accused of something which we, at least, think he didn't do. He must have had a dreadful life. We'll take our leave of you now and thank you again. Goodbye, Adrian. No doubt we will meet again."

* * *

"Interesting," Gabby said, pointing the key at the car.

"Very interesting indeed. I'd like to write some notes before we move off, if you don't mind. My head's buzzing and I know I shall forget everything in no time at all."

Pen hovering over her notebook, Amy spoke her thoughts out loud before jotting them down. "He was very sure Ahmed had nothing to do with the murder, but didn't offer any explanation as to why he was so sure. I'm guessing he knows something we don't.

"The CCTV tapes were changed at 9.30 p.m. that night. Duncan was right to pick up on that discrepancy. Adrian was quite firm that he never varied that routine. Yet in both Rutherwood's statement and his own statement, they speak of the time being 10.25 p.m.

"Vincent Palmer was gay which could have had something to do with the murder. Maybe. Maybe not.

"Our Adrian does indeed live in a very smart bungalow and a most expensive part of town. There certainly aren't many caretakers who could afford anything like this. I wonder where he got the money to buy it?

"EB is most probably Ed Bright, Ahmed's pal, and his father is a distinguished man – Sir Edward Bright, no less. That narrows down the field.

"Ahmed has a distinguishing scar on his forehead, so we have more than the name Singh to go on now.

"Ahmed and Vincent were close, making it even more unlikely that Ahmed would have killed his teacher. Is it possible that Ahmed asked Mr Vincent to look after the dagger for him?

"Adrian became very agitated when asked who might have murdered Mr Vincent. Is he hiding something?"

"I do believe, Gabby, that we have made a great deal of progress today. Thank you, my dear." Amy put the notebook in her purse. "Remind me that is where I've put it, will you, dear?"

Twenty-Five

2022

"Open up. Open Up."

Gabby awoke with a start and checked the clock. Six o'clock in the morning; it was still dark. No one in Magnolia was ever up at that time of day unless there was a real emergency. Her thoughts turned to Aunt Hetty and Uncle Max. Had Aunt Hetty had another heart attack or had something worse happened? Her heart thudding, she leapt out of bed. Grabbing her dressing gown, she fumbled to get her arms into it. "I'm coming, I'm coming," she shouted. Making for the front door, she reached for the key on the hook above the door and inserted it into the lock. The door was not locked. In the back of her mind, she remembered thinking she had to lock the door before going to bed. But had she? She couldn't recall doing so and she couldn't think straight with all the noise.

"Open up. Open up!" A fist was pounding at the door. She didn't recognize the voice, only its urgency.

"Okay, okay," she shouted. Flinging open the door, Gabby stopped dead in her tracks. "Who the hell are you?" she said. Tall, broad, and untidy, wearing a loose overcoat, he was, she guessed, in his forties. His arm raised with his fist locked tight,

179

he was ready for the next assault on the door. Alongside him stood a woman dressed in a navy-blue short overcoat and a baseball hat. Behind them, lined up on the steps, stood two uniformed police officers, one male, and one female. Three cars were parked untidily in the narrow lane – a plain black Audi saloon and two marked police cars, their flashing lights illuminating the Old Forge and the Mansion House beyond.

"Detective Sergeant Yates. With me, Detective Constable Manwell. Gabrielle Olsen, we have a warrant to search these premises," he said poker-faced.

Gabby took a step back and looked at the man as if he had come down from Mars. "You must be mistaken. This is Magnolia Court Retirement Complex. Why on earth would you need to search any of these properties, let alone this one? I'm sorry to say that you've had a wasted journey," she said as she started to close the door on him. Slowly it registered. They had addressed her by name. "I don't understand. This is ridiculous. I need to put some clothes on and then, and only then, can you come in and you can explain to me what this is all about," she said crossly. "And for heaven's sake, turn those lights off. Do you want to wake the whole neighbourhood? You do realize that there are elderly people on this site who need their sleep? It's enough to give anybody a heart attack."

Reaching into his pocket, he drew out a sheet of paper. "This Miss, Mrs Olsen, whichever it may be, is a signed search warrant. If you please, stand aside and we will get about our business."

"Mrs Olsen. You will not step one foot through this door until you tell me what this is all about," Gabby said angrily, her arms stretched across the open door. "I'll have you know I am quite familiar with police procedure and search warrants."

"Stand aside, Mrs Olsen, or I'm afraid I shall have to remove you bodily. It's your choice," he said, narrowing his eyes, leaving her in no doubt that he would do precisely that. Gabby stood aside. "Right, you lot, let's get on with it," he called.

"What are you looking for?" Gabby demanded. "I have a right to know."

"You have no rights, ma'am. Just let us get on with our job," he said, at the same time issuing orders. "Tracy, kitchen. PC Denham, lounge. PC King, bedroom. I'll take the bathroom," he said. "Stay right where you are, ma'am. If you move so much as an inch, we'll have to put you in one of the police vehicles while we get on with our job."

Pulling her robe tight around her, Gabby watched in horror as cupboards were emptied, rugs lifted, cushions unzipped, the bed stripped, and drawers rifled. Furious, she glared from one to the other. "You'll put everything back where you found it when you have finished. If there's one thing out of place, I shall be speaking to your superior. Check that. I shall be speaking to your superior anyway."

Seething inwardly and aware that all the protestations in the world were not going to make a jot of difference, she bit her tongue. They were going to do 'their job' come hell or high water. And then they'd leave. An apology was unlikely.

"Well, well, well," he said, emerging from the bathroom. "What do we have here? By my reckoning, there must be at least ten grams in this little packet. Not the most novel place to stash cocaine, wouldn't you agree, Mrs Olsen? Always the cistern. Why don't you people ever learn?" he said, grinning and waving a small polythene bag containing a white substance in the air. "Nice little haul. Who'd ever think that there would be dealers in a retirement community?"

"What the hell?" Gabby leapt to her feet, narrowing her eyes. "Whatever is in that packet is not mine and I have no idea how it got there. Cocaine? Me? For God's sake, I'm an investigative journalist, not a drug dealer. I don't touch drugs. I never have. I spend half my life tracking drug dealers down."

"Travel a lot, do we?" he asked.

"Of course I do; that's my job," Gabby snapped.

"And what might that be, Mrs Olsen?"

"I've already told you. I'm an investigative journalist. For your information – not that it's any business of yours – I've just spent the last six months helping – let me underline helping – the police here and in France root out the lowlifes who traffic men, women, and children across the channel," Gabby fumed. "And if you'll forgive me saying so your time would be better spent on similar assignments. Not marching into my home, at some God-awful hour, pulling my flat apart for a packet that most certainly does not belong to me. Do I make myself clear?"

"Mmm. That would explain it. The perfect cover for bringing drugs into the country," he said. "For your information, we had an anonymous tip-off from a reliable source that you were dealing. But you'd know all about reliable sources, wouldn't you?" he said.

"Of course, I do, and let me tell you that that is one reliable source that you should get rid of, right now. That is if you don't want to find yourself out of a job." Gabby shook her head in disbelief. "This is absurd."

"It all adds up to me, Mrs Olsen. Perhaps you'd care to step into the bedroom and put some clothes on. I am arresting you for the possession of a quantity of Class A drugs. You do not have to say anything but it may harm your defence if you do not mention when questioned, something that you later rely on in court. Anything you do say may be given in evidence," he said, turning to the female officer. "Please accompany Mrs Olsen to the bedroom and remain with her while she gets dressed."

Dumbfounded, Gabby walked slowly into the bedroom, her head buzzing with unanswered questions. Who? What? Why? Where?

* * *

"Max, Max, are you up there?" Stan shouted. Picking up a few chips of gravel, he gently threw them, one by one, up at the bedroom window. "Max, Hetty, wake up," he called again.

Hair dishevelled, eyes blurry, Max stumbled out of bed. "What time is it, Hetty?" he asked.

Hetty fumbled to find her glasses and squinted at the alarm clock. "Ten past six. Come back to bed. It's not even dawn yet."

"Someone is throwing stones at the window," he said, throwing it open. "Stan, what in heaven's name are you doing, man?"

"No time for questions, Max. Get your dressing gown and slippers on and come with me. The police are at Gabby's door, and they've gone inside," Stan called, evidently fearing the worst.

Max's head disappeared as fast as it had appeared. "It's Gabby. There's something wrong. The police are at the Old Forge. You stay here. I'm going down there with Stan...and don't worry."

Leaning heavily on his walking stick, Max hurried as fast

183

as he could to catch up with Stan. "I saw the blue lights coming up the drive. Just having my first cuppa," Stan said breathlessly.

* * *

Stopping short of the Old Forge, Stan and Max exchanged glances. Gabby was dressed and being escorted down the steps from the flat. "What's going on here," Max yelled. "That's my niece you've got there. I demand an answer."

Hands in pockets, Detective Sergeant Yates sauntered in their direction, stopping six feet short. "Gabrielle Olsen is your niece, is she? Well, I have to tell you, Mr—"

"Max Brightwell. And this is Stan Morrison, a friend, and resident."

"—Your niece has been caught in possession of Class A drugs. She has been cautioned and we are taking her down to the police station to interview her formally. What happens then will be up to her."

"Gabby? Drugs? Never. She doesn't even smoke. She hates drugs or anybody associated with them." Max wobbled and grabbed hold of Stan's arm for support.

Gabby stood beside the police car. "It's okay, Uncle Max, nothing to worry about," she called. "I'll get it sorted out. Just a misunderstanding. I'll be back before you know it. Go back to bed."

"Shall I ring Greg? He'll know what to do," Max asked.

"No, definitely not, Uncle Max," Gabby said emphatically. "He's got enough on his plate where he is and there's precious little that he can do stuck in India. He'll only worry and hop on the next plane home. I don't want him to do that. Just keep calm. And can you lock up the flat for me? The key is in the door. I'll see you later."

"Don't be so sure of that," Yates mumbled under his breath and grinned.

Gabby waved through the window as the car sped off down the drive, her brain working overtime.

Twenty-Six

2022

"I'm afraid there's going to be a reception committee," Andy said as he indicated left and turned into Magnolia. "Everybody's been so worried about you. They're all in the Great Hall propping up the bar. They won't rest easy until they know you're back safe and sound. Do you feel up to it or would you like me to make your excuses for you and drop you off at the Old Forge?"

"No, Andy," Gabby replied. "No excuses. They all deserve to know what went on, and there's something else I need to share with everybody. If I can see them all together, it's a bonus. At least I shan't have to tell the same story over again."

"I'll drop you at the door and then park the car," Andy said. "Be right with you."

Gabby planted a smile on her face, squared her shoulders, and marched in. "I hope I haven't missed the cocktail hour," she said, glancing around. "Sorry I'm late. Unavoidably delayed, or should I say unavoidably detained?" Andy had been right. Even the detested Paul and his lovely wife Ros had turned out. "Make mine a large one," Gabby called to Gerald behind the bar.

"Coming up, young lady. Ice and a slice?" Gerald reached for a glass. Gabby nodded.

"So, it's all sorted, is it? A misunderstanding?" Uncle Max asked anxiously, taking Gabby aside.

"No, it's not all sorted," Gabby whispered as she planted a kiss on his cheek and squeezed Hetty's hand reassuringly. "Let's just say that you might have me hanging around Magnolia for a while yet. Look, do you mind if I just tell everyone at the same time? I don't want there to be any misinformation or speculation. And there's something I need to tell everyone."

"That's fine, Gabby. You take your time. We're just relieved to have you back in one piece," Max said, clapping his hands together. "Can I have your attention, please, everyone? As you know, today hasn't been the best. Gabby wants to tell you about it herself, so charge your glasses, grab a seat, make yourselves comfortable, and we'll give her the floor."

A hush fell over the room as the residents dropped, one by one, into armchairs. Anxious faces looked up at her as she perched on one of the bar stools.

"What a day," she started. "I thought I'd get a lie in this morning, but it didn't quite work out that way. And my apologies to all of you who may have been woken up at some unearthly hour this morning by flashing lights. I guess you all know by now that the police visited me this morning with a search warrant, would you believe? They'd had an anonymous tip-off, so they told me after they had pulled the flat apart. Don't worry, I insisted they put everything back where they found it. The flat is quite tidy and nothing is broken or damaged…They found a small packet of cocaine hidden in the toilet cistern. I'm sure I don't need to tell you that it wasn't mine. Most of you know my views on drugs and nothing has changed. In my job, I've seen first-hand what they do to the buyers, the sellers, and the users. It was Detective Sergeant Yates who found it."

"I installed that bathroom, Gabby—" Stan interrupted, "—and I can tell you there was nothing but water in that cistern."

"I know that, Stan," Gabby said. "To cut a long story short, they were quite determined to charge me no matter what I said. In the end, I admitted to the charge and I'm out on bail."

"You did what? Why?" Max gasped. "That makes you a criminal. You'll have a criminal record. What about your job?"

"I didn't make the decision lightly, Uncle Max. I had plenty of time to think about it. I'll be called to appear before the magistrates' court, but that won't happen for a while. I needed to buy time, and I needed to get out of there," Gabby said.

"I don't understand."

"I need time to get to the bottom of what is going on. You see, not only did a packet of cocaine quite incredibly appear in my bathroom, but the dagger and the notebook disappeared. They were both there on my sideboard when I went to bed last night. I only noticed they were gone when I was being taken out to the police car. You can draw your own conclusions. Either, somebody entered my flat during the night, planted the drugs, and stole the dagger and the notebook, or..." Gabby hesitated, "the police planted the drugs when they searched the flat and, at the same time, stole the dagger and the notebook."

"The police wouldn't do such a thing. They are employed to uphold the law not to break it," Max said, shocked at her accusation.

"It has been known, Uncle Max, believe me," Gabby said. "There are bad eggs in any organization. I'm not saying it was them. When I opened the door to them this morning, it wasn't locked and I can't be one hundred percent sure that I locked it before I went to bed last night. I could – just could – have forgotten, so it is not beyond the bounds of possibility that I had a night-time visitor – someone with a key. I'm a heavy sleeper. I may well not have heard anything. I'm keeping an open mind. The fact remains that the drugs appeared and the dagger and notebook disappeared."

"Did you tell them about the theft? The police, I mean?" Uncle Max said.

"No, I followed my instinct and kept quiet about it. As I said, there are only two possible explanations," Gabby replied.

"Someone must have wanted that notebook very badly," Amy whispered. "Not the dagger; I think that's probably immaterial, but I could be wrong."

"And they'd probably want the copy I made of the notebook as well," Duncan grinned, "but they're jolly well not going to get their hands on that. That is safely locked away."

"And I have photographs of the dagger if we need them," Thomas added.

"And we still have the VHS tape, not that we know its contents – yet," Duncan said.

"What worries me is that whoever stole them knew precisely where to look," Gabby said.

"Well, tomorrow, we had better double up on our efforts and find out what this is all about. It's going to be all hands to the pump," Amy said. "We can't have our Gabby being hauled up in front of the magistrates' and being charged with something she didn't do. We now have no choice but to get on with it."

"I don't like it. It's too risky. Aren't we getting out of our depth? Time to get the police involved," Uncle Max said.

"Not yet, Max," Amy said firmly. "We've got some good leads to follow up on. I suggest Gabby stays in the background manning the command post while the rest of us get stuck in. We can't afford for her to have any more mishaps or be found in breach of her bail conditions."

The investigative journalist in her wanted to protest, but Gabby knew that there were times when no one argued with Amy.

Twenty-Seven

2022

Gabby scowled. The very last thing she wanted was another visitor this evening, however well-meaning they might be. Hair wet, no make-up, she looked dreadful, but it was no good pretending she wasn't in. "On my way," she called, pulling her dressing gown belt tight around her waist.

"See, locked this time," she said flippantly. "Oh, it's you two." She had wondered how long it would take Paul to get around to an apology.

"Gabby, sorry to disturb you," Ros said. "We could come back tomorrow if you like."

"No. That's fine. Come in. Take a seat. Sorry about my appearance," Gabby said coldly.

"It all looks very nice here, Gabby," Paul said sheepishly.

"We won't keep you long," Ros cut in, "but Paul has something he wishes to tell you, isn't that right, Paul?"

He nodded and sat down beside Ros on the sofa. Gabby pulled up a kitchen chair, crossed her arms, and waited. This she had to hear. "I want to apologize to you for my behaviour the other day. I was totally out of order. I promise you, that's not me. If I could take it back – every word – then I would.

I'd like to try to explain."

Gabby raised her eyebrows. She wasn't prepared to let him off the hook that easily. Most times she happily brushed off a spat and moved on. But when somebody's words gave her sleepless nights, she was less inclined to do so. And Paul had done just that. "I'm listening," she said sharply.

"I know how you must be feeling, Gabby, but please hear him out," Ros said.

Paul rubbed the palms of his hands over his face and smoothed his brow. He started talking, as if to himself, unable to look either his wife or Gabby in the eye. "I got myself into a bit of bother. No, not a bit of bother, a whole heap of trouble…"

Gabby listened carefully. As the story unfolded, her anger slowly dissipated. He was just one more in a long line of victims taken for a ride and whose life had been ruined by some money-grabbing cretin with nothing better to do than fleece the elderly. Didn't she see it every day in her work? Yes, she did. But it was rarely quite so close to home. She'd read about it and had heard second-hand accounts about how it worked, then stored it away in her mind as an area to cover in a future investigation. To say her heart went out to him would be an exaggeration, but no one deserved to be put through that. Just another victim.

"I'm so sorry, Gabby. Sorry for how I've behaved to you and sorry for what I've put my wife through. I've been a real pig for the past couple of months," he said, finally looking up.

"Apology accepted," Gabby said without reserve. "Maybe we can start again?"

"I wish that was all, Gabby, but there's something else I need to get off my chest," Paul said, glancing sideways at Ros.

Ros stared at him. "Something else? Something else you haven't told me, Paul? I warned you what would happen if you kept anything more from me, didn't I?"

Paul nodded. "My offer stands, Ros. I'll go right back and pack my suitcases, if that is what you want."

"Excuse me, but I don't want to get involved in your domestic affairs. I'm sorry to be so blunt, but it's been a long day. If you have something to say to me, say it, then go and sort things out between yourselves," Gabby said impatiently.

"I sold the Mustang to get some quick cash – to see us through. Afterwards, I went to the pub and got drunk, very drunk indeed," Paul started. "Another chap came in and sat next to me. We got talking. I downed pint after pint in quick succession. He seemed quite unperturbed about listening to a drunk prattling on. I told him about the dagger that Stan found and where he had found it. About how it was all your fault I'd had to sell the Mustang. That if you'd done as I wanted, I'd have had my cut from the proceeds – enough to keep us going for a while. And I told him about the notebook too and the man who was murdered. I went on and on. Couldn't answer his questions fast enough. You see, I thought we were mates by then. It was only much later, when I thought about it, that I realized he hadn't told me one single thing about himself, not even his name. I don't know how many I had. I don't remember him leaving. I don't remember how I got home." Paul stopped to catch his breath. "Say something, Ros. Say something."

"I'm speechless." Ros stood up and picked up her handbag. "I think I've heard more than enough. As if it wasn't bad enough before. Now I find out it was your loose tongue that's led to the dagger being stolen, and quite possibly, Gabby ending up on a charge. I don't think I can ever forgive you."

Getting swiftly to her feet, Gabby put her hand on Ros's arm. "I think, on this occasion, it's for me to decide who metes out the forgiveness. We're none of us saints, Ros, when it comes to spouting off after a few drinks. If I had a pound for every time I'd said too much, I'd be a rich woman. Paul was stupid and naïve, but nothing was said intentionally," she said, looking Ros in the eye. Any fool could see that they were in love, made for each other. "Think, Paul, think," Gabby said, turning back to him. "Did you mention the tape?"

"No. I'm sure about that. I don't think I even knew about it. And I didn't even know about the copy of the notebook until Duncan mentioned it earlier, so I couldn't have told him about that either," Paul replied.

Ros sat down again, a tear trickling down her cheek. Paul reached out and stroked her hand.

Gabby heaved a sigh of relief and smiled. "Well, that's one blessing. Two blessings, if I'm not mistaken," she said, noticing Ros had not withdrawn her hand. "Can you describe this man?"

Paul nodded. "I was almost sober when he walked in and sat at the bar, so, yes, I can. He was about six feet, maybe a bit taller, broad-shouldered. He had a full head of thick, almost-white hair, cut quite short. Very upright for a man of his age."

"And what age would you put him at, Paul?"

"Late seventies, early eighties. Fit, I'd say, and smartly dressed. Nicely tailored suit, expensive brogues," Paul said.

"Any other distinguishing features?" Gabby asked.

"Well spoken. Authoritative, if you know what I mean. And ears – yes, the ears, now I come to think about it—"

"Ears?" Gabby asked.

"They stuck out," Paul replied. "Can't think how else to describe them. I'm so sorry I can't be more helpful. If I think of anything else, I'll tell you straight away. Do you think it might have been him who stole those things?" Paul asked.

"No, not in person, but it's probably more than a coincidence you spoke to him," Gabby said.

"You are looking miles away, Gabby," Ros commented.

"I am. There's something about Paul's description that rings a bell and, for the life of me, I can't put a finger on it," she said.

Gabby checked her watch. "Right, Paul, it's getting late. I was about to ring Greg – get him out of bed yet again. Thanks for sharing your problems with me. I doubt I would have coped much better. First thing in the morning, you need to speak to Peter about the money. He was a banker, and he has contacts, contacts who will give him advice on how best you might recover some of that money. He may be quiet, but he's a miracle worker when it comes to anything financial."

"We'll do that, Gabby," Ros said. "We'll go and see him together first thing tomorrow morning and then we'll do the rounds and apologize to everybody else. We're going to be okay, thanks to you. Everybody has always said what a special person you are and they are right. Thank you."

Paul returned a half-smile. "Not everyone is as forgiving as you, Gabby. Do you think they'll overlook my behaviour? I wouldn't blame them if they turned their backs on me, but it's not fair on Ros. She's the innocent victim in all this. We've talked about it and decided that if needs be, we'll sell up and move on."

"Moving on where?" Gabby said, abruptly. "You're doing no such thing. Do you honestly think you're the only one around here who's done something they live to regret? I know these people far better than you. They don't pass judgement on each other. There's nothing they do better than rally together when one of them is down. But, if you'll take my advice, you'll tell them about the pension scam – lock, stock, and barrel. If nothing else, it might well prevent one of them from falling for the same mean trick. And I suggest you don't mention the unfortunate discussion in the pub. You've told me. That is what matters. I'll tell others on a need-to-know basis, and I promise you they too will understand."

"The least I can do, Gabby," Paul said. "And then with luck, I'll get on with what I should have been doing in the first place – that veggie garden needs work."

"Right, home you two, and I'm going to ring my husband, half-past two in the morning or not. Get a good night's rest. I may well be calling on you both for a bit of help," Gabby said, mulling over an idea that had that minute entered her head – one that just might help Ros and Paul feel part of the community again.

Twenty-Eight

2022

Wide awake, Jennifer lay under the covers and thought about the future. Dead to the world, and snoring gently, Duncan lay beside her with a look of perfect contentment on his face. It was the first night they had spent together. Too long in the tooth to worry about the proprieties of waiting until their wedding night, they had decided to start married life just a bit sooner.

She hadn't known what to expect, nor did she have any high expectations. More concerned about pleasing him, she had got undressed in the bathroom, removed her make-up, and slipped into new silk pyjamas. Checking herself in the mirror, she had been sorely tempted to reapply her make-up, but stopped herself. This was the real Jennifer – warts and all – and she just hoped he wouldn't be disappointed.

Undressing in the bedroom, Duncan had had no such reservations. Holding back from offering him help with his clothes or getting from the wheelchair into bed, she had simply watched with admiration as the whole process had been completed, smoothly and without incident, in a matter of minutes. A proud man, totally comfortable with his disability, he had never asked for help domestically, nor had it been offered.

Smiling, she remembered his arms around her, his fingers running through her hair, and the kisses that still tingled on her lips.

They'd talked late into the night about the wedding and the wedding guests. She remembered Duncan laughing as she counted them on her fingers and then when she ran out of fingers, on his. Twenty-eight guests in total: eighteen, including themselves from Magnolia and another ten with Jennifer's family. She'd tested him on all their names and ages. Jamie, Lynn, Olivia, Ed, Janine, Graham, Jay, Daisy, and Rubie and not forgetting Rory. He passed the test with flying colours.

The date had been set for Saturday 25th April, just over four weeks away.

Jennifer lay back and closed her eyes, her head full of her new love, the wedding, and all the other weddings scheduled to be held at Magnolia throughout the summer. There was just one that niggled her – Ian had promised he would confirm his late booking, but he hadn't.

* * *

"Good morning, Gabby. Duncan here. Did I wake you?"

"No," Gabby said, blinking through her sleep. It had been a late night or, more correctly, a very early morning – her choice. Tempted to ring Greg right after Paul and Ros had left, she'd resisted. It wasn't fair to keep waking him up in the early hours, so she'd waited until 1.00 a.m. UK time, reasonably sure that it would be time for him to start getting ready for another day. An hour later, after she had explained all that had passed, persuaded him not to jump on the first plane home, and given him yet another assignment, she cut the call and crashed out, mentally and physically exhausted. "I was just thinking about getting up," she lied.

"Good. Jennifer and I are having breakfast and there's something that you might be interested in. How soon can you get here?" Duncan asked.

"Urgent?" Gabby asked, looking around the bedroom and through into the lounge and kitchen where she had left clothes strewn everywhere, ironing waiting to be done, and pots in the sink.

"Give me twenty minutes, and I'll be there." A past master at showering in record time, throwing on clothes fast, and rearranging her hair, Gabby headed for the bathroom. The housework could wait. It wouldn't go away.

"Jennifer's here at my cottage. Can you get down here soon?" Duncan asked.

* * *

"There's tea in the pot and bread in the toaster if you want it, Gabby. Help yourself," Duncan said.

"Just tea, thanks. I've put on three pounds since I arrived here courtesy of Aunt Hetty's cakes and meals, Thomas's scones, and cocktails, so I'll pass, but thanks," Gabby said.

"Now, Jennifer, tell Gabby exactly what you've just told me." Buttering his toast, Duncan nodded reassuringly at Jennifer.

"Well, it's possibly something and nothing. Just being a bit paranoid. But I was expecting a call back from someone yesterday to confirm a wedding booking. He seemed keen.

But I haven't heard from him," Jennifer said.

"Not following you, Jennifer. He'll most likely ring today," Gabby said. "Worrying about nothing."

"No, no. Now I think back on it, something didn't sit right about it all. I met him at that very nice little tea shop in Stroud the day before yesterday.

"He was quite charming, even flirting with me," she said, turning back to Duncan. "But, of course, I took no notice whatsoever of that – kept the whole meeting entirely professional.

"He was looking for a wedding venue for his granddaughter. The booking that she had with another venue – Burleigh Court Hotel – had been cancelled. He as good as confirmed the booking on the spot, but I told him he had to confirm in writing by yesterday at the latest. By email, I said, would do fine and then pay the deposit. Well, I haven't heard a single word from him, not a phone call, or an email. I was going to ring him, but then I remembered that, other than his name, Ian Williams, I didn't have any contact details for him. Not an address. Not a phone number. I'd asked him for them when we first spoke on the phone, but somehow the conversation wandered off in other directions. By the time I remembered to ask him for his number at the café, he had gone," Jennifer said.

Gabby shrugged her shoulders, thinking about her comfortable bed and the sleep that she might be having. "It happens, Jennifer. Don't fret about it. There'll be some other couple delighted to take that weekend."

Duncan wagged his finger at Gabby. "You know me better than that. I don't haul anybody out of bed without a good reason. You need to listen to Jennifer."

"The thing is, I told him about the dagger and the notebook. I don't know how the whole conversation started, but I think it was him suggesting it must be very boring living in a retirement community. Of course, I couldn't let that comment pass. I told him life was never dull at Magnolia and...and then I told him all about Stan's find. I did exaggerate a bit, I have to admit. Not about the dagger, but the notebook. I can't remember my actual words, but I told him something to the effect that it was filled cover-to-cover with notes written by a man who had been murdered in the Old Forge. You know what I'm like when I get carried away."

"And did he ask you any more questions about the note-book?" Gabby frowned.

"No, he didn't, but I do remember bragging about you. I probably mentioned you were road-testing the Old Forge. And then I told him what a wonderful investigative journalist you were and that if anybody could get to the bottom of the mystery it would be you," Jennifer said, downcast. "It was me, wasn't it?"

"But you didn't mention anything about the tape?" Gabby asked, ignoring Jennifer's question.

"Oh, that? It had completely slipped my mind," Jennifer said.

"Good. Did you tell him that I was looking after both of them at the Old Forge?" Gabby asked.

"I did. It was just part of the story. I didn't mean to...Oh dear, Gabby. I'm so sorry," Jennifer said.

"Easily done, Jennifer. Can you describe this man?" Gabby asked.

"Quite tall. Beautiful, thick white hair swept back from his forehead and very smart. Well spoken. Quite handsome for his age. He must have been in his early eighties, I'd guess."

Gabby took a deep breath. It had to be. "You may think this a very strange question, Jennifer, but did you notice anything about his ears?"

"His ears?" Duncan grimaced.

"Now you come to mention it, I did. They were very pronounced, if that's the right way of putting it," Jennifer replied. "Is it important?"

Gabby nodded. "It's the same description as the man Paul met in a pub a few days ago. He and Ros came round to tell me last night. And Paul hasn't exactly been discreet about Stan's find either. I think this man, Ian Williams, contacted you about the wedding under false pretences. What he wanted to know was more about the dagger and the notebook."

"So, he wasn't looking for a wedding at all, you think?" Jennifer said. "He was so convincing."

"I don't think so. Whoever he is, he's clever and he's got contacts. People to do his dirty work for him," Gabby said, turning to Duncan. "You've got as near as damn it, a photographic memory. Cast your mind back and think where else you've seen a man who fits this description," Gabby said.

Duncan narrowed his eyes. "Drawing a blank there, Gabby. Doesn't ring a bell with me at all."

"Well, there's another mystery man for us. He'll no doubt show his face again some time. When he does, we've got him," Gabby replied.

Jennifer yawned. "I'm so sorry. Do you mind if I slip off? I've got a fitting with Hetty and Dot, and then I'm off to have a chat with Thomas and Gerald. We've asked them to be ushers at the wedding. They'll be perfect for the job."

"Do you want me to drop your case down later?" Duncan asked with a glint in his eye.

"You're such a dear," Jennifer laughed. "But I can manage it. Supper at mine at six?"

"Looking forward to it. Now you go home and get some shut-eye and don't worry," Duncan said.

"I spoke to Greg last night," Gabby said, helping herself to another cup of tea. "It's a dead end on tracing the silversmith, but we always knew that was a longshot. As it happens, he's got the day off today, so I've set him a new task. I've asked him to try and track down David McMasters, Ahmed's guardian, and put him in touch with me. That might throw a bit of light on matters.

"Going off on an altogether different tack, Duncan, have you had time to get the gen on this Sir Edward Bright, the father of Ed Bright?"

"I did. Name crops up all over the place. One-time MP, staunch Tory, owns a lot of property in Hampshire. One son – Ed. According to sources, they haven't got on for years, and he rarely visits the family home. The father isn't a particularly well-liked chap, by all accounts. Into his early eighties like the rest of them, and most of us for that matter, he's still going strong, just like his wife. They've got a big house and estate in the New Forest and they've just opened the gardens up to the public, three times a week in the afternoons. The lady of the house conducts the tours in person. Good feedback on Trip Advisor. Any good to you?"

"I think it might be," Gabby said. "It would be very useful to find Ed and talk to him. He may have information that could lead us to Ahmed. I can't help thinking he's the key to all this…It's a risk, but possibly worth taking."

"What is, Gabby? Trying to find Ed Bright?" Duncan asked.

"No," Gabby paused. "I'm thinking of Paul and Ros. They've had a rough time. You'll all find out soon enough. Paul's going to do the rounds to explain and apologize for the other night. When you hear his explanation, you'll understand. I'm thinking a weekend break would do them good and where better than the New Forest?"

"Paul and Ros?" Duncan said, clearly surprised at the suggestion.

"Gardens open to the public, you said? They're both mad keen about plants. Ros with her flowers, Paul with his veg. All they've got to do is ingratiate themselves with the lady of the house and ask a few pertinent questions. I'll run it past Amy and, if she agrees, I'll have a word with Peter about the finances. It needn't cost much. Some fuel and a couple of nights B&B," Gabby said.

"Worth a try." Duncan nodded approvingly. "My turn to change the subject now," Duncan said, checking some notes. "You asked me to see what I could find out about Stanwell and Walker, the two teachers Grzeskowiak mentions in his witness statement. Well, I can tell you one thing. You aren't going to get much out of them. Both dead. Stanwell died in a hit-and-run accident back in '95 in Lowestoft. Walker died in a fire in 2005 in Cardiff. Both accidental death verdicts," Duncan said.

"It's a bit like ten green bottles, isn't it?" Gabby laughed. "Amy wants to go and see Grzeskowiak again. I'm not sure about it. I think she's doing too much."

"Me too, but I wouldn't dare tell her that. She's on a mission and she's not going to stop until she's got the answers."

"Maybe I should go and see him instead?" Gabby suggested.

"Definitely not, young lady. Remember, you are keeping a

low profile and manning the control room here. Max would come down on us like a ton of bricks if you were to go gallivanting around there. If she insists on going, tell her Stan is going with her. Nobody is going to argue with him. And maybe take Andy as well," Duncan said sternly.

"Spoilsport," Gabby laughed. "But you're right. If it all goes tits up and the police get involved, then I'm right up shit creek."

"And with luck, that tape will be back tomorrow or the day after..." Duncan said. "Let's hope it doesn't turn out to be Eric and Ernie's Christmas show." Duncan chuckled.

Twenty-Nine

2022

"Feeling better today?" Greg grinned. It wasn't often anybody riled his Gabby, but this Paul had certainly managed to get her hackles up. "You've got that smile back on your face."

"Good day. Did I tell you that Paul apologized and explained what it was all about? No, forget that. I did tell you when we spoke last night. I was just so tired I couldn't think straight. Poor man. I've made a decision. I'm going back on the scams trail just as soon as I get back to work. There's a whole lot more to do in that quarter. And I'm thinking I might take Duncan and Amy with me. What a team we'd make," Gabby laughed.

"Careful what you wish for." Greg laughed. "Seriously, any progress?"

"Definitely. I think we've identified one of the key players, at least by sight. Not quite sure how he fits into it yet, but we're quite convinced he's pulling the strings. There's the small matter of motive and opportunity to deal with, but I'm pretty sure we're on the right track. I won't go into it right now, if you don't mind. You know me. I don't like to go for the jugular until I've got all the facts to hand."

"So, you're behaving yourself, are you?"

"Confined to barracks by a ninety-four-year-old lady and a mature Olympic wheelchair sprinter. Did you ever hear anything like it? The others are doing the leg work while I man the control room back here."

"How does that feel?" Greg said.

"Odd, but strangely okay," Gabby said. "I worry about them, but maybe I shouldn't. They're quite capable of looking after themselves."

"Good. I don't want to be visiting you in prison when I get back."

Gabby leant into the screen. "Have you got your feet up on the furniture? You do know that you are breaking house rules. If that was me doing that in our home, you'd soon give me that disapproving look of yours," Gabby laughed.

"I've earnt it," he said. "Just about worn out my shoe leather today tracking down your David McMasters. He retired about seven years ago. No problem finding the office headquarters, but tracking down McMasters was another thing altogether. He'd moved to Ramgarh. Hope you've got a good expense account. I'll be putting my bill in when I get back," Greg laughed. "You wouldn't believe how hot it has been here today – well into the nineties. You know they should give that Willis Carrier a medal."

"Willis Carrier?" Gabby frowned. "Never heard of him."

"He invented air conditioning. Back in 1902. A New England man. Thank God that taxi had air conditioning," Greg said.

"I'll store that gem of information up for the next pub quiz," Gabby laughed. "You didn't actually go and see him, did you?"

"The man left me no choice. As soon as I spoke to him on

the phone, he wouldn't take no for an answer. Nice chap. Married an Indian woman. Quite charming. Four children and thirteen grandchildren and they all live together in a quite magnificent house with views out across the mountains. We should go there sometime. We've got an invitation to go and stay," Greg said.

"Tell me, what did he have to say?"

"Well, first of all he hasn't set eyes on Ahmed since '85 when he put him on the plane for England, and hasn't heard from him either. I could see his eyes glazing over as he told me. Think he was pretty fond of Ahmed as a boy."

"Did Ahmed write to him while he was at school? Surely, they must have kept in some contact?" Gabby asked.

"David's got letters. Not many, but he let me read them. Nothing mind-blowing, but one bit of interesting information. He talks about two school friends – Ed Bright and Colin Reed. Pours his heart out in the letter when he finds that Colin died, and then again when Ed was expelled. There are photographs of the three of them together. He's loaned it to me. And he also mentions Vincent Palmer."

"Colin Reed," Gabby repeated. "He must be the CR in Vincent's notebook. There's mention of a funeral. That was the last bit of the puzzle, Greg. Well done you. Now we can put a name to every initial in that notebook. Can you scan that photo and send it to me?"

"Will do. And there are two school reports in David's collection. Both glowing. Academically brilliant, slotted into the school well, not a moment's trouble."

"Doesn't quite accord with the Headmaster's witness statement after Palmer was killed. If I remember correctly, according to Rutherwood, Ahmed was a troublemaker –

fighting with other boys and stealing. Doesn't stack up, does it?"

"Doesn't stack up at all. When we were at school, if you were punished, the teachers made damned sure that your parents, guardian, whatever, knew about it, and then you got a double dose from them too."

"David was quite proud of the boy," Greg said quietly.

"So McMasters was both guardian and benefactor?" Gabby said.

"No, he was Ahmed's guardian. He looked after all the paperwork and paid the bills on behalf of the benefactor."

"Sounds like an odd arrangement to me."

"It was. Ahmed's benefactor is a man called Sir Francis Carruthers, and a great friend of McMasters. Carruthers had an affair with Ahmed's mother – a woman called Indira – not long after her husband died, and Ahmed was the result of the relationship. He couldn't acknowledge Ahmed as his son. In those days, it would have been frowned upon, to put it mildly. Ahmed never knew who his real father was. Carruthers found out he had a terminal illness just after Indira had passed on. He wanted to make sure that his son had a future. That's when David took on the role of guardian and that's when Ahmed was packed off to St John's."

"So Carruthers must have been quite a wealthy man?" Gabby said.

"Very wealthy. A financier. Even owned his own bank. No family of his own. No siblings, no wife, no children. He'd made his business his life. And Ahmed had been named as his one and only beneficiary on his death."

"And the benefactor died?" Gabby asked. "So, Ahmed, wherever he might be, is worth millions and possibly doesn't know anything about it?"

"Not so fast, Gabby. Miracles of modern – or not so modern – science. Carruthers was persuaded to go to Switzerland for some previously untried treatment. The odds were one hundred to one against but…he survived and is alive and kicking today. Quite an elderly gentleman, into his eighties. According to David, he's never got over Ahmed. Still thinks that one day he will come waltzing back to India, and into his life. David thinks that's the only thing keeping him going. That, and one day, seeing Ahmed's name cleared. His will is just as he made it all those years ago. Everything goes to Ahmed. Ahmed knows nothing about that. They'd both heard about the accusations. The police contacted David back in the day, looking for him. Lots of questions at first and then, after a few months, nothing. Both Carruthers and David kept pushing the police to keep trying to find Ahmed, but they drew blanks and finally gave up."

"And the dagger?" Gabby asked.

"The dagger. It does belong to Ahmed, and it is valuable. It was passed on to him after his mother died. Yes, and Thomas was right, it is what is called a peace dagger. David found a photograph of it. It's the same one you showed me, I'm pretty sure of it. Been in Ahmed's family for generations, apparently. Strictly speaking, it should have been passed down through the male line, but there'd been some controversy in the family and Ahmed's grandfather had asked that it should go to Indira, and then on down through the male line. Ahmed, albeit born out of wedlock, was an only son. I did ask him how Ahmed came to have the dagger in England, and I have to say that he was pretty evasive about it, so I didn't push him on it. But he did say something interesting – that Ahmed treasured that dagger and would never have left it behind unless there had been a very good reason."

"So, you told him we found it, and that we'd lost it again?" Gabby asked.

"I levelled with him on a lot of things. I hope you don't mind. It was kind of quid pro quo. I told him it all started out with you trying to find Ahmed so the dagger could be returned to him and how that led to a raft of other issues...And that you were of the opinion that Ahmed was being wrongly accused...And that it was looking like you might be able to prove it. Did I overstep the mark?"

"Not at all. I'm quite convinced Ahmed had nothing to do with the murder, but proving it is going to be another matter. Let's keep our fingers crossed. I'd love to give him some real good news," Gabby said. "Is he going to tell Carruthers about your conversation with him?"

"No, he was quite clear about that. When and if there is some positive news, he'll tell him. Not before. Won't get his hopes up. We've agreed to keep in touch with each other."

"I'll make sure you're the first to know if anything breaks, Greg. I love you, and promise I'll buy you a new pair of shoes when you get home," Gabby said blowing a kiss at the screen. "Can't wait to see you. Goodnight."

Gabby flipped her laptop closed, checked the time, and reached for the phone. "Duncan, hi there. Thought you might be staying overnight with Jennifer. Love's young dream and all that. Up to no good..." she teased.

"That's for me to know and you to find out," Duncan laughed. "Haven't you got a bed to go to?"

"On my way. Just had a good long chat with Greg. Do me

a favour, can you? Use those remarkable skills of yours and find out all you can about a Colin Reed who was a pupil at the school. He's CR – the one who we think died."

"First thing tomorrow. I'm worn out. You know what it's like, Gabby – first love!" Duncan grinned and cut the call.

Thirty

2022

"Gabby, can you drag over a couple of comfortable chairs? This could be a very long session," Duncan said, positioning his wheelchair close to the computer desk in the corner of the Great Hall.

"I'm glad you decided on the big screen today. Small screens have a habit of making me go cross-eyed after an hour," Amy said, plumping up cushions and arranging them behind her back. "It's such a pity we don't spend more time in this wonderful room. It's a beautiful space but with the economies...Oh well, when we have wind turbines everywhere, solar panels on everything, nuclear power stations in every corner of the country, and we've fracked every square inch of ground, we'll be able to stop worrying about fuel costs, at least for a few more years and then the next generation will have to worry about it. I don't know which is worse. Sorry, Duncan, don't get me going on my hobby horse," Amy said.

"I didn't." Duncan grinned. "But if we're going to sit here for the next eight hours, we are not going to be cold. I've put the heating on – high. Are you ready, girls? The moment of truth."

Duncan powered up the computer and the forty-two-inch monitor and inserted the DVD into the external drive.

"Popcorn anyone?" Gabby said reaching into her handbag. "We might as well enjoy ourselves."

"Hmm." Duncan stared at the monitor and fiddled with the keyboard. "Blank so far. I'll just fast forward a bit."

"Maybe it won't be such a long session as we thought," Gabby said.

"Patience," Duncan muttered. "If that tape had been blank, I'd have been told about it. Now, what have we got here?" Duncan pressed stop as the first image appeared.

"That looks like the car park," Amy leant in. "It's much smaller than it is now but I recognize that oak tree on the far side."

"And there," Gabby said, pointing to the screen, "are the stone mushrooms. I've nearly reversed into those a dozen times."

"So, let's get our bearings," Duncan said. "We're looking at the car park and we can also see a bit of the drive up from the road. I'd say the camera was located fairly high up on the right-hand side of the Mansion House as you look at it from the front and angled towards the car park. It looks as though it could well have been a full moon that night."

"But not a werewolf in sight," Gabby added.

"Duncan, can you freeze it there and zoom right in? There's something right in the far corner. I can't quite make it out, but it could be a structure of some kind," Amy said, squinting at the screen.

"You're right. Whatever it is, it wasn't there when we moved into Magnolia." He zoomed in further. "It's pretty blurry, but I reckon there's a door on the front. Not big enough to be a garage door—and a couple of small windows at the front. Difficult to tell, but they might just be boarded up."

"Maybe a storeroom of some kind?" Gabby suggested.

"Possibly. Let's start it playing again. Maybe there will be a clearer image later," Amy said, sitting back and helping herself to a handful of popcorn.

* * *

Gabby checked her watch. Two hours had passed since they had started watching the DVD, and still nothing. Other than the odd owl that had flown across the camera, nothing had stirred. Duncan's head had dropped down onto his chest, his eyes closed, his breathing slow and regular. He was sound asleep. Her head resting against the cushions, Amy muttered a few words as her dreams took her to places from the past. Resisting the temptation to follow suit, Gabby munched the remains of the popcorn.

Blinking hard to remain awake, Gabby did a double-take. Something was playing out on the screen. They had action at last. "Duncan, Amy, wake up. We're in business. Duncan, rewind thirty seconds," she shouted.

Duncan shook his head. "Did I drop off?"

"You frightened the life out of me." Amy's head shot forward, her glasses askew. "I haven't been to sleep at all. I just had my eyes closed for one minute."

Duncan pressed rewind. "Stop it there. See what I see?" Gabby pointed at the screen.

"A car pulling into the car park. I'll zoom in...A Jaguar XJ6. Possibly black. Could be navy or grey," Duncan said. "One occupant, but that's about all I can make out. Can't make out the number plate."

"Let it run." Eyes fixed on the screen, Gabby tapped her fingers on the desk impatiently. "Five minutes and no movement. Whoever is in that car is waiting for someone. Well, pal," she whispered to the monitor, "we're not in a hurry. We can sit here all day until you show yourself. What time is it on the camera now?"

"11.45 p.m. Maybe midnight is the witching hour," Duncan whispered. "There!" Duncan started. "The car door is opening. It's a man I'd say and tallish. He's putting a hat on. He's waving in the direction of the Mansion House. Now he's locking the car door and heading away from the car towards...towards that building at the back of the car park. Hang on, I'm going in again. Look, I think he might be reaching into his pocket and taking something out. It has to be a key. He has the key to the building. I'm going to rewind a few seconds – to see if we can get a better look at him. Damn, we can only see his back and that bloody hat. Turn around, will you?" Duncan shouted at the screen. "The blighter's not going to show himself."

"Well, he's gone in," Amy said. "And he's left the door open so any minute now we should meet our other guest."

"And there he is," Gabby said. "Back view again. Wish they'd put the camera on that other side of the car park. Tall, unmistakable trilby hat, walking with a slight limp and a stick."

"And two more bringing up the rear. One of them is carrying a bundle of some sort," Amy said. "Zoom in on those two, Duncan...Oh, my lord, do you see what I see?" Amy gasped, her hands flying to her throat.

"It looks like a sack of some kind. I don't believe it. Is that a head hanging over his shoulder?" Gabby stopped in her tracks. "And could that be a school cap on the head?"

Duncan froze the screen as they all sat back in complete silence staring at the monitor in utter disbelief. "It's got to be a boy, small and light in weight. He's not moving."

"Drugged or dead," Gabby said quietly.

"Perhaps you ladies shouldn't watch this anymore. I can watch it and let you know what transpires," Duncan suggested reaching for the control.

Amy shook her head. "Oh, no. We've come this far. If I have to sit here for the next week to find the truth, that's what I intend to do."

"I can't walk away now, Duncan. It isn't going to change anything. We have to know," Gabby said. "Play on."

The door to the building closed behind them; a light went on inside. Duncan was right, the windows had been boarded up. The tape ran on, and on. Duncan, Amy, and Gabby sat patiently waiting for the four of them to reappear. An hour passed before the door was reopened and the light switched off. Now they were all in full view, their features indistinct in the dim light. The tall man in the trilby carried the bundle which was now capless and struggling with his captor. Two men followed on behind. The Jaguar man locked the door, put the key in his pocket, and returned to his car.

"Rewind, Duncan. Stop. Zoom in again," Gabby shouted. "I'd put my last dollar on that being Ed Bright. How did Grzeskowiak describe him, Amy? A little runt of a boy. Skinny as a rake. Ginger hair."

"The boy who was expelled and sent home the day after this tape was recorded," Amy said. "It's all in the notebook."

"I'd hate to think what happened in that room," Duncan said, his voice flat. "You hear these stories about boarding schools—"

"That poor child," Amy said.

"No one except them knows what went on in there. We can only imagine. It proves nothing specific. There are four of them. They'd back each other up," Gabby said. "We still haven't got enough."

"But we know who one of them is, don't we?" Amy said. "The trilby has got to be the Headmaster. The gait, the walking stick, his height. The man with the car is taking no chances. That damned hat. Do either of you recognize the other two?"

"No," Duncan said.

"Not a clue," Gabby said. "I need some fresh air for a minute."

"I wonder how many more there were." Duncan switched off the computer and closed his eyes. "It doesn't bear thinking about. Right here at Magnolia. It makes my skin crawl just sitting here no more than thirty yards from where it happened."

Amy leant across and took Duncan's hand. "It wasn't here at Magnolia. It was in a school long ago, before Magnolia was built. You can't think that way."

Duncan shook his head as a tear escaped his eye. "Is there no decency in the world, Amy?"

Throwing open the oak doors to the Great Hall, Gabby held her face up to the sky and took a deep breath; a deep breath of sweet, clean air, freshly mown lawns, and the promise of spring and summer to come. Maybe Uncle Max had been right. They should have simply turned everything over to the police and let them sort it out. 'The police,' she said out loud to herself. Turn everything over to yet another detective to bury as he or she felt appropriate? Not on her watch.

"Better now, dear?" Amy asked. "Duncan and I were just

thinking about the options going forward."

"No police," Gabby cut in sharply. "I'm sorry, but we have to plough on without them. I don't trust them after that incident the other morning. We now have a motive. Who wouldn't kill to get hold of this tape? That's why Vincent Palmer was killed. The tape was hidden up his chimney. Someone knew it was there, and somebody wanted it badly enough to kill for it."

"We both came to that same conclusion, Gabby dear. We are getting closer every minute," Amy said. "I agree, no police for the time being."

"We need witnesses. First-hand witnesses. We need Ed Bright to come forward to give evidence, assuming he is still alive. And there's another one we need to follow up on. That's Colin Reed," Gabby said.

"CR?" Amy asked wide-eyed. "And how did you get hold of that gem of information?"

"Greg. He had a long, long session with McMasters yesterday. I can fill you in on it later, but apparently, he let Greg read letters Ahmed sent from school. Our CR was Colin Reed and a very good friend of both Ahmed and Ed. Colin is dead but maybe his parents might be able to help fill in some of the gaps," Gabby said.

"So, you think CR was another of their victims, do you?" Duncan asked.

Gabby nodded. "I don't know, but it's quite possible. Vincent's book confirms that CR was sent home on...when was it, Amy?"

"16th April," Amy confirmed, checking her notes.

"And the funeral was when?"

"22nd April. Coincidence maybe, but in my job, we don't

believe in coincidences – there's always a link somewhere," Gabby said. "Duncan, can you work your wonders and see what you can turn up on Colin Reed?"

Duncan nodded. "Now we've got a name, I can do that. We still don't know who the other three are," he added.

"No, we don't. Let's concentrate on what we do know and leave what we don't know until tomorrow," Gabby said. "Ros and Paul should be down in the New Forest by now. Tomorrow they're going to the Brights. Maybe Ed will be there."

"Don't you think we should warn Paul or Ros about what we've just found?" Amy asked.

"No, better they know nothing then they can't say the wrong thing. All they need to do is find out where Ed Bright is, and we'll take over from there," Gabby said firmly.

"And in the meantime, my friends," Amy grinned, "I have a few words to say to our friend Adrian Grzeskowiak. Don't tell me he didn't know what was going on. If he thinks he's going to pull the wool over my eyes again, he is sadly mistaken. He'll wish he'd never been born by the time I've finished with him. Either that or he'll be our other witness," Amy said. "Tomorrow, Stan and I will be paying him an unexpected visit. And yes, I think it's a good idea that Andy should come too. I am going to enjoy this."

"We need to decide what we're going to tell your Uncle Max and the rest of them." Duncan pursed his lips. "Not an easy decision."

"I think we stay quiet about it for the moment as much as we can. It's a very upsetting subject," Amy said. "No one else knows that we have the VHS tape back. Let's keep it like that for the moment. Stan and Andy will have to be told if they are coming with me tomorrow, otherwise, I suggest we keep it to ourselves. Maybe when we have some good news, we can share the full story with everybody."

"I'm not planning to tell Jennifer either. You may think she's tough, but underneath that pretty exterior she's as soft as butter, especially when it comes to kids," Duncan said.

"Then we're all agreed," Gabby said. "I think we all need a strong cup of tea and a piece of cake."

Thirty-One

2022

"Keep your eyes on the road, mate," Stan shouted, covering his eyes. "That's twice you've nearly knocked a poor cyclist for six."

"After what Amy's just been telling us?" Andy exhaled loudly. "Gawd love us, I've heard about it, but never expected it to come knocking on our door."

"Yes, I thought it might come as rather a shock," Amy said. "That's why you're both here. Stan to man the front line, and you to be on standby in case we need you."

"You expect trouble, Mrs A?" Stan asked. Mrs A she had been from the very first day they had met, and the name had stuck.

"I don't rightly know. I am quite sure there's going to be a certain reluctance to cooperate with us, but whether it will end in violence remains to be seen." Amy smiled at Stan. "I'm just teasing you. If it gets even slightly out of hand, we will make a strategic withdrawal and regroup. We're nearly there, Andy. Just turn right here, and it's about the third bungalow on the right – the one with the green gate posts."

"I don't know how you can be so cool about this, Amy," Andy

said, pulling up outside the gate. "This is dynamite."

"It comes from living through a world war. I found myself in some very tricky situations in those days, but I lived to tell the tale."

"All that foreign office stuff you mean? One day, you'll have to tell us all about it."

"It's in the past, Andy. It's not a period in my life I like to dwell on. So many dreadful things happened," Amy said.

"Are we ready, Stan?"

"Whenever you are. If you wait a second, I'll come round and give you a hand to get out."

"Thank you, Stan. A little help goes a long way these days," Amy said.

"I'll knock on the door and you stand over there, Stan, out of sight. Be ready to get your foot in the door if he tries to close it on me." Amy said, pointing to the wall alongside the door.

Straightening her cardigan, Amy knocked on the door and stepped back carefully. "Adrian, how nice to see you again. I think we need to have another little chat."

"I told you not to come back 'ere. Don't you understand King's English? Now clear off before I see you down the path meself," Grzeskowiak replied as he started to close the door in her face.

Stan took his cue. Appearing from nowhere, he stuck his leg out and foot in the door. Had he not been wearing steel-capped builders' boots, it would have been painful. "No way to talk to a lady, mate," he said. "Now no more of your nonsense. The lady wants to speak to you, so move. Inside. Now."

Grzeskowiak eyed Stan and decided the odds were against him.

"I'll go into the lounge, Adrian. I know my way," Amy said, stepping through the door. Stan followed. "I suggest you sit down, Adrian. You may want to once you've heard what I have to say. And, Stan, you keep Adrian company on the sofa." Stan grinned; this was Mrs A in her element.

"So where were we?" she said. "Oh yes, you don't know who murdered Mr Vincent and you are quite sure it wasn't Ahmed. Correct so far?"

Looking daggers, Adrian didn't answer.

"Now if I were to tell you we've found the motive for Mr Vincent's murder, what would you say about that?" Amy paused. Still no answer. "And if I mention we found a tape and a notebook up the chimney of the Annexe together with a silver dagger, might that jog your memory a little more?" No answer. "If I were to tell you I have now watched that tape from end to end – and I am appalled to say it quite clearly shows there was a paedophile ring operating in that school – the school in which you were the caretaker, and not only the caretaker but head of security, what would you say to that?" No answer. "Well, Adrian, your silence tells me this does not come as news to you." Amy opened her handbag, took out a handkerchief, and blew her nose. "We're in no hurry."

"Don't know nothing about any of it." Grzeskowiak glared at her.

"The tape was the motive for Vincent Palmer's murder, wasn't it? One of the tapes that had been recorded on your security system. A tape you knew full well contained graphic evidence of what was going on at that school. One you desperately needed to recover from Mr Vincent, as you like to call him. I can only guess he refused to hand it over to you. So...You murdered him. Motive and opportunities galore.

You then falsified your statement to the police. One way or the other, Adrian, the police will take a very dim view of it."

"I told you, I didn't murder Mr Vincent, whatever it looks like," he barked. "Wasn't like that. God's truth."

"But surely that is why you're so positive Ahmed didn't commit the murder. It wasn't like what, Adrian?"

"I never murdered 'im. He was dead when me and Rutherwood went over there. Just like I said in me statement. And I don't know who did."

"Let's get back to the tape, shall we? Do you have any theories on how and why it got up that chimney? I'd love to know," Amy said. "I'm waiting, Adrian. You were responsible for the CCTV and therefore, I assume, for the safekeeping of the VHS tapes. You would have known precisely what was on those tapes and therefore, correct me if I am wrong, you would have been fully aware of the dreadful things that were happening to those boys, and yet you did nothing. Or were you part of the ring as well?"

"I've never touched boys. Wouldn't never touch boys. 'ad enough of that as a kid meself. I know what it's like to be played with. It leaves you scarred for life," Grzeskowiak said, shaking his head in disbelief at her words.

"The tapes, Adrian," Amy said quietly.

"I never watched the tapes. Sometimes glanced at the screen during the day, but never stayed up watching it at night. Aliens could have landed for all I knew. I 'ad to change the tapes. That were me job. And then one of 'em went missin'. I'd never have noticed if Rutherwood hadn't come knocking demanding that I 'and it over to 'im. It weren't there. Nearly went bonkers, 'e did. Threatened to sack me. So I told 'im Ahmed had been in a few times. That we'd played chess. It 'ad to be 'im. No one else ever came to Keepers. And then I felt guilty landing Ahmed in it, so I told Rutherwood he 'ad probably been put up to it by Mr Vincent. I couldn't think why else 'e'd do it."

"So, you honestly didn't know what was on that tape?" Amy looked Adrian square in the eyes. "And had Mr Rutherwood ever demanded you hand over tapes before?"

"Couple of times, yes. And, no, I didn't know what were on the tapes. After Rutherwood was gone, I got thinking about it. See, I had me suspicions that something were going on in that school. I should've spoken up sooner but I 'ad no real evidence. Talked meself into keeping me mouth shut in the end. Worked out that if Mr Vincent were on to something, 'e'd be the one to sort it out."

"And what were those suspicions based upon, Adrian?" Amy asked.

"I was the cleaner – mostly cleaner. Couple of times 'e sent me up to the old storeroom to clean it. Top to bottom and plenty of bleach, 'ed always say."

"The storeroom?" Amy asked.

"Up at the back of the car park. Where the games stuff were stored mostly. You didn't ask questions with Rutherwood. One day, I found a school cap while I were cleaning. Thought nothing more about it at the time. And then I started to ask meself why 'e wanted an old storeroom cleaned like that."

"You didn't report your concerns to anyone?" Amy asked.

Grzeskowiak shook his head. "Who? Rutherwood? The fuzz? They'd 'ave thought I were mad. Probably lock me up and throw away the key…It's the truth as God's me witness."

"It had better be," Stan said, clenching his fists, "Or you'll have me to deal with next time you hear a knock on that door."

Amy frowned and glanced across at Stan. Stan nodded. "As

it happens, I do believe you, but I'm certainly not condoning your silence in any of this, Adrian."

"So, if Mr Rutherwood knew what was on that tape, he would have had a motive for killing Mr Vincent, wouldn't you say?" Amy said.

Grzeskowiak shrugged his shoulders. "Mebbe, but it was 'e and me who found Mr Vincent dead. Without a word of a lie. What I said in me statement to the fuzz was true."

"Think back. What I am going to ask you now is very important. Did you see a school cap lying on the floor beside Mr Vincent's body, or a boy's school exercise book on his bed after you and Mr Rutherwood had discovered the body? Take your time."

Grzeskowiak closed his eyes and rubbed his forehead. It might have been thirty-seven years ago, but that picture of Mr Vincent lying there was as clear as a bell. "No, I don't remember seeing either of 'em. I ain't never gonna forget seeing that room."

"I thought not," Amy muttered to herself.

"Be honest with me, Adrian. Did you suspect Rutherwood might have murdered Mr Vincent all along?"

Adrian dropped his head. "It crossed me mind, but I couldn't work out 'ow 'e might have done it. Like I said, it were 'im and me who found Mr Vincent. Rutherwood with 'is gammy leg weren't no match for Mr Vincent. He might have been skinny, but 'e were all muscle. I seen 'im throw a few punches in 'is time. Don't stack up..."

"Unless there were two of them..." Amy let the words drift in the air. "And Ahmed? You ruled him out very quickly? Was that for a reason?" Amy pushed on.

"Just know...knew 'im. He just wouldn't. He weren't that

sort. Not a bit of anger in that lad and with what 'e's been through, you'd 'ave thought there would be. There weren't. Got to know 'im real well. 'e trusted me and I trusted 'im."

"I've got just one more question, Adrian, and then we'll leave you in peace. What time did you change that tape on the night Mr Vincent was murdered?"

"Like I told you, nine thirty like always. Never varied."

"So, why did you say in your statement you had just changed the tape and also that you arrived at the Annexe at ten twenty-five? What did you do for fifty-five minutes between the time Mr Rutherwood knocked on your door and the time you arrived at the Annexe?"

"It were five minutes after I changed the tape that we got to Mr Vincent's."

"Do you wear a watch, Adrian?"

"Ain't never 'ad one. Clock in Keepers were all I ever needed."

"So how did you know that it was ten twenty-five when you arrived at the Annexe?"

"Rutherwood told me it were." Grzeskowiak shuffled uncomfortably on the sofa. "Took me for a right mug, didn't 'e?"

"The question is why would Mr Rutherwood tell you it was ten twenty-five when it wasn't? There's a reason and I have the feeling it's key to us getting to the bottom of the whole thing." Amy frowned. "You couldn't have mistaken what he had said to you, could you? Maybe you are, and were at the time, a little hard of hearing? I can't say I have noticed that you are while we've been chatting."

"No, why you asking?" Grzeskowiak frowned.

"You didn't hear the disturbance at the Annexe and then you

228

say in your statement that you didn't hear the police arrive fifteen minutes later. That's strange, Adrian."

"Didn't 'ear no scuffle or noises coming from the Annexe. And didn't 'ear no police arriving later, cause I crashed out when I got back to Keepers. Out like a bloody light."

"You crashed out? Do you normally crash out so easily?" Amy asked.

"No. Didn't think nothing of it at the time, but I 'ad an 'ell of an 'ead in the morning. Rutherwood gave me a whisky in 'is office – to steady me nerves, so 'e said. Then told me to go back to Keepers. I can take me whisky..."

Amy nodded. "I think we'll leave it at that for today, Adrian, but there might be more questions."

"So, what happens now, Mrs A?" Grzeskowiak asked. "You going to talk to the fuzz?"

Amy smiled. Up until that moment, it was only Stan who addressed her as Mrs A. Strangely, she felt quite at ease that Adrian should do so as well.

"Not until we have a few more answers," Amy said. "And we've yet to find Ahmed, but we will. Anyway, Adrian, not to worry. I'm very pleased for your help on this occasion."

"Then they'll arrest me?" Adrian said.

"Not if I have anything to do with it. Your worst crime, as far as I can see, is not coming forward with your suspicions at the time. That was a mistake on your part, but not a crime," Amy said, picking up her handbag.

"You need my 'elp, you ask for it," Grzeskowiak said as he opened the door and held out his hand to Stan. "And you, mate."

Thirty-Two

2022

"Come on, Paul. We need to edge our way discreetly up to the front of the group. It's the last part of the garden tour coming up," Ros whispered, taking the lead. Paul straightened his tie for the fourth time, and put his hands behind his back rather than in his pockets – a habit Ros deplored. He trotted, shoulders back, behind her.

"And this last part of the garden is entirely peonies and concludes my tour for the afternoon," Lady Isabelle said, sounding every bit the lady of the manor. Dressed in a long-sleeved cream-coloured linen suit, she wore her hair in a chignon. "We have one of the best collections of peonies in the country here at Dartford Hall and fine examples of most varieties – the anemone, the single, the Japanese, the semi-double, the double, and the bomb. As you'll see, quite a few of them are enjoying this early spring weather and blooming already. Connoisseurs come from far and wide to admire my collection." Ros listened intently.

"Do you have the Festiva Maxima or Duchesse de Nemours, here, Lady Isabelle?" Ros called out.

"My, someone knows their peonies." Lady Isabelle looked

around for the questioner, finally alighting on Ros. "Yes, we do have both of those varieties. No good collection would be complete without them. They're a little behind some of the more popular varieties, but if you look over to your right, you'll see they occupy the whole of that bed," she said, pointing in the near distance. "They take up a great deal of my time. My personal project, you know. I don't let any Tom, Dick, or Harry near my peony beds. We start all our plants off in the greenhouse," she added, glancing towards the house.

Ros followed her glance and gulped. It was more like the Orangery at Kew gardens than a greenhouse.

"By far my favourite varieties," Ros said. "And so rare. I'd love to use them in my wedding bouquets, but they are so difficult to source." Ros knelt on the grass and gently cupped a blooming white peony. "The fragrance is quite exquisite. I do think a bridal bouquet should be both beautiful to behold and fragrant at the same time. Such tight, neat, and perfectly-shaped heads, and such beautiful pastels. Even an artist would be hard-pressed to capture their beauty on canvas. You do indeed have one of the finest collections, Lady Isabelle." Ros sighed contentedly. "Ros, Ros Gardiner by the way," she said, offering her hand. "This is one off my bucket list. What a magnificent collection. I am quite overwhelmed."

"How kind of you to say so."

"I do apologize, Lady Isabelle," Ros said, grabbing Paul's sleeve and pulling him forward. "This is my husband, Paul. He's not so much a flower man as a vegetable man. He's a darling following me around all these gardens. Never complains. I've made wedding bouquets for quite a few society ladies – always using peonies. Of course, I couldn't possibly mention them by name. It wouldn't be etiquette," Ros said conspiratorially.

"Really," Lady Isabelle replied, her attention elsewhere. "You'll have to excuse me. Now the tour is over, I need to make sure my guests leave the premises."

"The garden is open in aid of a homeless charity, so if you feel able, a small donation would be most welcome as you depart." Lady Isabelle herded her guests back towards the main entrance. "Was there anything else, my dear?" she asked, turning back to Ros.

"No, no, nothing," Ros stuttered. "I just find your house and the gardens quite awesome. It's so wonderful to know that a national monument like this is lived in and family-run. It's exceptional these days, isn't it? So many sold to the National Trust because of the cost of maintaining them."

"It has been in the family for several generations. How much longer is another matter altogether. It is not, and never has been, a national monument. It is simply our home," Lady Isabelle said tartly.

Paul stood back and listened. He could see where Ros was going, but somehow, he didn't think she was going to pull it off.

"That's sad, Lady Isabelle," Ros said.

"What is sad?"

"That all this might not stay in the family." Ros struggled to keep the conversation going.

"That is life. Now – what was your name – Ros? I'm very sorry, but Sir Edward and I have some very important guests coming to tea. I'll say goodbye."

Paul glanced at Ros.

"Could I beg a small favour of you, Lady Isabelle, before you go?" Ros asked, reaching in her handbag for her phone.

"Would it be at all possible for Paul and me to spend a little more time in the garden? I'd love to take a few photos of the peonies."

Lady Isabelle hesitated. Strangers wandering around her garden unsupervised. It was unheard of, but there again the woman did seem to know her peonies, unlike most of the visitors who couldn't distinguish a peony from a rose. "Just half an hour, then. I'll ask the gardener to escort you. Good day, Ros, and good day, Peter."

"Paul, actually." It almost looked like he was about to touch his forelock. "Very kind of you, your ladyship. Much appreciated."

"Kenton, over here," she called. An elderly gardener put down his spade and made his way towards them. "Please escort this lady and – er, gentleman – around the peony beds and answer any questions they might have. They'll be leaving in half an hour."

"Thank you so much," Ros called after her as she started to make her way back to the house.

"You struck lucky," Kenton said. "She don't normally let people stay on after a visit. Peonies, hey? Bet she's been telling you that all these here peonies are her work. It's me who does all the work. It were me who planted the first peony in this garden and that were a few years ago. Give her her due though, she does love them."

"I can see that," Ros said. "She's very proud of them and seems to know quite a lot about them."

"Only what I taught 'er. Now, where do you want to start?"

Paul smiled. It took a lot more than Lady Isabelle to beat

his Ros.

"You're a mine of information, Kenton. Great photos. Thank you. Where ever has the time gone? We'd better be making a move before you get into trouble. Do you happen to know if there's a café nearby where we could get a cup of tea?" Ros asked.

"Brockenhurst is the nearest. And you'll be lucky if you get into any of them cafés. Heaving it is at this time of the year. I were just thinking about a cuppa myself. I can put the kettle on if you fancy it. My cottage is on the edge of the grounds. Good to have some company. You can leave through my back gate. She won't see you go. The car park is in that direction too. I'll square it with her ladyship. Tell 'er you didn't outstay your welcome."

"Good cup of tea, Kenton. It's very welcome. We've got a long drive back and that'll keep us going until we get home," Paul said, stretching out in an armchair. "Comfortable little cottage. Do you live here on your own?"

"I do that. The wife passed away ten years ago. She used to work up at the big house. Did most everything for Lady Isabelle. She knew how to handle 'er alright."

"She does seem as though she might be a bit of a tyrant, if you don't mind me saying. A bit short on please and thank you."

"Take no notice of that, me. Its 'er who owns the place – lock, stock, and barrel. Sir Edward married into the money. Plain old Edward Bright 'e were before 'e met 'er. Clever mind. Got his knighthood through services to industry. Don't ask me what. Known 'er since she was a kid. My dad were gardener 'ere before me – lived in this very cottage. We used to play together as kids – me and Isabelle that is. None of the Lady Isabelle in those days. She's lonely, that's 'er trouble, ever since—"

"I sensed that," Ros interrupted. "She said something about the house having been in the family for generations and then 'how much longer is another matter.' Don't they have any children to carry on from them?"

"Not as you'd notice. Not anymore. One – one boy – well 'e's not a boy anymore. Must be fifty or more. Sad case. Sent 'im off to boarding school when he was no more than a nipper. Nice kid. No airs and graces. Reckon 'e spent as much time up 'ere with me and the missus as 'e did up at the big house. Didn't 'ave much confidence in 'imself. Small kid 'e was and ginger hair after his mum. Mind you, don't let 'er 'ear me saying that. She'd 'ave my guts for garters. As far as she's concerned, she's a redhead." Kenton took a sip of his tea. "It was always nice to see 'im back for the holidays. I remember once he brought a friend back with him. Nice kid 'e was too. No airs and graces about 'im either. Foreign. They was best of mates."

"Did something happen to him?" Paul asked.

"Search me. We never did find out. One minute 'e was normal. The next minute 'e were off the rails. And, when I say off the rails, I mean off the rails. Got sent 'ome – expelled – for stealing. Can you imagine 'ow that went down with 'is knobs? Ranted and raved at 'im 'e did, but young Ed – that was his name – wouldn't say a word. Didn't speak. Didn't defend 'imself. Nothing."

"So what happened then, if you don't mind me asking?" Ros said.

"Sent 'im to a local day school. Didn't settle down there either. 'e wasn't the kid I knew. 'e just didn't care. Didn't care about anything or anybody. Stopped coming down to see me and the missus. She was right upset about it. When 'e weren't out and about with some very shady characters, 'e stayed in his room. Even took meals in 'is room. Went on for years. Almost gave old Isabelle a nervous breakdown. None of us was sorry when 'e announced 'e were moving away. Sixteen 'e was. A waste – 'e wasn't stupid. Far from it. He was good at figures. Always 'ad been."

"But he does come to visit his parents, doesn't he? A beautiful home like this. Who wouldn't want to spend time here?" Ros said.

"'e comes back. That's between you and me. But never to the big house. It were some years before I saw 'im again after 'e left, but 'e turned up on my doorstep. Needed some money, 'e said. Just a short-term loan to get 'im out of a bit of bother. Well, what can you do? I gave 'im the money. 'e did pay me back. And now and again, I still 'elp 'im out."

"That's kind of you," Ros said. "I suppose he couldn't or wouldn't ask his father to help him?"

"Old Sir Edward's now washed 'is 'ands of 'im altogether. The old man found out that he's now out on probation. Don't know 'ow, but he did. That was it. Don't speak about it, they don't. And Ed? I've tried my best to get 'im to talk to them but 'e won't. Always on the move is young Ed – Lowestoft, Brighton, Bournemouth, Bristol, Swindon, Cardiff, and now 'e's in Birmingham. I only know that cause 'e rang me and asked me for some more cash. I've lost count of how many places."

"Maybe you might go and visit him sometime. He might

appreciate it," Paul suggested.

"If 'e weren't shacked up in Spring Hill, I might just do that. I'm not planning to walk those streets in the day let alone at night. No, he'll turn up 'ere again soon. You mark my words."

Paul looked at Ros and pointed to his watch. "Sorry, Kenton. Completely lost track of time. It'll take us a few hours to get back. We've taken up too much of your time already. Thanks for the tea. And we'll keep our fingers crossed for Ed."

"And thank you so much for our peony tour. I shan't forget that in a long time," Ros added. "Back gate?"

"That way," Kenton said, pointing to the end of a narrow strip of garden.

* * *

"Peonies, Ros?" Paul grinned.

"Peonies. A girl's best friend," Ros replied.

"Since when did you know anything about peonies?"

"I don't. I didn't. Thank you, Google."

Thirty-Three

2022

"Thought you were confined to barracks," Andy said, opening the car door. "Front or back?"

"Don't mind," Gabby said. "There'll be more room for Stan at the front."

"Just a shopping trip, today. I got my release papers signed by Uncle Max, Duncan, and Amy. I didn't quite plan on spending so long at Magnolia and I could do with some new jeans and a few tops," Gabby said, a glint in her eye.

"Why don't I believe you?" Andy laughed. "You're up to something. You've got holes in those jeans and that top looks as though it was five bob in a charity shop. If that's all you've got left to wear, maybe shopping is a good idea."

"I'll have you know these jeans are the height of fashion. I paid a small fortune for those holes. And this is a Primark top." Gabby looked down at her jeans and grimaced at the coffee stain and her threadbare knees. They weren't her style at all, but they were perfect for the occasion. "Here comes Stan, so we can get going now."

Stan opened the passenger door and squeezed into Andy's small runabout, pulling the seatbelt over his shoulder as he sat down. "What are you up to, Gabby?"

"Who me? Stan, how could you say such a thing? You know full well that you're taking me shopping." Stan shot a glance across at Andy and raised his eyebrows.

"Left or right at the bottom? Give me a clue." Andy started the engine and drove slowly down the drive.

"Whichever is the quickest way to Birmingham," she said, pulling out her mobile. "I'll get Google maps going and give you directions as we go."

"Bullring is it? Car park right beside Moor Street. Me and Stan'll go and have a dig around the markets while you go girly shopping," Andy said, knowing full well there was more to come.

"We're going to Spring Hill," Gabby said. "One hour and eighteen minutes; sixty-two miles according to my phone."

"Spring Hill?" Andy turned to look at Gabby. "Think I might need my ears syringing. You don't mean *the* Spring Hill, do you? Just down the road from Winson?"

"The very same. Now you know why I'm wearing jeans with holes in them and this crappy T-shirt. You don't want to stand out in a crowd around there."

"Just as well I didn't put my suit on," Stan said. "I'm hoping you'll tell us on the way why we're going there. Would it be better if Andy pulled over?"

"Nothing shocks me anymore mate – daggers, paedos on the doorstep, and murder. It can't get much worse. Okay, Gabby, you've got my attention," Andy said. "And you, Stan, you don't need to hold on to that door handle for grim death."

"Paul and Ros came up trumps yesterday, and with a bit of Duncan's magic thrown in, we've got an address for Ed Bright. So we're off to pay a call on him," Gabby said.

"In Spring Hill? What's someone with a dad like that doing hanging out in a place like that?" Andy said.

"According to our source, he's pretty work-shy, to put it mildly, always in trouble, 'a waste of space'. And did I mention he's out on probation? My guess is he doesn't get up too early in the morning, so we're going to take him by surprise."

"Right up my street," Stan laughed. "Max will eat us alive if he finds out. I suppose Duncan and Amy know what we are up to?"

"Amy wanted to come herself, but she actually admitted she was feeling quite worn out after everything that's happened the last few days. She took some persuading to let me loose, but I won in the end. As for Duncan – well he knows me well enough. I'm pretty good at getting out of scrapes."

"No pressure, then." Stan grinned.

* * *

Gabby looked back to see Stan puffing and panting as they climbed yet another set of steps; predictably the lift was out of service. "How many more, Gabby," Stan called, wishing he had offered to stand guard over the car and let Andy do the climbing.

"This is it," Gabby said, stopping outside Number 34. "Bit grim, hey? This door looks as though it's been kicked open more times than it's seen a key."

Gabby hammered on the door and stood back. Stan hammered even harder. "Get lost. Piss off," a voice shouted.

"Nice turn of phrase. Don't think our Ed is too keen on visitors," Stan said. "Get your arse out here or I'll kick this door down. You've got five seconds."

The door opened on a key chain and a face glared at them through the narrow opening. "What do you want?"

"Ed Bright?" Gabby stepped forward from behind the wall. "We're friends of Ahmed Singh. It's very important that we talk to you," Gabby said. "It would be better if we could talk inside."

The door closed again. Gabby looked at Stan, shrugged her shoulders, and held her arm out ready for the next assault on the door. "Wait," Stan whispered, as they heard the keychain released. A small-framed man with steely blue eyes and long, straggly red hair looked at Gabby and then at Stan. "What about him?"

"Can we come in?" Gabby asked as she stepped through the door, Stan following close by. "Stan lives at Magnolia Court and so do my aunt and uncle. It's a retirement complex, built on the same land as St John's a few years after the school closed down."

"Find yourself a seat if you can. Throw the stuff on the floor," he said. "What's that got to do with me or Ahmed?"

"I'd be happy to explain if you can make the time. A week ago, not much more, we found some stuff we believe had been hidden before the school closed..." Gabby started at the beginning. Ed listened, his expression unchanging as she described the contents of the video and suggested he was the victim caught on camera.

"I've had a lot of years to live with it," he said. "Shall I show you something?"

He led them into the single bedroom, little more than a box room. Gabby ignored the rank smell of stale tobacco, unwashed clothes, and urine; instead her eyes were drawn to the long wall behind the bed. It was covered from ceiling to floor, and from end to end with newspaper cuttings, photographs, and handwritten notes; a lifetime's work. "Not bad for an amateur, wouldn't you say?"

Gabby moved close and studied one picture after another.

"This one?" she asked.

"Stanwell. Taken 1995, Lowestoft. Nice place. Good hostels down that way. Nasty-looking bloke, wasn't he? Ex-army. Pity the bastard got knocked down by a hit and run."

"This one?" Gabby moved on.

"Walker. Another ex-army. Taken 2005, Cardiff. Never did like that place. Too bloody Welsh for me. Died in a fire. Poetic justice is what I say. Play with fire, you get burnt." Ed grinned. "And just in case you're wondering about it, I've got rock-solid alibis. Some might say they both lived too long. I'd say they lived in fear for a very long time; knew what was coming but didn't know when."

"Recognize this one – it's Rutherwood, isn't it?" Gabby said.

"Clever bastard. Gone into hiding. Hope nothing bad happens to him when he surfaces. You can't hide forever, my son."

Gabby shifted her gaze away from him. Deep down she wanted to congratulate him on a job well done, but it would go against all her principles and her values; justice was a matter for the police and the justice system. Or was it? she thought to herself, her eyes and thoughts moving along the rogue's gallery."

"Number four?" Gabby said. "Bloody hell."

"Leave the best until last." Ed grinned. "I'm saving him. It's what keeps me going. Not that I'd personally lay a hand on a hair of his head, you understand, but there's plenty of others out there who'd be queueing up to do it. Surprised, are you? Rutherwood always thought he was top dog. Stanwell and Walker were his puppy dogs, but this one – the biggest bastard of them all."

Stan stood back, watching and listening as the whole sorry story came out.

"Col, he was a good guy. We were good mates. Me, and Col, God rest his soul. Back then it was the three of us, thick as thieves, me, Col, and Ahmed. You've heard about Col?" Ed asked.

Gabby nodded. "Suicide," she said.

"Bloody murder more like," Ed exploded, showering Gabby with his spittle. "And let's all have a minute's silence for Davy as well. He disappeared the previous year."

"And Ahmed, was he abused too? Is that why he ran away?" Gabby asked?

"Raped, you mean. That's the word. Raped. A small slap is an abuse. We were raped until all we wanted to do was crawl under a stone and die."

"You didn't tell anybody?" Gabby asked.

"Sir bloody Edward Bright, you mean, and Lady Isabelle Bright, pillars of the community? Don't talk daft. They wouldn't have believed a word of it anyway. Bad things didn't happen in their circles, or didn't you know that?" He was angry. "I don't know about Ahmed. I read the papers like everyone else. Boy kills teacher. Boy disappears. What do you think?"

"I think it's a possibility, but unlikely," Gabby said. "Could Vincent Palmer have been involved at all?"

"Palmer." Ed roared with laughter. "You're having me on! He was about the only decent bloke in that school. No way

243

would he ever have tried anything on with Ahmed or any other boy. Me and Col spent time with Palmy as well. Never. It wouldn't happen."

"So, if Ahmed didn't kill Vincent Palmer, who did?" Gabby said.

"You seem to have set yourself up as the ace detective, so you tell me."

"Rutherwood's certainly in the frame," Gabby said.

Ed shook his head. "Rutherwood isn't the brains; I told you that. And he's not one for the dirty work. Work it out and get back to me when you do."

"Ahmed's the key. I'm sure of that. We need to find Ahmed. Did you keep in touch with him?" Gabby pushed for the one answer she needed.

"Ahmed wanted to get lost. Just like I wanted to get lost. The answer to your question is no. I respected his wishes." Ed turned on his heel. "I should charge for my guided tours," he said.

Gabby sighed. It was looking sorely like another dead end in the search for Ahmed. Just one more push..."Did he ever mention anybody, anybody at all, that he knew in the UK, anyone he might have wanted to meet up with? Surely there must have been somebody."

"You don't give up, do you, lady? I have to admire the progress you've made. What'll you do if you find him?" Ed challenged.

"I'll nail the bastards who killed Vincent Palmer and I'll nail every one of those bastards who thought they could get away with raping children," Gabby said, stamping her foot hard on the wooden floor.

"You wouldn't spoil my fun, would you?" Ed grinned.

"Ahmed talked about a couple of Brummies he'd met back in Jaipur. Bill and Nancy Hathaway. In their forties, so he said. It's a name that sticks – Shakespeare's wife was Ann Hathaway, but you'd know all about that wouldn't you? He kept the man's card in what he called his precious box. The address was somewhere in Edgbaston. That's all I know."

"Did you know Ahmed owned a dagger?"

"I did, he kept that in his precious box too for a while, then he moved it somewhere. Pity, I could have done some damage with that."

"Will you come forward as a witness if we can prove who killed Vincent Palmer and why? For Ahmed's sake. He's been out there on the run for thirty-seven years. He deserves closure."

Ed lit a cigarette and blew a ring of smoke over Gabby's head. "There might be a deal..."

"I promise you: if I find Ahmed and the truth and have all the evidence to back it up, I will not go to the police without talking to you first. It'll be your call."

* * *

Stan opened the door, let Gabby pass, and closed it behind him. "Shit, was that what I thought it was?"

Gabby nodded. "Yes. A man who has wasted his life on revenge and can't or won't stop until they're all dead or locked behind bars. We've got to stop him from doing anything else stupid, ruining his life even more. Let's hope the wheels are still on the car."

Thirty-Four

1985

Legs pumping, blood pounding in his head, Ahmed ran for his safe place. Puffing and panting, his mind in a fog, he reached up and grabbed the first branch. It felt familiar and strangely comforting. Swinging his legs up, he hooked them around the branch, ignoring the searing pain of the rough bark against his bare shins. Climbing higher and higher, until finally he reached a strong branch high in the canopy of leaves, Ahmed thanked the moon and cursed the moon. Would it be his saviour or his downfall – a beacon of light that would reveal his presence? Time had no meaning. Loud voices calling his name, torch beams arcing to the left, to the right, in front, and behind. Holding his breath, he shook uncontrollably.

The sound of wheels crunching on gravel startled him. Way down below, he saw a dark coloured saloon pass by and drive down towards the gate. His thoughts turned to Ed. It was their tree. It was Ed who had shown him the footholds that led up to the treehouse, as they had always called it. Since Ed had gone, he had turned it into his own refuge, one he had shared with nobody, one he often occupied on a Sunday morning when the rest were at the service in the Great Hall.

It was here he shared the week with his mother and spoke to her of his dreams for the future. He fought the tears but still, they fell. He was alone. Alone in this faraway country with nowhere to go and nowhere to hide.

Ahmed closed his eyes and rested his head against the branch, turning his thoughts to his beloved Jaipur. It had been a warm sunny day in high season. The tourist coaches poured into the city. He was up early, dressed in clean clothes, his feet clad in sandals, and he was on his way to the Rambagh Hotel. The day was full of hope and expectation. He was taking Bill and Nancy on a tour of the city. They had asked him to take tea with them at the Rambagh. His mother was at home waiting for him to return in time for his bookwork. Tears flooded down his face soaking his neck and the collar of his pyjamas but still, he ignored them. They would soon dry in the warm morning sun. Ahmed glanced at his watch, the one Mr McMasters had given to him before he left India that never left his person. It was gold and shiny, waterproof, with luminous hands.

It was almost an hour since…The words wouldn't come. If he didn't think about them or speak of them, then maybe it had not happened and was no more than a nightmare. In the distance, he heard the squeal of tyres. A dark saloon raced up the drive followed by three police cars, sirens breaking the quiet of the night. Headlights and blue flashes lighting the drive as they raced past and up towards the school. Vincent was dead. There was no one to protect him any longer. He had to get away, as far away from this place as possible.

A cloud passed over the moon, darkening the sky. Feet first, hands feeling his way, Ahmed scrambled quickly down through the tree. Missing the last hold, he fell hard to the ground, his ankle turning as he fell. Wincing with pain, he ran to the next tree. Taking deep gulps of air, he pressed himself hard up against the trunk of the next tree on the far side of the house. Another cloud, another tree. Another cloud, another tree, until finally, the gate was in sight. A white saloon with blue flashing lights was parked at right angles to the gate. Close now, so close that he could almost smell the driver. Ahmed dropped to the ground and then slowly lifted his head in the direction of the car. A uniformed policeman stood leaning against the far side of the car, talking into a microphone. "Nothing, guv. No sign of the kid." The man's words carried in the still night. The car door opened. The man climbed back in. Ahmed watched and waited. The man leant his head back against the headrest and was motionless. Five minutes, ten minutes, the man did not move. It was his chance. The only chance he might have. Ahmed crept slowly forward on his hands and knees. On and on and until he reached the other side of the gates and the safety of the hedgerow. Fighting his way into the darkness beyond, brambles tore at his body, shredding the pyjamas he wore. Flimsy, knee-high leaves brushed against his ankles and legs, leaving a burning trail on his skin. Ahmed curled up in a ball and nursed his painful body. Vincent's words came back to him: 'You got to be tough to survive in this world. Never feel sorry for yourself. There are a million people worse off than you are.' When the next cloud shrouded the moon, he mustered his courage, dragged himself out of the bushes, and hobbled across the road, up the bank, and into a field beyond. Mindlessly he pushed on and on until finally he could bear the pain no longer, lay down on the wet grass, and drifted into a deep sleep.

Far away, he heard a voice. "It's a kid." A soft, gentle voice. And then another, harsher. "Leave him. Let's get out of here before we get caught. Do you see that watch? It'll be no good to him when he's dead."

He knew they were talking about him. Fingers wrestled with the strap, undid the clasp, and loosened the watch from his wrist. Blindly, summoning all his remaining strength, Ahmed shot his elbow out towards the voice. "That's mine. Give it back," he shouted. Caught unawares, the boy fell back on his knees, clutching his crotch.

"You little bastard, I'll teach you," the boy yelled, jumping to his feet, arms drawn back, fists clenched.

"Leave him, Silas. Give it back. That watch belongs to him. Don't you ever learn? You lay one finger on him and I swear I'll lay you out beside him. That's a promise, not a threat."

Silas threw the watch down on the stony field and ground it under his boot until the glass cracked and shattered. "He's welcome to it," he laughed, turning on his heel before glancing back. "See you back at camp."

"My name's Byron." Picking up what was left of the watch, he spoke quietly. "I know somebody who may be able to fix it. What happened to you?"

Ahmed sat up. "There are people after me. They've just killed one of my teachers, and now they're after me. They'll find me when the sun comes up. I'll be next. I'd be better off dead," he said, Vincent's words once more thundering in his ears. "I'm in big trouble. I've got to get away…"

Byron laughed. "You've been rolling about in nettles, haven't you?" he said, shining a torch on Ahmed's ankles and legs.

Ahmed nodded. "Is that what they were?"

"Stay right where you are. I'll find some dock leaves and

we'll soon take the sting out of that lot. I can't do much about those cuts and bruises, but we can make you a bit more comfortable. That ankle is swollen badly."

Ahmed lay back. There was still a vestige of hope. The gods had not deserted him completely.

"Where have you come from?" Byron asked, rubbing the leaves on Ahmed's legs and ankles.

"St John's. The school. Do you know it?" he replied.

"Seen the signpost. We've passed by a few times. A big old house up at the top of the drive. A couple of miles away," Byron answered. "How old are you?"

"Thirteen," he replied. "And you?"

"Fifteen, going on sixteen."

"Was that your friend?"

"One of my brothers. He has a bad streak. Gives the Roma a bad name," Byron replied. "You're Indian, aren't you? We hail from the same country. Our roots are in India. They called us gypsies. The name stuck. Can you walk?"

Byron put his arm around Ahmed's shoulder and hoisted him onto his feet. Ahmed winced. Byron took his weight. "I'll bend down. Pull yourself up onto my shoulders; I'll carry you."

"Where?"

"Back to camp. It's a mile further up on the common. Let's get you back there and cleaned up. You can tell my father what has happened and then he'll decide what will be done," Byron said.

"Will he send me back?" Ahmed whispered.

"He'll do the right thing," Byron said as he set off across the field. "We're Lovells – the family – my father is the leader: Duke Lovell. He's a fair man."

* * *

"They'll be here not long after dawn. We need to be packed up and ready to move out. They've got an eviction order. There'll be no arguing with them. I want no violence. We'll come back to Rodborough again next year," Duke said. "The boy comes with us. They'll be looking for him. We leave at five."

"How long will it take us to get there?" Byron asked.

"To Birmingham? At a gentle pace, five or six days. The boy needs time to rest and recover."

"And we pray that he remembers the address as well as he says he does. Is that right?" Byron said.

"It was printed in his memory," Duke said. "Not a moment's hesitation. I just hope he will not be disappointed when we get there. People say things they don't mean. You'll ride upfront with me in our vardo, Ahmed inside. John will follow on with the women and children. Silas will bring up the rear."

Thirty-Five

2022

"Taxi ready and waiting, ma'am." Andy stood beside the car and saluted. "Two gorgeous ladies today. I'm spoilt. Sweet-talked Uncle Max again, did we?"

Gabby glowered. "After giving me the third degree – where was I going, who was I seeing, how was I getting there and how was I getting back – he finally capitulated. Amy turned up right in the middle of the conversation, chipping in to say that she'd make sure I behaved myself. The cheek of it. I hadn't intended to mention today's trip to her, thinking she'd be better off having another quiet day, but you know Amy. She wasn't going to be left out. According to her, the Hathaways will be far more likely to open up to a person of similar years. Never argue with Amy. I should know by now," Gabby said. "So, yes, two gorgeous ladies today. Dressed for the occasion, Andy?"

"Pulled out my old cricket blazer just for the occasion. Still fits a treat. Not often I get to go to Edgbaston," Andy said, smoothing the wrinkles out of his jacket. "I always had a hankering to look round that place. And I see you've swopped those holey jeans for something a little more appropriate.

Nice suit. Did you buy it in Spring Hill?" he laughed. "Stan's coming along for the ride. We might drop into the grounds while you two ladies are busy. He's just gone to collect Amy and then we'll be off."

"Great," Gabby said, checking her watch. "Let's hope the traffic is kind to us."

"Here they come," Andy said, hopping into the driver's seat and fastening his seatbelt. "Everybody ready? Then we're off."

Sitting side by side in the back of a car, it was a while before either of them spoke. "Luck seems to be on our side so far, Gabby. Let's hope it doesn't run out on us today. It's quite rare that people stay in the same house for so many years," Amy said.

"I checked it out on Street Maps. It's a lovely property and in a very smart road. I wouldn't want to move if I lived there. They must have help to maintain it. The garden alone is over an acre. If Ahmed met them before he came to England, and they were in their forties then – at least according to Ed – they'd be in their late seventies or eighties," Gabby said.

"It may be a wild goose chase, you know. How would Ahmed have got himself to Birmingham and found that address?" Amy said. He was often on her mind. The thought of a thirteen-year-old, probably terrified about what might happen to him, running away with nowhere to go and no more than the clothes he stood up in, sent shivers down her spine. She'd said a short prayer for him every night before she went to sleep.

"This is it, ladies," Andy said. "And we won't have to worry about the wheels here. More likely that someone will come along and tow this old banger away for spoiling the look of the neighbourhood."

"I've got the mobile on, Gabby. If you need anything, let us know. We'll hang around for a while just in case there's nobody in. We won't be far away. And when you're done, call. And Mrs A, you take care, you hear me?" Stan said, opening the door for her and giving her a helping hand out of the car.

"I hear you, Stan." Amy smiled. "Take my arm, Gabby. It looks like a good long walk up this driveway. I'll try not to put too much weight on you."

"Someone likes polishing," Amy said, admiring the shiny brass doorknob and letterbox. "You can almost see your face in it. Reach up and ring the bell, there's a dear."

"Coming," a cheery voice called as the door opened. "Hello. What can I do for you ladies this morning?"

Gabby's face dropped. She was no more than thirty if a day. "We were hoping that we might find Mrs Hathaway here, but it looks like we may have made a mistake."

"No mistake. The right house. I'm the live-in carer, Hilary. So how can we help you?"

"Mrs Hathaway and I have a mutual friend," Amy said. "He suggested if ever I was passing by, I should look in and say hello. My name is Amy Wilson. She won't know the name, but I'm sure she will be pleased to see me. And this is my friend, Gabby. Would it be possible for me to have a few words with her if she is in?"

"She's in alright. I've just got her dressed and in the conservatory. Come on in."

"And Mr Hathaway? Is he at home, too?" Amy asked, stepping into the hall.

"Mr Hathaway's not so well these days. A bit forgetful, you know what I mean? He stays up in his room most of the time. He's happy there," she said. "Can I get you some coffee? I've just given Mrs Hathaway hers. I'll take you through now… You've got visitors. Isn't that nice? This is Amy Wilson and her friend Gabby. They're friends of…Who did you say you were friends of?" she asked, turning back to Amy.

"Ahmed Singh," Amy said. "I understand you may have met him many years ago. In Jaipur? Would I be right? He would have been a boy then, possibly no more than twelve years of age."

"I'm not sure that I know that name," she replied. "Why do you ask?"

"May I call you Nancy?" Amy asked. "His name cropped up a few weeks ago and we decided we had to find him. He ran away from a school called St John's College. Magnolia Court, my home – a retirement complex – was built on the land a few years after the school closed. Ahmed was accused of something awful. Of murder. It was a very long time ago when he was no more than a child himself. A few things have recently come to light that lead us to believe he had nothing to do with it. That evidence was planted and that he was falsely accused. Ahmed disappeared after that night. I fear the whole incident might have left him scarred for life. If we could find him – if indeed he is still alive, we might be able to help him close that dreadful chapter in his life."

"How did you find my husband and me?" she asked.

"From a school friend of his. According to this friend, he kept your husband's business card in what he called his precious box. He must have been very fond of you both."

"Would it help if we shared the whole story with you?"

Gabby interjected.

"There is no need for that, my dear," Mrs Hathaway sighed. "I know most of it already."

"So, Ahmed did find you?" Amy said.

"He was delivered to our doorstep by two gypsies. Duke was his name, and he had a son called Byron. They were kind and caring men. They'd looked after Ahmed when he had most needed it. He looked so small and ill. The light had gone out of his eyes. We couldn't turn him away. It was days before he was able to tell us the full story. He was an honest boy. He took us out on a tour of Jaipur when we were there visiting. It was our twenty-fifth wedding anniversary. We spent a wonderful day with him, but we never thought we would see him again, and certainly not in those circumstances. And not long after he arrived here, there were the newspaper articles. The police were searching for him in connection with a murder. It wasn't just in connection with. There was no doubt that he was being accused of it."

"To be abused and then accused of murder, I can't imagine what state he must have been in when he arrived here—" Gabby said.

"What? No. He wasn't abused. He'd narrowly escaped that, unlike his friend, " she said. "Well, of course, we didn't know what to do. He couldn't stay with us forever. Our first thought was to help him get out of the country – back to Jaipur, but it wasn't that simple. He didn't have a passport and he was quite adamant he couldn't return. He'd made a promise to his guardian, and through his guardian to his benefactor, that he'd return only when he had achieved his qualifications. He was a proud boy."

"So he stayed here with you?" Gabby asked, gently.

"For several weeks, yes. He didn't leave the house. We kept people away while we worked out our options. There are a lot of Indian families around these parts. Bill met many of them through his business. We knew many of the families well – shared their successes and their tragedies too. There was one Indian family who had recently lost an only son, almost the same age as Ahmed. The Abdullahs. We decided to invite them round for dinner. That was when they first met Ahmed. Bill told them his story; he knew he could trust them. It was the mother who came up with the idea. Ahmed could take the place of Aahil, the son they had lost, and he could live with them. They would move to a new neighbourhood where nobody had ever known Aahil. They would find a new school that would accept Ahmed with Aahil's identification papers. Aahil would live again in a new skin..."

"But surely Aahil's papers wouldn't be valid after his death had been registered," Gabby said.

"You'd be surprised how few people check papers properly. It was a risk. We all knew one day it might all come out. We just prayed Ahmed could have a life – at least for a while. And that is exactly what happened."

"How very generous of you both. To find him again, look after him, and then let him go," Amy said, tears pricking her eyes.

"He keeps in touch. He is very good like that. Bill looks upon him as the son he never had. We're very proud of him," she said, a smile crossing her face.

"Did he achieve his qualifications? Did he return to India in the end?" Gabby asked.

Mrs Hathaway shook her head. "No, he didn't feel he could go back there while there was a cloud still hanging over his head, and, of course, he didn't dare apply for a passport in Aahil's name."

"But he could if his name was cleared," Amy said quietly. "We've been in contact with his guardian – a Mr McMasters. We explained everything to him. He'd so like to see Ahmed again. I promise you, Nancy, we can and will clear his name. Will you tell us where he is?"

Sitting quietly with her arms neatly folded in her lap, Amy waited patiently. If the answer was no, they would respect Nancy's wishes and leave. It was her decision and hers alone. Either she would take the secret to her grave or she would share her knowledge with them.

Slowly, she started speaking. "There is nothing in this world that Bill would want more than to see Ahmed's name cleared. He may not remember much these days, but he hears everything I tell him. If I could tell him his wish had come true, he would die a happy man. Ahmed, as I have already told you, goes by the name of Aahil Abdullah. He is one of the leading paediatricians in the country. He works out of London."

"Thank you, Nancy. You will have to trust me when I tell you that we will be discreet in our enquiries and even more discreet about the information you have shared with us. We'll keep in touch."

Stan listened. Andy drove. While Amy slept, Gabby recounted the conversation to them as they headed back to Magnolia. It was beyond incredible, but it had happened. They were so, so close...

Thirty-Six

2022

What goes around, comes around, and now it's my turn to step up to the mark. That's the way it works around these parts and I haven't got any problem with that. This one was right up my street. Sam, I said to myself, you've made the grade at last. Sure, we'd been kept informed about the whole thing but, I have to admit, I had been feeling a bit left out of the action.

Gabby, Duncan, and Amy had been doing most of the running with Stan and Andy riding shotgun and, right at that moment, were away staking out a house. Don't ask me what that's about, but no doubt another part of the puzzle. Thomas and Gerald had done their bit. Ros and Paul had just returned from a mini-break in the New Forest. Peter was busy sorting out Paul's finances. The girls had been spending every waking hour preparing stuff for Jennifer and Duncan's wedding. And I was just sitting there – pretty much a spare part.

I wanted to be in on it. I'll never understand how men can do that to kids. I signed the Hippocratic oath way back when. There's one bit that talks about not playing God. When it comes to stuff like this, I wish I could. I'd hang them by the balls if I had my way. There's still the small matter of bottoming out who killed Vincent Palmer.

Gabby came right up and knocked on my door. She gave me the run-down, but not quite all of it. She saved the best for last. She's cute. The right person for the job, she had said, looking at me with those big brown eyes of hers. Your job, Sam, she said, is to use your connections to find and speak to Ahmed Singh, and get him to talk. He's Indian. He works in the NHS. He's a top man. Are you serious? I said. Deadly, she said – and you know when Gabby's being serious. It won't be easy, she said, he's been living under a different name for the past thirty-seven years…No pressure.

Give me a clue, I said. She gave me a copy of a photograph taken from a newspaper thirty-seven years ago. A school photograph. He's got a scar on the top left of his forehead. Kicked by a mule, she said. You can imagine what thoughts were going around in my head right then. A kid with a scar, thirty-seven years on and working for the NHS. If it weren't for the Indians that had come over here over the years, there wouldn't be any NHS. But I didn't say as much.

And then she spoke the magic words. He goes by the name of Aahil Abdullah. It was a while before I said anything. There was no way she could have known our paths had crossed on more than one occasion.

I first heard him at a medical conference. Must have been ten years since. He stood up there in front of a thousand experts in the field and presented a book that he had written – The Complete Guide to Paediatric Infectious Diseases. I'd already read it, cover-to-cover, but never heard the man talk about it personally, or his motivation for writing it. He'd lived in India as a child, he said, and witnessed too many kids ridden with disease. He said he'd made it his life's mission to make a difference. The man was a walking, talking encyclopaedia. Awesome, that's the only word.

And then a couple of years later, I had a real difficult case at University College, London. It wasn't often I couldn't diagnose what was wrong with a kid, but this one just beat me. I remember reaching for Abdullah's bible and reading it again, word for word, right through the night. Nothing, no clues. So I rang the great man himself. We talked about the kid. We examined the kid. We drew up a plan and tried every damned thing we could. It was three months before we cracked it, or should I say, he cracked it. Aahil Abdullah. Right up there with Bob Marley.

I know him, I said to Gabby. And you think that he is Ahmed Singh?

I know he is, she replied. There's no doubt about it.

We'd kept in touch with one another in London. I shared information with him. He shared information with me. And I still had his phone number. We weren't what you'd call buddies, but we respected each other, so I rang him, suggested we hang out, and catch up, and that I was planning to be in London the following day. A man like that's always super busy. It was a long shot, but I hit lucky. The following day I was on a train working out how the hell I was going to approach the subject.

We met up in the rooftop bar of the Hilton on Park Lane. I found a quiet, comfortable corner and ordered a grossly inflated rum cocktail while I waited for him to arrive. He drank water, sparkling water. I never knew him to drink anything else. We exchanged the usual niceties, talked about the latest medical finds, and then I told him I'd retired to Gloucestershire – Stroud – Magnolia Court. I could see it didn't ring any bells, so I threw in the name St John's College as well.

His eyes darkened and I swear the scar on his forehead glowed red, but he said nothing so I ploughed on. I told him how we'd found him – via Nancy Hathaway and with Bill's blessing – why we were looking for him, and that we had evidence that could clear his name once and for all. I could see he knew exactly what I was talking about. For good measure, I threw in that we had found his dagger. I told him we needed to know precisely what had happened that day and why he had run away from the school. I didn't tell him the whole story – no mention of the tape we'd found or the notebook. Couldn't put words into his mouth. This had to be his story, uncluttered by my version.

Still, he didn't say anything. By that time, I was beginning to think it was a wasted journey. In for a penny, in for a pound. Isn't that what you Brits say? I told him we'd spoken to Ed.

This was the story he told me. Faltering at times, I could see that he struggled and that it brought back painful memories, long since buried.

"It was lights out at nine each night. I'd got behind with my homework for Vincent. I'd been playing chess in the evenings with the caretaker, instead of concentrating on my studies. I was trying to finish my homework, covers over my head and in the torchlight. There was one problem I couldn't solve. It kept me awake. Round and round in my brain. It was nine twenty when I decided I'd pay Vincent a late-night call. There was a window in the boys' toilet that was never locked, big enough to get through if we wanted to avoid being seen in the corridors. And, with the help of an upturned plant pot, easy enough to get back in. No one saw me leave. I was in my pyjamas and slippers.

"He wasn't at all pleased to see me. Blew my head off before giving me the one clue I needed to get my work finished so I could get some sleep. That was Vincent. I'd been there a couple of minutes when we heard footsteps coming up the steps up to his flat. He knew we'd both be in big trouble if anybody found us there at that time of night. So he told me to go in the bathroom and stay out of sight until they'd gone. I hid behind the door and flattened myself against the wall just in case anybody opened the door to check.

"The walls were thin. There were two voices; one I recognized and one I wasn't so sure about at the time. I recognized the Headmaster's voice, Mr Rutherwood. He wasn't the nicest man at the best of times, but I could tell from his voice he was angry. He wanted Vincent to hand over a tape. I guessed what he was talking about. It didn't take a genius to work it out. A few days earlier, Vincent had asked me to get inside Keepers Cottage and tell him everything that I saw. That's when I started playing chess with the caretaker. I told Vincent about the screen, the VCR recorder, and the tapes lined up on the shelves. He quizzed me at length about the tapes.

"Vincent didn't seem concerned. He wasn't afraid of anybody, especially Rutherwood. They were old sparring partners. And then the other man spoke. He called him Vinnie. Vinnie, he said, we've been friends for years. If you know what's good for you, you'll just do it. Give us the tape and we'll walk away now. No games.

"I remember Vincent saying: Are you threatening me? And then: What's Rutherwood doing here?

"It went quiet for a few seconds, then Vincent suddenly got very angry and started shouting at this man, the friend. How could I have been so dumb? he said. You're in this right up to your neck. That's why you warned me off. You bastard. It all makes sense now. You'll not get that tape from me. And you'll not find it here either. It's in a safe place. Somewhere where nobody will get their hands on it until I'm ready. And then watch out, I'll nail you – both of you.

"It was Rutherwood who spoke next. Maybe we should talk to your little friend, Singh?' he said. See what he's got to say for himself."

I could see the terror in his face. He was reliving every moment of it. He was slowing down, trying to find the words. He continued.

"Nice tight little ass, Rutherwood said. We can soon loosen his tongue and a few other bits as well...Better game than that little runt, Bright, or Reed, for that matter."

Man, was he choked up this time. It was painful to watch. We took a break. I ordered coffee. He hardly touched his.

"I was thirteen. Pretty naïve, but not entirely. Ed was my friend. Colin was my friend too and they both as good as disappeared overnight. I knew something bad had happened to them and I remembered how often Vincent had told me to watch my back. I wanted to tear out of that bathroom and kill them both, but I was frozen to the spot. Vincent had told me to stay put. So, like the coward I was, I did just that.

"Where's the tape? they kept saying. Vincent wouldn't tell them. He kept saying what was going to happen to them when it all came out. And then something happened. I heard a dull thud and Vincent moaning. I'll never forget that sound. I could feel his pain. And then another and then silence. Vincent wasn't moaning anymore. I looked at my watch. It was nine twenty. I couldn't think straight. I just wanted to cry, to get out of the bathroom and see what I could do to help him, but they were still there. I could hear drawers being opened and closed and then feet scurrying around the room.

"And then Rutherwood said: I'll get one of my men to fetch the boy. He'll talk, then we'll have a bit of fun with him, and then we'll make him disappear. They were talking about me.

"I heard their footsteps as they went down the steps. Rutherwood with his cane, and the other man. When I came out of the bathroom, Vincent was lying there in a pool of blood. His eyes were open. I knew he was dead and I knew I might be next. I couldn't go back to the dorm to get anything – they were looking for me. I wanted to find the dagger that Vincent had been keeping safe for me. He'd hidden it somewhere, but he wouldn't tell me where. It was for my own good, he'd said. I knew I didn't have time to search for it. I ran as fast as I could down the drive and climbed up into one of the magnolia trees.

"Gypsies found me and took me in. And then they passed me into the safe hands of the only two people that I knew in England. By that time, the hunt was on: the hunt for Ahmed, the boy who had murdered his teacher. Ahmed disappeared."

"You didn't see this other man?" I asked.

"No, but I'd know that voice anywhere," Ahmed said. "I hear it every night. And I know his name. I heard Vincent call him by his name…"

And then I asked him the sixty-four-million-dollar question. Would he be prepared to tell the police everything he had told me and give evidence in court if necessary? I knew it was a big ask. It would all come out, one way or the other. That the real Aahil Abdullah had been buried thirty-seven years ago. That he had been practising medicine under a false name all those years. It was too important a story for it not to.

It was my turn to get choked up then. Do you know what he said to me? It would be a small sacrifice to save a few children from that same fate.

It was a huge sacrifice. No thought for himself. Man, was he one in a million.

Thirty-Seven

2022

Duncan had volunteered himself for the job. Calling Colin Reed's parents was not a decision they had taken lightly, but if Ed was correct in what he had said, they had a right to know. Amy had wanted to make the call herself – women, she said, had a way with words that men did not. They'd batted it backwards and forwards until Gabby had intervened and suggested Amy's time would be better spent helping her put together the report for the police – he should be the one to make the call.

He'd slept little that night, going over and over it in his mind. What should he tell them? What should he leave out? The whole business had cut him to the quick and left its mark. Finally, exhausted by his thoughts, he had fallen asleep none the wiser.

* * *

It was a very rare occasion when he poured himself a whisky at ten in the morning, but that morning, before sitting down and writing out some notes, he had.

"Hello, John Reed." The man announced himself. Duncan hesitated and caught his breath. He was sorely tempted to cut the call before another word was spoken. It was too late. He had begun and now he would finish.

"Mr Reed? You won't know me, but my name is Duncan Gillespie. I don't rightly know where to start." Scrunching his notes into a tight ball, he threw them into the waste paper bin. This had to be from the heart. There was no other way. "Please don't hang up on me," he said. "I'm not going to sell you anything. No scams. Nothing like that. I need to talk to you about Colin. If you want to put the phone down right now, I shall not be offended and I won't call you again."

Silence. Duncan took another deep breath and waited.

"Our son died thirty-seven years ago, Mr Gillespie, whoever you are. We laid him to rest many years ago. I'll thank you for not bringing it up again," he said.

"I know how painful this must be for you, Mr Reed. Just the very mention of his name. Losing a son is a terrible thing and it gets no easier as time goes by."

"What do you know about losing a son?" he snapped. "I don't know who you are and what this is about, but it has to stop right now."

"That's where you are wrong, Mr Reed," Duncan said quickly. "I too lost a son much the same age as your Colin – an accident. There's never a day that passes when I don't think about what he would be like if he were alive today. I don't talk about it because I can't bring myself to do so." It was the truth and one that he had never shared with a living soul from the day it had happened, including Jennifer. "I do understand, Mr Reed. Only too well."

"What do you want, Mr Gillespie?" Duncan heard the man's

voice soften and imagined his eyes glazing over.

"I want your son to rest in peace in the knowledge that justice has been done," Duncan said quietly.

Silence.

The past flooding back, Duncan carried on. "When I lost my son, I blamed myself for all the things I didn't do during his lifetime, for all the things I thought I had done wrong, and for all the things I should have done differently. For all the things I didn't say while he was alive. Tell me you don't feel the same." Duncan spoke from the heart.

"I'll never forgive myself," he said. "Colin should be alive today."

"Maybe I can help you find a way to forgive yourself. What I have to tell you will be hard to hear." Duncan paused. "Have you got somebody with you? You may need to sit down."

Mr Reed responded with a simple, "Right."

Duncan continued. "We have reason to believe your son was abused at St John's College. Not just abused, but probably raped," Duncan said. "I am sorry to put it so bluntly, but there are no other words."

Silence.

"He committed suicide, if the newspaper reports are correct. I believe he committed suicide because of what happened to him at school," Duncan added.

More silence. "How do you know this?" The tremble in his voice was unmistakable.

"I, together with a few of my friends, have been unwittingly drawn into untangling this mystery. We found what might prove to be evidence of a paedophile ring operating in that school. We believe Colin was one of their victims."

Duncan gave him some time to take in what he had said.

"Are you okay, Mr Reed? Shall I continue?"

"Go on," he answered, clearing his throat.

"I need to ask you some questions," Duncan said. "It will help us pin this on the perpetrators. We know Colin was sent home at short notice and suffering from acute anxiety, or so we are led to believe. Did he say anything to you when he got home?"

"Nothing, not a word. He hardly spoke. He'd changed when he arrived home. He was a lovely boy, full of life and hope. He was everything to us. And suddenly, we couldn't get through to him, and neither could the doctor. He was scared, scared of his own shadow. In my heart I always knew that there was more to it than we had been told...I'll answer any questions you may have."

"Thank you, Mr Reed. That is very helpful. May I ask you – how did Colin get home?"

"One of the teachers – Stanwell was his name – drove him back. Couldn't do enough to help. He said Colin had been struggling at school, anxious about his work, and anxious about forthcoming exams. He'd never mentioned anything to his mother or me about it. We'd spoken to him on the phone just a few days before. He seemed fine. Mr Stanwell was kind and contrite, saying he hadn't noticed the downward spiral until it was too late. Colin, so he said, had been taken ill in the night and moved into the sick bay. By morning, he was almost delirious. They'd called a doctor who'd diagnosed anxiety, depression, call it what you like, and said that everyone felt that Colin would be best looked after by his parents. That's when Mr Rutherwood called me and said that one of the teachers was bringing him home.

"When he jumped off that cliff, we blamed ourselves. Colin

was a home boy really. He'd never wanted to go to a boarding school, but I put my foot down. Then he seemed to settle down – even seemed to enjoy being there – so we stopped worrying about him."

"Did Rutherwood come to the funeral?" Duncan asked.

"No. I did send him an invitation out of courtesy, but he didn't show. Another teacher came. Vincent Palmer. A good man. Colin used to speak of him a lot. They got on well…You say you've got evidence?"

"Irrefutable evidence that another boy was abused a month after your Colin was sent home – yes, we have. A video recording taken from a CCTV system and a witness statement," Duncan said. "That boy, now a man, is willing to give evidence. We can't be one hundred percent certain that the same happened to Colin, but there is a wealth of circumstantial evidence that points in that direction. Maybe we can prove it, but I can't promise right now," Duncan said. "One way or another, they'll be going down for child abuse."

"Who would do such a thing to children?" he asked, sounding desperate for an answer.

"I've asked myself that same question every day since we found out what went on. I wish I had an answer for you, but please, believe me, you must not blame yourself in any way."

"What do you want me to do? I've told you just about all I can," he asked.

"When the formal investigation starts, the police will hear your story. Just tell them what you have told me," Duncan said.

"When?" he asked.

"Soon," Duncan replied. "They'll have all the evidence in their hands in a matter of days."

"Duncan? You said your name was Duncan Gillespie? Thank you, Duncan, for setting the record straight. It would be nice to meet up sometime – talk about our boys together."

Thirty-Eight

2022

The Silver Dagger

An investigation of the ownership of a silver dagger found
16th March 2022 at Magnolia Court, Stroud, leading to:
An investigation into the unsolved murder of Vincent
Palmer, 5th June 1985.
An investigation into a hitherto unknown paedophilia ring
operating out of St John's College, Stroud, 1985.
An investigation into the theft of a dagger and a notebook,
21st March 2022.

Report by Gabrielle Olsen
30th March 2022

*"My name is Gabrielle Olsen. I am a freelance investigative
journalist. In the past three years, I have undertaken assignments
relating to people trafficking, drug abuse, privacy of information,
and prostitution. I became involved in this investigation on March
17th 2022 when I arrived to visit my aunt and uncle, Mr and Mrs
Brightwell, residents of Magnolia Court Retirement Community,
Stroud."*

A gem as always, Amy – bless her heart – had spent hours

checking the facts and dates and organizing everything into chronological order. It was now down to her to bring the whole story together in a cohesive and convincing report – one that could not be ignored when finally, it was handed over to the police. Three times she had started writing the bones of the report, and three times she had deleted them. At that moment, other than presenting her own credentials, she had written zilch.

Gabby rubbed her forehead hard, ran her hand through her hair in frustration, and reached out blindly for her cup of now stone-cold coffee. How much should she tell and how much should she leave out? There were so many people who needed to be protected. Her sources, most particularly Duncan and his extraordinary network of contacts and ability to search out information from the darkest of places. Aunt Hetty and Uncle Max, and all her friends at Magnolia who had conspired with her to progress enquiries under their own initiative without, arguably, proper recourse to the police. Adrian Grzeskowiak who, by his own admission, had suspected foul play at St John's College but failed to speak up at the time. Ed Bright, on his own quest for revenge, whose actions, if known and proved, would almost inevitably lead to his imprisonment. And the Hathaways and the Abdullahs who had, albeit out of the generosity of their own hearts, technically broken the law.

As an investigative journalist, it was her job to uncover and expose, irrespective of feelings and emotions. It was her job to be wholly detached from the stakeholders. Instead, she found herself drawn into so many of their lives and tragedies. That was her dilemma.

Weighing up the options, she made her decision – she would follow her instincts and conscience. The report would be comprehensive, but it would not tell all.

"Chronology of events

Magnolia Court was built on the grounds previously occupied by St John's College, a private school for boys.

*On **16th March 2022**, in the course of clearing a chimney in the Old Forge (a recently rebuilt outbuilding within the grounds of Magnolia Court), Mr Stan Morrison, a retired builder, and resident of Magnolia Court, uncovered three items that had been hidden within the original outbuilding:*

- *A bejewelled silver dagger of significant value and of Indian origin.*
- *A calf-bound leather notebook, the contents of which reference dates during the first six months of 1985.*
- *A VHS tape clearly dated 16th May 1985, time 9.30 p.m. to 5.30 a.m.*

All three items were found carefully bound in the same strong polythene bundle, sealed against the elements. Together the three are referred to as 'the find' in this report.

I volunteered to take responsibility for the safekeeping of 'the find' in the Old Forge.

An examination of local newspaper articles related to the year 1985 revealed that a teacher at St John's College, Vincent Palmer, had been murdered on 5th June 1985 in a building within the confines of the school and referred to as the Annexe. The same building in which Vincent Palmer resided. (For copy, see Appendix A.)

Given that the notebook was found in the Annexe, we concluded that it was most likely the property of Vincent Palmer and had, quite probably, been written in his own hand.

The land together with the then-existing buildings was acquired in 2003 from the St John's Trust by a developer following the closure of the school some eighteen years previously. No development took place between the period 1985–2003 when the construction of Magnolia Court began. Based on the location within the grounds and descriptions examined, it is believed that the Annexe and that which is now named the Old Forge, are the same building. Used by the residents of Magnolia Court as an open garage and storage area from 2003 up until 2021, the refurbishment of the Annexe started in May 2021 and was completed in late February 2022. The original right-hand wall encasing the chimney breast was left in situ while other walls – beyond repair – and the roof were replaced in their entirety. Subsequently renamed the Old Forge, it now provides visitor accommodation on the first floor with an enclosed garage and storeroom below, adjoined by a wooden staircase closely replicating the layout of the original building.

The same newspaper article that reported on the murder of Vincent Price also described the disappearance of a pupil of St John's coincident with the time of death of Vincent Palmer. The statement given to the press by Detective Superintendent Garry Seymour, the Senior Investigating Officer, named Ahmed Singh and stated that the thirteen-year-old boy should not be approached; a clear indication that the boy was viewed as a critical witness or a possible suspect for the murder. According to an unnamed source, Ahmed Singh had been receiving twice-weekly extra-curricular lessons from Vincent Palmer. (See Appendix A.)

A subsequent newspaper describing the closure of St John's School in July 1985 noted the cause of closure to be that of structural damage to the main building. The architect/surveyor who carried out the initial survey on Magnolia Court confirms that there was no such structural damage. Thus the school closed down for reasons other than those stated. (See Appendix B.)

Based on the origin of the dagger (India), that Ahmed Singh had arrived not less than six months previously from Jaipur, India, and that Vincent Palmer and Ahmed Singh were 'believed to be close', it seemed reasonable to assume that Ahmed Singh might have once owned the dagger.

The focus of the investigation then turned to establishing the current whereabouts of Ahmed Singh to return the dagger to him. No record was found that Ahmed Singh had been tried or convicted in the case of the murder of Vincent Palmer. Indeed, records showed the Vincent Palmer murder to be an unsolved case and all files had been redirected to the National Archive in 1995.

An unnamed source, active during the period of the murder, was able to produce copies of two of the witness statements written immediately following the murder. These were the witness statements taken from Mr William Rutherwood, then Headmaster of St John's College, and Mr Adrian Grzeskowiak, the then caretaker of the same. Other names mentioned in the witness statements were those of Messrs Stanwell and Walker, both teachers at St John's College, along with the name of David McMasters, Ahmed Singh's guardian, resident of Jaipur.

We decided to pursue the whereabouts of Mr Rutherwood and

Mr Grzeskowiak in the belief that one or the other might have information leading to the current location of Ahmed Singh. We discovered that Mr Grzeskowiak had not moved far following the closure of the school and still resided in Stroud. Mr Rutherwood proved to be more elusive.

In the company of Amy Wilson, resident of Magnolia Court, I visited Mr Grzeskowiak on **20th March 2022** at his home. I explained that we were trying to locate Ahmed Singh. He confirmed that he remembered the boy as a pupil at the school. They had been friendly with one another, the two of them enjoying the occasional game of chess. He also confirmed that he had neither seen nor heard from Ahmed Singh since his disappearance on 5th June 1985. The subject of Vincent Palmer's murder on the same day came up in our discussion. Mr Grzeskowiak was adamant that Ahmed Singh was uninvolved in the murder. Mr Grzeskowiak was forthcoming in describing his responsibilities as caretaker, which included his responsibility for running and managing the CCTV system. He took those responsibilities seriously, effecting the change of VHS tapes at regular eight-hour intervals, always at the same time: 5.30 a.m., 1.30 p.m., and 9.30 p.m., a routine that never varied. (See Appendix G, Timeline.) Mr Grzeskowiak recalled a strong friendship between Ahmed and another pupil by the name of Ed Bright and considered him a worthwhile contact in our pursuit of Ahmed. I thanked Mr Grzeskowiak for his co-operation and left.

Up until that point in time, we had not considered the notebook to be of any great significance. As our enquiries progressed, we became aware that names that were cropping up elsewhere in our investigation might have been those referred to by initials only in the notebook: AS, Ahmed Singh; AG, Adrian Grzeskowiak, and

EB, Ed Bright. (A copy taken of the pages contained within the original notebook may be found in Appendix C. Note: the original notebook was subsequently stolen.)

Neither had we considered the VHS tape to be of any great significance. Following Mr Grzeskowiak telling us that a CCTV system was in operation on the school grounds with footage recorded on VHS tapes, we revised our thinking. Having no access to a VCR player, we decided that the tape should be converted to DVD so that we could watch it and thus establish its relevance or not as the case may have been. Duncan Gillespie, resident of Magnolia Court, was able to organize this for us.

At this point, we had no verifiable reason to believe that 'the find' might be material evidence in the murder of Vincent Palmer. Thus, we spoke about it openly and shared our findings with all of the residents of Magnolia Court. It later became apparent that they in turn had innocently shared that knowledge outside of Magnolia Court.

*On **21ˢᵗ March**, I was awakened by members of the police force, led by Detective Sergeant Yates, bearing a search warrant for the Old Forge. An anonymous call to them had suggested that I was in possession of drugs. A small quantity of cocaine was found in the Old Forge which was where I had been staying since my arrival at Magnolia Court. It did not belong to me. I was cautioned, taken to the police station, and charged. As I was taken down to one of the waiting police cars, I noticed that the dagger and the notebook were missing from the place that I had left them the previous evening. (Note the VHS tape had already been sent off for conversion.) I did not inform the police at the time.*

The same day, Paul Green, retired greengrocer, and resident of Magnolia Court, came to see me to tell me that he had had a long conversation about 'the find' with a man whom he met by chance in The Ale House in Stroud town centre. The conversation had taken place on 19th March.

On the day following my arrest (22nd March), Jennifer Buchanan, resident of Magnolia Court, recounted a meeting she had had with a gentleman on 20th March. Magnolia Court provides a complete wedding service which was the key purpose of her meeting with him. The gentleman showed a keen interest in Magnolia Court and 'the find'. Notwithstanding a clearly stated requirement that he should get back to her within twenty-four hours, she had heard nothing from him.

Descriptions of the two men were identical. The man whom Paul Green had met in the pub had not offered his name. The man whom Jennifer Buchanan had met named himself as Ian Williams but provided no contact details.

On 21st March following my release on bail, I spoke to my husband, Greg Olsen, who, at the time, was working in Jaipur. I asked him if he could try to locate David McMasters, a retired solicitor, and Ahmed Singh's guardian – again to try to ascertain the whereabouts of Ahmed. (Note: David McMasters was referenced in Mr Rutherwood's witness statement.)

On 22nd March, I had a subsequent conversation with my husband in which he told me that he had met with McMasters who confirmed that he had neither seen nor heard of Ahmed Singh since his disappearance. In the course of the conversation, Mr McMasters revealed that Ahmed had had an exemplary record at the school – a statement that was at odds with that made by Mr William Rutherwood in his witness statement to the police. Mr McMasters also showed my husband letters that had been written by Ahmed and sent from the school. In them, Ahmed made many references to two of his school friends – Ed Bright and Colin Reed – the latter with the initials CR, also referenced in Vincent Palmer's notebook. The letters confirmed that Colin Reed had left the school at short notice and subsequently committed suicide. Ed Bright had been expelled for no reason that Ahmed could understand. Both had left overnight. Neither had said goodbye to him. Mr McMasters was also able to confirm that the dagger was indeed the property of Ahmed Singh. Mr McMasters loaned both the letters and school report to my husband who has since mailed them to me. (See Appendices E and F.)

*On **23rd March,** the new DVD and the original VHS tape were returned by post and delivered to the hands of Duncan Gillespie. I then watched the DVD in the company of Amy Wilson and Duncan Gillespie. It is a recording of a child being carried into a storeroom that lay beyond the original St John's College car park followed one hour later by the footage as the struggling child is carried away. From the description of Ed Bright given to us by Mr Grzeskowiak, we concluded that the child might well have been Ed Bright. Four men were caught on camera. The first, we knew from photographs in the 1985 newspaper articles – was Mr William Rutherwood. The second and third we were later able to identify from research into military archives as Mr Brian Stanwell and Mr Ian Walker, teachers at St John's College who had previously served alongside Mr William Rutherwood in Cyprus during the '74 troubles. We were unable to identify the fourth man who drove a dark coloured*

Jaguar. The original VHS tape and the converted DVD are now handed in as evidence.

I asked Mrs Amy Wilson to revisit Mr Grzeskowiak in the hope that he might be able to throw some light on how the VHS tape might have reached the hands of Vincent Palmer. Mrs Wilson visited Mr Grzeskowiak in the company of Mr Stan Morrison, resident of Magnolia Court. Mr Grzeskowiak was visibly shaken when Mrs Wilson revealed to him the contents of the tape. Adamant that he did not know what was on the tape, he shared with them his suspicions of foul play that he had had during his employment at St John's College. On more than one occasion, including the day following the expulsion of Ed Bright, he had been told by the Headmaster to clean the storeroom with bleach. He had not questioned Mr Rutherwood's instruction for fear of losing his job. Nonetheless, he had been concerned that something untoward was going on.

During the same visit, Mrs Wilson took the opportunity to clarify a few matters concerning the witness statement that Mr Grzeskowiak had made after the murder. Two interesting and highly relevant facts arose from that discussion; their importance will become clear later in this summary of events:

- *There are significant discrepancies in the times stated in both witness statements. Mr Rutherwood states that he first knocked on Mr Grzeskowiak's door at 10.25 p.m.. On reflection Mr Grzeskowiak is convinced that it would have been more like 9.35 p.m., remembering that he had that moment changed the VHS tapes. He recalls Mr Rutherwood checking his watch and telling him that the time was 10.25 p.m., a time that stuck in his mind when later he was interviewed by the police.*

- *Mr Grzeskowiak does not recall being asked in his interview about the presence of a boy's cap and exercise book at the crime scene. Mr Rutherwood writes that he clearly remembers such. Mr Grzeskowiak refutes that statement.*

*On **25th March**, I asked Paul Green and his wife Ros, to take a trip to the New Forest. To be precise, to visit the gardens of Sir Edward Bright and his wife, Lady Isabelle, and in so doing, to engage one or other of them in conversation to track down Ed Bright – so far, the most promising lead in our quest to find Ahmed Singh. While they did not get the opportunity to talk personally with Sir Edward and his wife, they did talk to a long-term employee of the family. Their visit exceeded my expectations and they returned with an address at which we might find their son in Birmingham.*

*Together with Stan Morrison, I went to the address in Birmingham and met with Ed Bright on **26th March**. Reluctant at first to speak of the matter, he then spoke at length. During the conversation, he confirmed that on the night of 16th May 1985, he had been raped by four men. (According to the notebook, an EB was formally expelled from the school the following day.) He confirmed their names to be Rutherwood, Stanwell, Walker, and Seymour, Detective Superintendent Garry Seymour. In his possession, he had photographs of all four men. Bearing distinctive facial features which age could not hide, I recognized Seymour as being the same that Paul Green had met in the pub, and with whom Jennifer Buchanan had met for a business meeting."*

"Garry Seymour. Garry Seymour," Gabby said out loud, thinking back over the past two weeks. A cunning, scheming, despicable apology for a human being, little did he know that his past had caught up with him and he was about to get his just deserts. It couldn't come too soon.

"Ed Bright was also of the opinion that Colin Reed (deceased – verdict suicide) had been subjected to the same treatment, and that there may have been other victims before them. When asked why he had not spoken out after the incident, he replied that he was terrified of how it would have been received by his parents and the impact that it might have on his family name. Finally, he furnished us with the name of two people to whom Ahmed might have turned when he disappeared on the night of 5th June – Bill and Nancy Hathaway, who at the time had lived in Edgbaston."

Gabby took a deep breath. There was so much more she could, and maybe should, include in the report about Ed, but she had made a deal. Her word was her honour. The rest would remain between herself, Ed, and Stan.

"On 27th **March**, *in the company of Amy Wilson, I visited Mr and Mrs Hathaway at their home in Edgbaston. We spoke with Mrs Hathaway – her husband was unwell and rarely left his room. Once more we explained our quest to find Ahmed Singh, adding, for the first time, that we believed we had evidence that might clear his name. Mrs Hathaway provided us with the information we were looking for. Ahmed Singh was now known by the name of Aahil Abdullah and was practising as a senior and highly respected paediatrician within the NHS.*

With suspicions aroused that Seymour might be implicated in far more than the abuse of children, I asked Stan Morrison and Andy Finmere, both residents of Magnolia Court, to keep watch on the residence of retired Detective Superintendent Seymour, beginning on the evening of 27th March. The following day, they reported back to me that Seymour had received two visits from Detective Sergeant Yates, the same detective who had arrived on my doorstep with a search warrant.

At my request, Sam Brown, a retired specialist in infectious diseases and a resident of Magnolia Court, met with Aahil Abdullah in London. Aahil explained in detail the events of the evening of 5th June 1985, stating that he was present in the Annexe at the time of the murder, although was concealed within the bathroom. He will testify to the fact that Vincent Palmer was murdered by two men – Rutherwood and Seymour, the latter addressed by name by Vincent Palmer during the argument. He will also testify to the fact that he heard Rutherwood tell Seymour immediately after the murder that 'he could not have done a better job himself'. Ahmed's testimony will show how Rutherwood and Seymour conspired to ensure they both had alibis at the time of the murder. Ahmed has agreed to come forward and give evidence."

Gabby reread her previous two paragraphs. She had deliberately missed out the details of how Ahmed had been taken in by the Hathaways, and then by the Abdullah family. If it all came out in the course of the ensuing investigations, it would not have been at her instigation. She could but hope that it did not.

"For the record, I asked Duncan Gillespie to speak to the parents

285

of Colin Reed to establish if there was any known reason for their son's suicide. This he did on **29ᵗʰ March**. *There was none that they knew of. He had left St John's College and had been returned to the family on 16ᵗʰ April 1985 (as recorded in Vincent Price's notebook); a child they hardly recognized and who spoke not one single word to them. Mr Reed mentioned that Colin had been driven home by one of the teachers – Mr Stanwell.*

The silver dagger has never been recovered, nor the calf's skin note-book belonging to Vincent Palmer. I believe that once knowledge of the existence of the notebook became known, the perpetrators of the crime were prepared to go to any length to recover it in the belief that it contained sufficient evidence to have them sent down. I believe that the theft of the silver dagger was collateral damage only. The existence of the VHS tape was not revealed to anybody by either Paul Green or Jennifer Buchanan. Neither Rutherwood nor Seymour would have known that it was part of 'the find'. I further believe that the cocaine found in the Old Forge was planted there to serve as a warning to me to discontinue my investigations.

In summary, we accuse Rutherwood, Seymour, Stanwell, and Walker of rape and abuse of Ed Bright. We accuse the same four of the rape and abuse of Colin Reed, leading to his death by suicide. We accuse Rutherwood and Seymour of the murder of Vincent Palmer thus totally absolving Ahmed Singh (Aahil Abdullah) of any involvement in the murder. I accuse Detective Sergeant Yates of planting evidence leading to my arrest and my being unlawfully charged."

Sitting back, Gabby scanned the pages checking that the key facts had all been adequately covered. A simple quest to find the owner of the silver dagger had turned into a chapter of treachery, murder, and abuse.

Finally, she listed the appendices to the report:

Appendix A: The Newspaper Report on the murder of Vincent Palmer.

Appendix B: The Newspaper Report on the closure of St John's College.

Appendix C: Photocopies of each page of Vincent Palmer's notebook.

Appendix D: Photographs of the silver dagger, together with a valuation certificate.

Appendix E: Letters written by Ahmed Singh to David McMasters – January 1985–June 1985.

Appendix F: Ahmed Singh's end-of-term school report from St John's College.

Appendix G: Timeline of events relating to the evening of 5th June 1985, based upon the testimonies of Adrian Grzeskowiak and Ahmed Singh.

Appendix H: Photograph of Messrs Rutherwood, Stanwell and Walker, Cyprus 1974.

With the report completed to the best of her ability, Gabby heaved a sigh of relief. It was all there. At least more than enough to whet the appetite of the Chief Constable.

Satisfied there was no more she could do and that she had protected her sources as best she could, Gabby inserted the now bound report into a large, padded bag and dropped the VHS tape and the DVD in with it.

Taking no chances, she would deliver it personally into the hands of the Chief Constable. She could do no more.

Thirty-Nine

2022

A week had passed, and she had heard nothing. Gabby had started on a new assignment – one that was close to her heart, particularly after hearing Paul's story. With the economy in near-freefall and inflation at an all-time high, a new network of scammers had sprung up from nowhere targeting seniors, and bombarding them night and day with offers: pensions, investments, energy deals, fake pills, low-cost holidays, and so-called free tickets…And warnings – warnings that their bank cards had been used, that services to their homes were about to be cut off, that their computers had been hacked and that parcels, unordered, were awaiting redelivery. The newspaper chief had said she was on mission impossible. Red rag to a bull. Gabby redoubled her efforts. There were times when she wished that Duncan was there, beside her, worming his way into the dark web. Fortunately, her technical backup team was one of the best in the country. She was lucky.

Recently returned from his extended trip to India, Greg was suntanned, his hair bleached almost blond by the sun, and even more handsome than ever. Working from home in their own separate offices was a godsend. Other than when they were away on their travels, they had been able to spend so much more time in one another's company.

"Hi, how's it going?" Greg poked his head around the door.

"Good," Gabby said, grinning as he started nibbling her ear.

"Time for a break? All work and no play and all that…" he said.

"Give me five." Gabby closed down her browser, luxuriating in his lips on her neck at the very same moment that her phone started to ring.

"Ignore it. Whoever it is will leave a voicemail. Right now, we have more important matters to deal with," Greg teased.

Gabby checked the incoming number. "I don't think this can wait. It's the Chief Constable. I was beginning to think he'd never ring…Don't go away," she said as she accepted the call. "You have? That's marvellous news…Tomorrow? Just let me check my diary." Gabby put her hand over the speaker and turned to Greg. "What are we doing tomorrow? Are you free? Fancy a quick trip to Magnolia?" Greg nodded. "That would be fine, Barry. I'll look forward to it, and, yes, I'll let everybody know. Would two-thirty suit? Brilliant, and thanks."

"Progress?" Greg asked.

"You better believe it, Gregory Olsen." Gabby whooped. "That was the one and only Barry Hardcastle, Gloucestershire Chief Constable, sounding mighty pleased with himself. He even suggested we all meet up at Magnolia. Now, how's that for a coup?"

"Nothing less than I would expect, my darling. Right now, I've got my mind on another coup, and it won't wait." Gabby grinned. Why not?

* * *

"Right, it's all hands to the pump, Max. We've got twenty-four hours to get ourselves prepared and ready for the Chief Constable. He's coming here tomorrow afternoon and we're to get everybody together in the Great Hall. I do wish Gabby would choose better times. Do we give him a late lunch or an early tea? Two-thirty is neither one thing nor the other, right in between everything..." Hetty said.

"Slow down, young lady, or I'll be calling the fire brigade," Max laughed. "Anyone would think the Queen was coming here to celebrate her platinum."

"That's not until June," Hetty replied. "And I wouldn't be at all surprised. Right now, nothing would surprise me. If I get hold of Dot, we can do some baking this afternoon. And I could ask Jennifer to help in the kitchen as well...Perhaps not. Ros, yes, Ros will help. And I could ask Gerald and Thomas to bake some of their special scones. I'll ask Jasmine to make a couple of plates of sandwiches. And I'll see if Dinah can spare a little of her time, but I know she's worried about leaving Emanuel at the moment. Poor dear, he doesn't look at all well. Jennifer...I'll ask her to check everything is just right for Greg and Gabby at the Old Forge. They'll be staying again, but just for the one night. Amy is looking a bit tired, so I won't bother her. And you men...I want everything spick and span; not a speck of dust anywhere in the Great Hall. Dennis had better cut the lawns again. I didn't like to say anything to him, but his cricket pitch lines have all but disappeared under the growth. Tell Andy to rake the gravel on the drive and in the car park..."

"It's only the Chief Constable, Hetty." Max sat down and folded his arms.

"There's a first time for everything, and it's the very first time that the Chief Constable of Gloucestershire has graced Magnolia Court with his presence. We need to make a good impression. Ask Duncan to check up on etiquette for addressing a Chief Constable and make sure he briefs everybody. I do hope Gabby and Greg arrive in plenty of time, ready to greet him when he arrives. She's the only one who's met him. Now, away with you..." Hetty said as she scrambled into her jacket and set off on her rounds.

* * *

Gabby couldn't help but smile as she walked into the Great Hall. They were all there, even Emanuel, dressed up in their Sunday best. Aunt Hetty had been busy indeed since her call yesterday. Afternoon tea had been laid out on the long table, plates of sandwiches and cakes carefully covered with cling film. "I hope he's hungry," Gabby whispered to Greg. "Otherwise I'll never hear the end of it. And if I'm not mistaken, that will be his car coming up the drive right now, unless we're expecting anyone else. I'll pop out and meet him. Let's hope they don't all bow when he comes in!"

* * *

"After you," Gabby said as she opened the door. "Be warned, they might have gone a little overboard with their hospitality."

"I shall consider it a compliment. Fabulous setup, and this Mansion House...I might come here more often," he replied.

Gabby held up her hand. "Everyone. Could I have your attention for just a second? It is my pleasure to introduce Barry Hardcastle, Chief Constable of Gloucestershire."

Looking every bit the confident and polished senior policeman that he was, Barry took off his hat and wedged it under his arm. "It is not often I have the pleasure to meet such an enterprising and resourceful group of people. I feel quite humble to meet you all. If anyone is looking for a job in the police force, please don't hesitate to ring me at any time," he said with a broad smile on his face. "May I say: thank you all."

"Let's all find a seat, shall we?" Gabby said. "And then Barry is going to bring us up to date on what has happened over the past week."

Gabby caught sight of Aunt Hetty nudging Uncle Max. "Barry, hey? Our Gabby on first-name terms with the Chief Constable. How splendid is that?" She was glad for the buzz in the room. She didn't think Hardcastle had heard her aunt's comment, though she forgave her excitement.

"I guess the starting point is for me to thank Gabby for her comprehensive report and to thank all of you for your sterling efforts in ferreting out so much information. Quite remarkable, if I may say so. It's made our job so much easier. I'd almost say you've left us with very little to do other than make a few arrests," Barry laughed. " But in all honesty, it has been a full-on week bringing all the strands together, taking new witness statements, finding people, and finally, pressing charges. I wouldn't normally share information about a case like this, but today I am going to make an exception, partly because you probably know almost as much about it as we do. I'll be leaving out anything that I think might prejudice the case and I do have to bear in mind that we may need to call on one or two of you as witnesses at the trial. I would, however, appreciate it if, for the time being, you could keep what I say within these four walls."

"You have our word on that," Max said, speaking on behalf of all the residents.

"First of all, let me tell you that Garry Seymour has been formally charged with the murder of Vincent Palmer. With a search warrant in hand, we entered Seymour's house and found what we believe might be the murder weapon.

"We have also arrested William Rutherwood. He has been charged with accessory to murder. We found material evidence related to the assault of two boys – Ed Bright and Colin Reed – in the houses of both Rutherwood and Seymour. That same evidence confirmed your theory that Stanwell and Walker also took part in indecent acts. Stanwell died in 1995 in a hit-and-run accident; Walker in 2005 in a fire."

Gabby exchanged a fleeting glance with Stan. Neither of them said a word.

"And I'm sorry to say we found evidence that the abuse of boys didn't stop when the school closed down. Combining this material evidence found with Ed Bright's testimony, and the content of the VHS, the CPS had no hesitation in charging Seymour and Rutherwood with the indecent assault of the two boys.

"As you all know, Ahmed Singh changed his name to Aahil Abdullah roughly six months after his disappearance from St John's College. A person of interest in the murder investigation, he also knew that the police were not batting on his side. Ahmed had seen Seymour around the school and knew him to be both a school governor and a senior officer in the police force. Seymour had visited the school on several occasions in his role as Detective Superintendent and had spoken to the boys about the evils of drugs and knives and the like. As well as hearing his name spoken by Rutherwood,

Ahmed recognized his voice.

"Ahmed was helped to change his identity by two very kind and caring families. Along the way, they broke the law, but the CPS has agreed not to press any charges."

Gabby squeezed Amy's hand.

"Turning now to the theft of the dagger from the Old Forge: DS Yates has admitted to the theft and admitted to planting the cocaine. He and Seymour go back a long way. Shall we leave it at that? We take a very dim view of corruption within the police force. He will be dealt with accordingly. Bottom line is that all charges against Gabby for possession have been dropped."

"That's a relief," Gabby whispered to Greg. "At least you're not married to a criminal."

"Turning now to this famous timeline on the night of the murder. I would have to admit it took one of my very best officers to finally get to grips with the significance of the timeline in Gabby's report. We had a better understanding following Ahmed's statement. Critically, he remembers Seymour telling Rutherwood that, after 'dealing' with him, he would return to his own home. Rutherwood was then to ring later that evening and report the incident directly to him. He would then report the call to the station.

"Ahmed said that the murder took place at 9.20 p.m. Rutherwood in his statement claimed that he had heard the argument at 10.20 p.m. Grzeskowiak has confirmed that he had just changed the tapes when Rutherwood knocked on his door. It would have been 9.30 p.m. He now remembers Rutherwood repeatedly telling him at it was ten twenty-five when the two of them arrived at the Annexe. You know what they say – say it once, say it twice, and a third time and it is the truth. A simple but effective deception by Rutherwood that worked at the time.

"The purpose of manipulating time was simply that Seymour could not be seen to be on-site when the murder was reported. If he had been on the premises at or around the time of the murder, then he might well have been treated as a witness. By delaying the call by one hour, Seymour had been able to get home before Rutherwood made the call to him. By calling him directly at 10.30 p.m., Seymour was able to return to the scene as Senior Investigating Officer. SIO. He then had complete control of the case. He was able to make all the decisions concerning the investigation. In the event, he dropped the case far sooner than would ever happen in normal circumstances. We found little of interest in the National Archive. We can only assume Seymour made most of it disappear. Quite where you found those two witness statements, Gabby," he said, turning to her, "I don't know and I respect that you cannot reveal your sources."

Duncan and Gabby smiled.

"And finally, the moment I have been waiting for," the Chief Constable said, reaching into his briefcase. "The silver dagger, returned to the residents of Magnolia Court, for onward delivery to its rightful owner, Ahmed Singh. Who shall I pass it to?"

Gabby stood up. "Uncle Max, please. I wouldn't trust myself with it again."

"What more can I say? Give yourselves a round of applause." Barry stood up and started clapping.

"Tea, everyone. Help yourselves and I'll look after Barry," Hetty said.

* * *

"I'll see you to your car," Gabby said, leading the way.

"Thanks, Gabby. Good work as always," he said.

"Just one final question. Between you and me, what was that evidence you found in Seymour and Rutherwood's houses?" Gabby asked curiously.

"Photographs. They took action photographs and kept them."

"Bastards," Gabby said.

Forty

"A piece of cake, Amy? We've got enough left over from yesterday to feed an army," Hetty said, picking up the knife.

"Just a cup of tea this morning, if you don't mind. I think I overindulged a bit yesterday," Amy replied. "I've been thinking, thinking about a lot of things over the past few days."

Max grinned. How many times had he heard that? He knew Amy almost better than she knew herself – could read her like a book. She hadn't dropped in for either a cup of tea or a cake, or to chat about the weather.

It looked like Hetty shared the same thoughts. She glanced at Max, cut the cake, and passed a slice to him. She poured the tea, and handed cups and saucers to both of them.

"There are a few things still niggling me about this whole episode and they won't rest. I've always been able to rely on the two of you to give me an honest answer," Amy said.

Straight away, he was on guard. He'd known her for almost twenty years. In all those years, once her mind was made up about something, neither he nor anybody else was likely to change it. If she really and truly wanted their advice, then it must be serious.

"Whatever it is, Amy, we're more than happy to listen and offer you our opinion," Max said.

"Where to start...You know, so many lives were turned upside down all those years ago and now, thirty-seven years later, they've been turned upside down again. Of late, for very good reasons. I do understand that. People get stuck in their ways and then even comfortable in a different existence – because it gradually becomes a safe and familiar place to them. Some may want to break out but feel afraid to do so for fear of getting burnt all over again. Others may feel it best that the past is left in the past. What I'm trying to say, my dear friends, is that it may be over for us, it may be over for the police, but it's not over for them. Maybe I am not explaining myself very well, but do you see where I am going?"

"Not precisely, Amy, and that's being honest. Are you thinking of Ahmed?" Max asked.

"Him, and others," Amy said, with a faraway look in her eyes. "Sam's been talking to Ahmed quite regularly. He's a little worried that he seems to be avoiding some conversations completely."

"About going back to Jaipur, you mean?" Hetty asked.

"That's one conversation that he's avoiding. Another concerns David McMasters and his benefactor. He did at least confide to Sam that he would never forgive himself for not trusting his guardian with the truth after all he had done for him. And as the years pass, as we all know, it becomes so much more difficult to right a wrong. In the end, you convince yourself that it is destiny, that it was never meant to happen. Of course, Sam didn't mention that he knew about the guardian or the benefactor, or indeed Ahmed's immense future wealth. That was just information we happened to pick up along the way and was not ours to share. He was quite right not to mention it, but I wonder…And he doesn't even know he has a father, very much alive and living in Jaipur."

"He's a grown man, Amy. He'll make the right decisions in his own time," Hetty said quietly.

"But will he? That's the question. I know – because Sam told me – that Ahmed feels very guilty he didn't dare to come forward all those years ago. He's been told by somebody – maybe the police – that the abuse didn't stop when the school closed. He took it very badly, blaming himself for the suffering of other boys. It's such a mess."

"You're right about that, but I'm not at all sure there is a great deal we can do. They'll work it out," Max replied.

"And then there's Ed Bright. Stan is such a dark horse, you know. I knew about Duncan and the Hell's Angels, and all the good work they did to help keep kids and teenagers on the straight and narrow, but I didn't know that Stan has been doing much the same thing. Buddying, I think they call it. He's been doing it for years. Well, he has now buddied up with Ed. They've met up several times over the last week. Stan says Ed still feels very bitter towards his parents. No doubt he needs someone to blame. Probably blames the whole world for being born in the first place. He's had such a terrible life. He hasn't spoken to his parents and I doubt anybody else has either. So there they are rattling around in that huge house of theirs, as Ros describes it, with no heir to their kingdom and totally unaware. He's their only son. If they knew…"

"Gabby said that he was a pretty tough and determined young man – more than capable of looking after himself," Max said, reflecting on the conversation with his niece. "But

I do remember her using the word 'sad' when she described him. That was the way she saw him."

"And it doesn't stop there. There are the Reeds as well. Duncan says they still blame themselves for sending Colin to boarding school in the first place. He never wanted to go and, to this day, they believe that he resented it. It couldn't be further from the truth if you listen to some of the stories Ed has told Stan. They called themselves the three musketeers – Ahmed, Colin, and Ed. The high jinks they got up to hardly bear repeating, but there's no doubt they had so much fun. Can you imagine how much that snippet of information might mean to them? Colin loved being at that school, but nobody has told them that…The list is endless.

"We can't forget Vincent Palmer's sister, either. That very first newspaper article said that she was his next of kin. It was a long time ago, but has she spent almost all of her life believing Ahmed killed her brother and got off scot-free?"

"It'll all come out when the trial starts, Amy. It'll be front page headlines, I'm afraid," Hetty said.

"Precisely, Hetty. You've very cleverly put your finger on it. The newspapers will dig and dig and everything will be public knowledge. Wouldn't you rather hear the truth from a reliable source first?" Amy sat back, her case made.

Max smiled. As usual, Amy had manoeuvred them into her corner without the slightest effort. "So, what are you suggesting?"

"I'd like to call them all myself and explain what needs to be explained. Fill in the gaps. I may be wrong…By the time I ring, they may well all be speaking to one another, in which case, there will be a very short conversation – but I will then feel able to rest easy."

Max and Hetty looked at each other. He wondered whether they had done enough. Or was Amy right that they had an obligation to complete that which they had unwittingly started? "I can't speak for Max," Hetty said, "but I do understand what you are saying and if that is what you wish then you have my blessing."

"I couldn't have put it better myself," Max said.

* * *

Stan picked up his shopping bags and closed the front door carefully behind him. He locked it and, with nothing to hurry for, strolled over to Amy's cottage, savouring the fresh morning air. A gentle breeze, hardly a cloud in the sky; yet another perfect spring morning. With the prospect of Jennifer and Duncan's wedding to look forward to, and the Vincent Palmer saga behind them, he felt at peace with the world.

"Mrs A," Stan called through the letterbox. "Andy and I are on our way into town. Is there anything you want? Anything at the chemist or the supermarket?"

Standing back, he looked up at the bedroom window and called out again. "Mrs A, is there anything you want in town?" The curtains were still drawn. Stan checked his watch. 10.30 a.m. – Mrs A had a routine that rarely varied. The bedroom curtains should have been drawn back and the small top window opened. The window was shut tight. The curtains were drawn. His heart missed a beat. "Are you there, Mrs A?" he called louder. A sixth sense told him that something was wrong. He tried the front door. It wasn't locked. Mrs A always locked the door at night and never unlocked it until after she had dressed.

Stepping into the cottage, he called out again. "Mrs A, you're getting me worried now. Where are you?" Still silence. The kitchen was tidy, the last cup and saucer washed, and left on the stainless steel draining board. Cushions were plumped up in the sitting room, and magazines and books stacked up in neat piles, almost as if she had been expecting a visitor. Nothing was out of place.

Stan climbed the stairs so as not to disturb her if she had overslept, all the time whispering her name, expecting at any moment for her to appear at the top of the stairs in her pink nightdress. "Mrs A." Stan knocked quietly on her bedroom door. There was no answer.

Silently pushing the door open with his finger, he saw her clothes were neatly folded on a chair beneath the window, her slippers on the carpet beneath. Turning his eyes to the bed, it concerned him to see she had had such a disturbed night's sleep – the bedclothes were pushed back from her body, her feet exposed to the cold. Stan crept forward, whispering all the time. "Mrs A. It's me – Stan. It's late, Mrs A, and time you were getting up."

Slowly, he slid to his knees beside her and reached out for her hand. It was cold. A surge of grief overwhelmed him and he cried. Time stood still as he remembered her every kindness. It was almost more than he could bear to say goodbye to this lady. Time passed. He would never know how long he had knelt there, stroking her hand and talking to her about the old times. Thanking her for inviting him to buy Henry's cottage and welcoming him, with open arms, into the Magnolia community. She was one of a kind – irreplaceable. God was a lucky man to have her. "Rest in peace, Mrs A," he said. An envelope lay on the floor beside the bed where it had fallen. Written on the envelope were the words: 'To my wonderful friends. We will meet again soon.' Inside the envelope was a letter.

"To all my wonderful friends, my family, at Magnolia Court. Do not grieve for me. I have had the most wonderful life with you over the past twenty years – the very best years of my life except, of course, those few joyous years I shared with Gerard so long ago. I'm ninety-four and my time has come. How odd it is that you know when your time is close. I felt it yesterday. I felt God calling me and I saw Gerard holding out his hand to me, and waiting to welcome me into my new life with him. I do not regret anything. I have done all I set out to do in this world and I am very content.

"I am tired this evening. My handwriting is not as it should be, but I am sure you will overlook that this one last time. This afternoon, God allowed me the time and gave me the strength to complete a very important task. Max and Hetty will understand. I spoke to them earlier today about it.

"Duncan, you were so kind in finding all those telephone numbers for me with no questions asked. I think you knew.

"This afternoon I spoke separately to Ahmed and David Mc-Masters, Ed Bright and his parents, Mr and Mrs Reed, and even to Laura, Vincent Palmer's sister. I was right in my intuition. I spoke to each of them about matters I believed would help heal old wounds and give them the strength and the will to move forward. We spoke at length. They were all grateful for my call.

"Gabby, my dear, I promise that I was discreet in the knowledge I imparted and the words I used. I didn't want that lovely Chief Constable chasing me through the pearly gates!

"Duncan, we joked – was it only yesterday? – about inviting them all to your wedding and letting them sort it out for themselves. You know me, Duncan, I have never done things by half. Well, I

did just that and they have all accepted the invitation verbally. I hope Jennifer will not mind. I do apologize; it slipped my mind completely to ask how many might be in their parties, but I know you will all cope – you always do. Duncan, you will have to send out the formal invitations. I am so sorry I won't be there in person, but I will most definitely be there in spirit. I know you will both be very happy – together as one.

"Stan, I want you to know that I have always thought of you as a son. You are the kindest man and you have a heart of gold. You have been a rock to me for many years. I shall miss you.

"My fingers are stiff now and my eyes tell me it is time to sleep, otherwise I would leave each of you a personal message, but it would be the same for all of you. My wonderful friends. Thank you and God bless you all.

"PS I'll say hello to Henry and Charmaine.

"Yours forever,

"Amy."

Forty-One

2022

Saturday 25th April. Oh my gosh, that's a day that will live long in my memory. Jas and me, we still can't stop talking about it. What started in the planning stage as a small wedding – with family and friends only – turned into quite a spectacle. Amy had us guessing right up to the ninety-ninth hour. If it had been our wedding, we'd have been tearing our hair out, but they just took it in their stride and dealt with it. No sweat.

The wedding first. Awesome. The theme – magnolia. Well it had to be, didn't it? Jennifer and the bridesmaids – three of them – wore matching silk taffeta dresses in cream with the slightest tint of pink in the fabric. None of it was shop-bought. Hetty and Dot slaved over their sewing machines for months, translating Jennifer's designs into the real thing. Talk about *Sewing Bee*.

Duncan wore a sage-green jacket over a cream shirt with a pink bow tie. Max, the best man, wore the same. Jamie – the first time I had met Jennifer's son – he wore the same. Thomas and Gerald, the perfect ushers, wore cream jackets over sage shirts and both wore pink-and-white spotted bow-ties with matching top pocket-handkerchiefs. Talk about colour coordinated. The only thing that was missing was the blossom on the magnolia trees, but it was April. Even Dennis couldn't persuade the trees to keep flowering that long. Ros made the bridal bouquet, the buttonholes for each of the guests, the centre piece for the Great Hall, and the table decorations. White peony Bartzella, Belleville freesias, and jasmine. Don't ask. I can't tell a dandelion from a buttercup, but each was a work of art.

The service was held in the Great Hall, with six rows of four chairs on either side of a central aisle. I'll do the math. That was seating for forty-eight people. Twenty-eight seats at the front were reserved for family and friends – the other twenty – well, we just didn't know, or at least didn't know for sure, who might turn up. Thankfully, we'd built in a good contingency. Suffice to say that by the time the bride came in, there were just a couple of seats empty.

The day before, we had set up four tables of ten and one of eight at the other end of the Great Hall in readiness for the wedding breakfast. Then, supervised by Jennifer, the girls got to work on them. You couldn't fault a thing. Stunning.

And the weather forecasters almost got it right that day. Blue, cloudless skies, no wind, and seventy degrees Fahrenheit. Sorry, but where I come from, it's Fahrenheit, not centigrade. When I say almost, it must have touched eighty that morning while we were standing and sitting on the terrace outside the Great Hall. Maybe Amy had a hand in that as well, or was it climate change?

We were all on duty that day. Greg and I were to meet and greet Ahmed and the Indian contingent. I won't tell you that we weren't a little bit nervous. You see, neither of us knew what Amy had told Ahmed or David McMasters. For sure, neither of us had felt it our business to fill Ahmed in on the fact that his benefactor was also his father. Not such a small detail to overlook. But it works both ways. Ahmed hadn't told me that he was married with a wife and four kids – well not kids – two of them well into their twenties; the other two, teenagers. I'm damned sure Amy knew. The little witch! It took us a while to unravel who was who, but we worked it out in the end. You could see the bond between father and son and even the likeness in their features. Greg recognized McMasters immediately, escorting the rest of Ahmed's family towards us. Luckily – we found out later – McMasters had left his own family back at home in India, although I'm sure that if push had come to shove, we'd have fitted them in too.

Paul and Ros and Stan were on meet-and-greet-the-Brights duty. Boy, was Paul in a state the night before. One hundred percent convinced that Lady Isabelle would eat them alive for breakfast, that was if she remembered them at all. Not a bit of it. Old Lady Isabelle almost fell out of the Bentley in her haste to greet Ros – like long-lost friends. Well, Paul, he just stood back, completely overwhelmed, his eyes on stalks. Not only had Sir and Lady turned up in the latest model Bentley, but a Mustang had pulled up and parked right alongside them. Stan made a beeline for the Mustang. By deduction, I worked out this was young – well not so young – Ed Bright in the driver's seat. Sir Edward pumped Paul's arm until I thought sure that it was about to fall off and then led him towards the Mustang. The next thing – predictable, of course – the bonnet was up and all I could see were three well-padded bottoms lined up in a row, heads buried deep in the engine. Stan stood apart and admired the Bentley. Three guests were expected and three arrived. Thank you, Amy, for that one.

I didn't recognize the occupants of the next car, but again by deduction I guessed that it might be the Reeds. Looking a bit lost, they parked a little way away from the Bentley on their own and slowly made their way up towards the terrace. Gabby was right on it, introducing them to the residents and, of course, to Ahmed and Ed. All I could hear was laughter. The Reeds' faces were a picture of happiness. I can only assume Ahmed and Ed were filling them in on a few things that they didn't know about their son. All good, mind you. Colin was right there with them in all but body.

Laura, Vincent's sister, had tendered her apologies, but not without writing at length about how happy she was to know that, at last, the men responsible for her brother's murder had been caught and charged. She wished Duncan and Jennifer every happiness in their new life.

As far as we knew, we had a full house. Those of us who weren't driving sipped champagne – as you do on special occasions at Magnolia – or drank Buck's Fizz or fresh orange juice poured straight for Ahmed and his family.

Just when I thought there couldn't be any more surprises, I did a double-take, wondering if the champagne hadn't gone to my head. Seriously? Was that a huge white horse pulling a gypsy caravan up the drive? Automatically, I glanced at Dennis and knew precisely what he was thinking. It was bad enough watching him grimace as the big heavy Bentley glided up the drive, displacing gravel left and right as it came. But a horse and cart, as well. I could almost see him reaching for the rake.

"I'll go," Gabby had said, as if we had gypsies visiting Magnolia every day of the week. But she was just that bit too late. Like a flash of lightning, Ahmed was halfway down the drive. The next thing we knew, he was up and sitting alongside the driver. It was only later that Gabby shared that bit of the story with us. This was Byron Lovell, the Romany gypsy who had rescued Ahmed the night he ran away from school. The Lovell family took care of him until they could get him to Bill and Nancy Hathaway in Birmingham. God moves in mysterious ways. How anybody could have found him after all these years beats me. The hand of God? The hand of Amy?

By that time I wouldn't have been in the least bit surprised if the Queen's carriage bearing the Queen herself hadn't turned up – getting a bit of practice in for the Platinum Jubilee. I wouldn't have put that past Amy, either. But no, there was no national anthem announcing the Queen's arrival, only the roar of motorbikes as four bikers on their Harleys turned in through the gate and drove in perfect diamond formation up towards the house. Clad in black leathers from top to toe, they were enough to put the fear of God into anybody. Hell's Angels, they turned out to be and gentle giants of mature years. Parking the bikes, they stripped off their leathers and walked towards us. Duncan spun his wheelchair, put it into gear, and raced off to meet them in his very own Harley. A small wedding surprise orchestrated – yes, you guessed – by Amy.

It was ten to twelve by then. The celebrant was patiently waiting on the steps of the Mansion House. Max was getting decidedly twitchy and wondering how he might tear Duncan away from his friends. If it hadn't been for Gerald and Thomas taking command and issuing orders, the bride would have been standing at the altar long before her betrothed and the guests had taken their seats.

A hush fell over the room as we awaited Jennifer's arrival and for the service to begin. We'd none of us been privy to Jennifer and Duncan's choice of music and hymns. 'Bring Me Sunshine', the signature tune to *The Morecambe and Wise Show* echoed throughout the hall. We knew the words by heart and we all joined in. It couldn't have been more fitting. It epitomised everything about Magnolia and the wonderful friendships that we shared. We sang about happiness. We sang about joy. We sang about new days. It encapsulated the joy of Duncan and Jennifer's wedding, the sad passing of Amy and Henry before her, and filled our hearts with gladness.

We were so carried away with singing that we almost missed Jennifer's arrival. They all looked awesome. Duncan turned his wheelchair to face her and held out his hands. You could have heard a pin drop. In the seconds that followed and as the celebrant stepped forward to greet them both, a door creaked, and a gentle breeze drifted in through the Great Hall. We knew. The fragrance of lavender filled the room. So very familiar.

"I do," Jennifer said. "I do," Duncan replied.

The wedding breakfast was something to behold. The girls had surpassed themselves. No wonder we'd hardly seen anything of our wives for the past week.

Jennifer literally glowed as Jamie spoke of her as the very best mother and grandmother in the world, welcomed Duncan into the family, and hoped that he could cope with the six grandchildren that came as part and parcel of the package. Duncan, as always, was one step ahead. The latest Pokémon video games were already loaded up on his computer.

The best man, Max, kept it short. Extolling the virtues of

Duncan himself and a never-ending list of his contributions to the community, he stayed well away from the story of the silver sting which would forever remain unspoken outside of Magnolia.

And then Stan stood up, notes in hand, and spoke from his heart about Mrs A. Words that he had written late into the night, words that we would all have spoken had it been one of us delivering them in his place. I'd only known Amy for a few years, but it was long enough for me to have grown to love her. Forgetful as was her right at ninety-five years of age, she was always feisty, determined, kind and considerate – a legend in her own right. 'Can't' was a word that I had long since eliminated from my vocabulary. Everything was possible. Nothing was impossible. You just had to believe in yourself.

Stan reached under the table and put a brown leather package on the table. "Amy had one dying wish," he said and then laughed. "Well, that's not entirely true; she had dozens. When I found that parcel up the chimney in the Old Forge, it was Amy who said that the silver dagger should be returned to its rightful owner so, on behalf of Amy, I'd like to hand it back to Ahmed." Stan drew the dagger out of the leather pouch, walked across to his table, and carefully laid it on Ahmed's palm.

What happened then we could none of us have anticipated. Ahmed handed it back to Stan and addressed all of us. "And it is my wish that this dagger – this peace dagger – should remain at Magnolia Court in perpetuity to keep you and all who follow in your wake healthy and safe and safeguard you from all evils. It is my gift to you for giving me my father and my freedom to return to India."

It now sits on a small cushion of green velvet in its own alarmed, lit, glass cabinet in the Great Hall. It will be there long after we have gone.

I should stop now before I exhaust myself and everyone else, but there's a small thing that happened that day that I didn't hear about until later. A gift of kindness. David McMasters had presented Ahmed with a watch the day he left Jaipur to come to England. It had been broken the day he ran away from St John's. It was now repaired and immaculate; Byron had kept it all those years, knowing that one day he would return it to Ahmed.

Humour me. One more thing I've got to mention and the reason that Paul spends so much time at the Old Forge these days: the Mustang. Sir Edward Bright only went and gave Paul the keys to the Mustang – his 'small' way of saying thanks.

Boy, was that a day.

About the Author

From a corporate career to carer, from carer to being cared for - a survivor of breast cancer, Angela reinvented herself as an author and playwright back in 2015. She has made it her mission through her writing to be the voice for those whose needs are often ignored or are excluded from society for reasons outside of their control. The Silveries, the residents of Magnolia Court retirement complex, are close to her heart representing a community that is young at heart, fearless and bound by friendship. The Silver Dagger follows on from The Silver Sting with The Silver Dollar.

An active member of the Stratford Playwrights' Group, Angela loves writing plays and has recently taken to the stage in Stratford-upon-Avon starring in her own play.

In her spare time Angela enjoys travelling, DIY, gardening, craftwork, cooking and entertaining friends and family.

Also by Angela Dandy

The Silver Sting (Book 1 in The Silveries series)

The Silver Dollar (Book 2 in The Silveries series)

The Silver Dagger (Book 3 in The Silveries series)

California Dreaming - (The Silveries series novella)

The Gypsy Killer

If you enjoyed this book, you can sign up to Angela's newsletter on her website: www.angeladandy.com

Lightning Source UK Ltd.
Milton Keynes UK
UKHW040828260223
417684UK00005B/161